Always Never: The Disappeared

By Michael Cooke

For as much as we remember nothing before the first breath, a lifetime, briefly interrupting the eternity time of before, of after, a time with no scientific explanation. "I was, what I was." The grain of sand in the desert of the unremembered, the forgotten, the has been's. Why is it that an existence, once departed causes so much distress to those remaining? An imperfect emotion of eternal separation, a none existence of a present past. An ability to shed tears, the outward expression for that no longer existence. We say the only certainty of life is death, that certainty without an expectation of the last breath, unprepared to be switched off, of the next moment of which we have no knowledge. "I was what I am no more." That last breath welcomes in the unknown tomorrow. What did I forget to do before I am no more?

Copyright notice
Cooke, Michael J
Always Never: The Disappeared
Copyright ©2018, Cooke, Michael J Print book edition (8th Edition)
All characters and events in this publication, other than those clearly in the public domain, are fictitious and any resemblance to actual persons, living or dead, is purely coincidental.

ALL RIGHTS RESERVED. No part of this publication may be reproduced, stored in a retrieval system or transmitted in any form or by any means without the prior written permission of the author, nor be otherwise circulated in any form of binding or cover other than that in which it is published and without a similar condition being imposed on the subsequent buyer.

The author worked for many years during the Cold War in both America and the Soviet Union.

CONTENTS

Chapter One - Students	2
Chapter Two - Humanity	20
Chapter Three - Shooting Stars	37
Chapter Four - Five Eyes	49
Chapter Five - Apollo 10 Moon Music	69
Chapter Six - Mushroom Fire	90
Chapter Seven - Urals in Russia	114
Chapter Eight - Seven Year Hitch	131
Chapter Nine - Dark Web	165
Chapter Ten - End of the Beginning	183

Michael Cooke

*Dedicated to those who
died too young*

CHAPTER ONE - STUDENTS

Nearly a wonder of the world that time of mid-summer in St Petersburg, Russia, called White Nights. Daylight at nighttime as the population of young lovers walk along the bridges over the River Neva, time of no consequence when for once parents knew exactly where the teenage children would be. Many an adult remembers their first walk over the bridges in that twilight daylight of nighttime. The first taste of that love that St Peterburgers have for their city of beauty. Bright moonlight dancing off the golden rooftops of churches and Palace's alike. Romance in the air. Walking arm in arm were Vladimere with Anna, last year university students both studying nuclear physics. It was the study of 'neutrinos' that brought them together, a total disbelief that 'neutrinos' pass through solids! They can go in the Earth and come out the other side, continuing their journey forever, for both of them an incomprehension that millions of 'neutrinos' pass through their body every second. Scientists agree they have existed from those very first moments of the so-called 'Big Bang'. They would play games as they walked, pretending to guess what 'neutrinos' thought as they passed through objects. Did they react differently if passing through a good person to passing through an international arms dealer? Did they always travel at the same speed, never slowing down for thick, heavy objects, their speed somewhat less than the speed of light?

Vlad (shortened Vladimere) looked every centimetre a nuclear scientist with his John Lennon spectacles, his Fidel Castro beard. Anna looked every centimetre a catwalk model never afraid to flaunt her physical attributes. Tonight her pencil thin figure somehow squeezed into a mini red dress that left little to the imagination as she dispensed with all undergarments claiming that the straps/elastics were unsightly. Many a conceited male underestimating her ferocious brain power, she liked the 'put down' laughing at male self-importance, together they had one scientific purpose in life, attempting the impossible, to 'catch' a 'neutrino', a moment of creation from the 'Big Bang', or did they exist before in that period scientists call 'Plank Time', that which existed before the 'Big Bang'.

Tonight they walked in a group with other scientists from the Nuclear Physics Faculty, open minds exchanging theoretical ideas not polluted by the needs of conformity, the never ending climb up the greasy pole of academic promotion, back scratching inferior minds. More on the periphery with the centre of attention a young man named Peter, extolling his theory on the possibility of the accepted time taken for the light to travel from the Sun to the Earth as being inaccurate, that 8 minutes 20 seconds (that commonly accepted time scale) is at best an average as the Earth follows an elliptical orbit around the Sun, at the closest point light takes 490 seconds to reach Earth, at the most distant, 507 seconds. His favourite soundbite to say if the Sun disappeared on Earth we would not know for eight minutes, followed by, everywhere you look when you look into the Heavens we are looking back into past time. Reaching the salient moment of his speech, a loud splash washed the important words away. One of the group commented that Vlad and Anna must have returned to the University.

On the steps of the Sydney Opera House a menagerie of final year

Physics students were celebrating having submitted their Final Papers, only the final exams left which were six weeks away, "as always any excuse for a party." With the first rays of sunlight on a new day embracing Sydney Harbour Bridge, the sophisticated talk of the drunken, speaking many decibels above normal had 'Graham' disputing with his girlfriend, 'Alice' as to whether the term 'Light Years' had any meaning to the man on the Sydney treadmill of life. Alice reiterated that simple fact that light travels at a constant speed of 299,792 kilometres per second. What does that mean to the average motorist who, if lucky, might travel at 70 miles per hour? How can anyone understand 299,792 kilometres a second? Try then to explain that a beam of light in one year travels 9,460,528,000,000 kilometres (or 5,878,499,871,000 miles). Light Years are the standard measurement for defining a distance in the Universe. The nearest star to Earth, Proxima Centauri, is 4.22 Light Years from Earth. The nearest large galaxy, Andromeda, is 2.5 million Light Years away.

Overhearing this a girl called Ruth asked for quiet. "I have a question. Has anyone of us travelled 299,792 kilometres in our life so far?" No one responded positively. Now the drunken conversation moved on to each trying to work out how far they had travelled in their life to date. Even the most ardent backpackers struggled to get much over 24900 miles (one journey around the Earth's circumference.)

"How parochial, we are?" said a voice from within the group. Already those life-giving rays of the sun were getting hotter. Another fine sunny day forecast. Somehow no one had noticed that Alice and Graham had already left. When breakfast came the next morning, with none having seen the couple, an inevitable inquiry started. Police and parents notified of the 'lost'. Later in the day, the twenty-four-hour rolling news started reporting on 'the lost.'

Munich in the middle of the night (two or three) in the morning can be a very quiet place unless a tap is drip, drip, dripping in the bathroom. Helga could not sleep. Her partner, Thomas, could not sleep. That constant drip, drip. They had tried the obvious; making love, then a hot drink, a game of cards. Nothing could obliterate that more deafening dripping. Where had it come from this night of all nights when needing clear heads for lectures early that morning? Helga was a tall, well-built lady (good child bearing hips). Thomas, slightly taller at 6ft 3ins, just starting to show a stomach expanse due to his love of beer. In the extra long king-size bed they had plenty of snuggling up space, but tonight what was wrong with that constant tap dripping. Their relationship started in the few months before university on one of those long hot summer days in the Munich forests. At first, it was their common interest in hydrographics (water transfer printing) as applied to airplane interiors. Now both wide-awake, Helga decided to practice the next talk on Thomas (he had heard it before), her talk titled, "A cube of water or the visible Universe." It was based on one of those strange anomalies that can be produced when playing with numbers (she likes it as it made a nonsense of her fellow astrophysics friends talking about how big the universe might be). She would start with thanks to the clever people at 'NASA'. Quote, 'Of stars and drops and water' moving outward from the solar system, the next closest star to Earth beyond the Sun is Proxima Centauri at a distance of 4.22 light years. It is one of among billions of stars in our Galaxy, the Milky Way. The Milky Way is a pinwheel of stars 2000 light years 'thick' and 100,000 light years in diameter. It holds over a hundred billion (100,000,000,000) stars. The next closest spiral galaxy is M31 in the constellation Andromeda. It is nearly 2.5 million light years away. M31 is near the limit of naked-eye visibility. The Hubble Telescope extends the limit of visibility out to 10 billion (10,000,000,000) light years. From Hubble, we estimate that there are about 50 billion (50,000,000,000) galaxies in the observable universe and if each galaxy contains a hundred billion stars, then the observable contain 5,000,000,000,000,000,000,000 ('5' followed by

21 zeros or 5 septillions) stars. By contrast a cube of water, one inch on a side contained about 600,000,000,000,000,000,000,000 (6 followed by 23 zeros or six hundred septillion) molecules. There are 120 times more water molecules in the cubic inch of water than there are stars in the observable Universe, to emphasize she repeated, "There are 120 times more water molecules in the cubic inch of water than there are stars in the observable Universe."

Helga always enjoyed preaching this North American Space Agency (NASA) use of abnormal figures to make the individual think, but most of humanity does not think beyond the ant-like rush to own things, like money, which has no value other than a piece of paper or copper coin. <u>It made the point that the Universe of human thinking must have water.</u> How often Helga would mock the friends of the science courses when an announcement would be made of a discovery of a planet here or a planet there, could not support life because there appeared no sign of <u>'water'</u>. Thomas always enjoyed that part of her talks when she would berate those scientists/engineers who were still unable to provide any meaningful space transport to start real travel around this minute Solar System in which the Earth revolved around the 'Sun Star'. 'Salt into wounds' next, you people are not even scratching the surface of space travel. The one big project 'The International Space Station' is only 205 miles above Earth, which in reality is the building block of space travel. Beyond 205 miles, nowhere into the vast unknown does humanity now travel.

Therefore a fundamental question. If the big powers spend billions upon billions of their currency on military projects, with the greatest military asset as the control of space, for what reason are they not up their controlling their enemies? Helga liked the impact of this question. Why in the general population there existed no discussion on this basic judgment of humanities progress. Gravity keeping feet on the ground? In this great era of technological advance, like the internet, why is a politician not wanting control of space, when control of space around the Earth gives control of Earth, super power or individual, all controlled from up there.

Helga, in uncontrollable dialogue, continued. Why the constant failure of the super powers, the super individuals? What do they know which creates their none ability to meaningfully enter into 'Beyond Earth?' Many reasons have been offered for the inability to explore which is totally contrary to the explorative make-up of humankind. If this thinking had been in the minds of the early explorers when would the discoveries of the America's, the discovery of New Holland (Australia) be made? Who or when would someone get to the South Pole? When would the islands in the Pacific Ocean be discovered? Where has the explorer vision gone? Has it been replaced by watching sci-fi films? Exploring by doing nothing, while sitting comfortably? Like the Vulcan Mr. Spock in Star Trek, 'it is illogical,' that the explorer desire has been lost before the birth of space travel. Money cannot be the problem as any government can create 'new money' at will giving it a fancy name like 'Quantitative easing.' Ironic they can produce money from thin air then not use it to explore into thin air. What fact does the elite share to keep humanity on Earth poisoning itself with Carbon Dioxides? Is it a chemical within Carbon gases that dulls the brains exploring thirst? Like people question where do all the cancers come from? Is that within carbon gases? Helga, having reached the pinnacle of her lecture started winding the lecture down. Thomas knew the end words by heart, then applauding as if a real audience. Having not heard that drip, drip, dripping during the rehearsal, the sound returned even louder.

Thomas made the suggestion to go out walking rather than continue to listen to the deafening sound. 'Let's walk down to the river.' Munich's Isar River, which is fed with clean, fresh water from the Alps, is more of a river playground than a commercial river (like the Rhine). Even nudity has been allowed along the river since the 1960's, on a hot summer day, many a birthday suit of every shape and size will be on display, sucking up the rays of that life-giving Sun, unless of course skin cancers get caught.

Twenty-four hours later, they could not be found. Various witnesses came forward confirming they had seen Helga and Thomas walking by the banks of the River Isar.

Nikoliev, a major ship-building city in the Ukraine, is well off the Ukrainian tourist routes, dwarfed by the near neighbour Odessa with the tourists flocking to the Black Sea resort. Odessa is a city of wealth where businessmen from all around the war-torn Black Sea countries meet for those 'military arms deals', funding all those Bentleys, Mercedes, Rolls Royces, creating unending traffic jams. Even a Porsche registration 001 (not 007). Look at any map of those countries around the Black Sea with their requirement for military equipment. The Ukraine, free from the 'Soviet Union', now a population split between those in the West anxious to enter the protection of the European Union, those in the East expressing a wish to return to Russian influence. Then, of course, the Americans taking the opportunity to expand their sphere of influence directly to the Russian-Ukrainian borders. Even a story that the head of the C.I.A. is spending time in Kiev helping the Ukrainian military. Then the crime of the shooting down of the airplane on route from Amsterdam to Kuala Lumper over the Ukraine on 17 July 2014, whose missile downed MH17? Where the real truth is lost into propaganda. What airline in the world would fly over a war zone full of missile launching facilities? How much money was saved by not flying around the area of military action? What value is a human life to a commercial airline? Profit not people. The author well remembered flying around, not over war zones in the Far East, adding hours to journey time from London to Hong Kong.

Nikoliev, with a vast ship-building complex (military) with an associated specialist University. Here studying ship construction, were Peter and Anastasia, who had lived and studied in Nikoliev from the days they were born. Born they were within minutes of each other in the same hospital, Anastasia a few minutes before midnight, Peter a few ticks after midnight, nearly twins by time, with different parents they assumed. Not quite the same block of Soviet-style flats, in uncompromising dirty grey, close enough to attend the same schools.

Boys will be boys while girls will be girls, until those teenage years when they met as individuals for the first time when taking part at the end of school celebrations heralding the start of the long, long three month summer holidays. That happened in 2012 when the European Nations had a football tournament in Poland and the Ukraine. They found themselves at odds with their friends having no interest in the football tournament. With a group of like-minded students, they set up a group to study practical problems of 'Wind Travel in Space'.

Not a random selection, a quest for information following one of those semi-political lectures they listened to at school when their last year study group had to endure a political rant on the stupidity of American minds. From a visit to America (sponsored by the American Exchange Programme) the teacher had watched an episode of a science fiction programme called 'Star Trek, Deep Space Nine' in which a fictional character builds a 'sailing ship' to travel in space wind. The complete lecture a diatribe on American impracticability of none science. Far from the students looking at the stupidity of 'space sailing ships' a group, including Peter and Anastasia, formed to study the idea. At first, they met in secret, not wanting to be labeled as 'none-conformists'.

However, at University those remaining in the group were able to study the theoretical practicality. Someone in the military shipyard heard of the project, providing funds for the new group of 4 to continue the project. (Someone, somewhere, could see the military advantage of a fleet of sailing ships conquering space). Fanciful, perhaps, only a few hundred years ago they thought the Earth was flat; go too far and fall off the edge into oblivion.

The group were meeting for a midnight barbeque on the

banks of the River Inhul. A hot, sultry night, lying on their backs, star gazing, with the inevitable bottle(s) of cheap beer. In excitement, Peter exclaimed, 'there is a shooting star.' He pulled Anastasia to her feet, hand in hand; they raced to the water's edge.

Those two left behind heavily embraced in passion then had trouble explaining how they had not noticed for over thirty minutes that Anastasia and Peter had not returned. The girl claimed to have heard a loud splash, when questioned, totally unable to add any fact to the 'splash' information.

A journalist from Pravda in St Petersburg reporting on the disappearance of Vladimere and Anna heard of the Nikoliev incident. On arrival, after talking to the two witnesses, established that both couples had disappeared at the very same time, the convincing fact that the shooting star with exact timings for those brief moments it flew into the upper Earth atmosphere. The journalist managed a front page headline joining the two disappearances together, 'Alien Abductions'. It was well read; the journalist had made a step up the greasy pole of the reporting hierarchy.

One of the wonders of the world remains the Tajmahal Palace Hotel in Bombay, renamed Mumbai, left over from the days of the British Raj, the British occupation of India. It remains a fabulous structure combining Indian traditional Palace style with spectacular British construction design. A walled city palace nestling on the banks of the Indian Ocean, the sea breeze softening the stagnant heat of a bustling city. Around those protective palace walls, every kind of human deformity begging for scraps from the affluent residents.

Paying for a night's residence could keep a beggar in beggar luxury for a year. Here, then, the downside of the 'Taj', all those deformities crowding around the unfortunate visitor out for a walk, give a few rupees to one, the crowd enters the realm of stifling, escape into the city walls, then a necessity of life. How to decide a lucky recipient of those meager rupees, the one legged child leaning on a crutch? The mother sitting in the dirt, clutching a starving child with the balloon stomach awaiting the explosion of death? That old soldier, obviously blind, standing in the rags of a once proud army uniform still with two ribboned medals, tarnished from age?

So many deformities to choose from, are they all real or is there a gang master reaping the rewards of the unfortunates? How or who gets the nearest of best locations close to the entrance gates? A pecking order for beggars. Is the starting point next to the refuse bins, the food waste bins must be a prime spot to collect the slops falling out of the undersized refuse collection lorry? Where do all those food leftovers of the affluent guests go? Somehow, someone will make money out of those leftovers. Could they be given to the hungry beggars for a gift (No!)? Profit for someone more important.

'Let the beggars beg, but do capitalists beg as well? Perhaps beggars to bankers, main customers, main suppliers or do we call that commercial negotiations?' Into the Taj that summer came Chad (boy) and Chhab (girl) both from families of the new rich Indian elite, still with a caste system, their families had known each other in business from the Colonial times. Therefore they had contacts. Each through their families had found summer work both working nights on the 24 hours room service team.

Their English impeccable. Both at University at Newcastle (England) medical school. Their families were thrilled not thinking of future marriage only thinking they would be friends together in the cold North-East of England; they say the sun never shines; the north wind blows directly from Siberia to Newcastle, where it always rains. A bad weather sacrifice to receive the best medical training their families insisted.

After the first year in halls of residence, the fathers decided to invest in a new building of upmarket semi-penthouse flats. Plenty of room for them to be separate and together. Here a romance blossomed with now a wedding planned for fifteen months time after final examinations. Those family contacts already assuring them of good houseman (person) contacts at the major teaching hospital in Mumbai.

They were very much peas from the same pod. Tall, slim, intelligent, she the socialite of the 'two peas'. He a man of sporting ability in both cricket and polo. Most guests had no idea of their background or profession, she, in particular, finding it hard to endure the rude, arrogance, of those nobody tourists. One of those events found her letting off steam during their very early morning break. The offenders this time were a couple from Helsinki (Finland) drunk to the eyeballs on duty-free whisky.

Chad, having calmed her excessive temper entered into that conversation he knows would alter her mood. Medically they both believed that the future of medical procedures to be nano, smaller than micro, surgical tools, medicines, that could be placed within the body. Medical practice going from 'microsurgery' to 'nanosurgery'. The new frontier of none intrusive major medical procedures, producing super fast recovery periods. A through put of patients not dictated by hospital beds occupied for days with recovering patients, a future hospital without ward upon ward of patients only wanting to return home, not spending day after day in recovery. With the Nobel Prizes announced in 2016 acknowledging such a future, their determination as pioneers cemented convictions of a future.

As soon as that 'break time' arrived (officially a meal break) they would exit the palace of decadence to walk inside of the sea wall. Chhab clinging on the arm of Chad. Love and happiness oozing out of very breath they exhaled, a secure, happy future for a lifetime. Chhab pointed excitedly as a shooting star raced across the indigo coloured sky into oblivion.

Judged by Indian standards, the reward for the missing couple enormous with two families offering a joint reward for any information as to where they had gone. With a Police Chief related to the family of Chhab, no expense of manpower allowed to interfere with intense searches of property. Literally crowds around at the time tried to explain that one minute they were walking along, and instantly they were gone. The wildest explanation from that old soldier, who reported that they had left riding a shooting star, but he was blind.

Rio De Janeiro continued to get back into the old ways as the last reminder of the 2016 Olympic Games were removed from public sight. Yes, the stadiums remained, the athletes, the excitement, television crews on every street corner, had all gone. Hotel bedrooms now plentiful and at bargain prices. For many Brazilians, the legacy would be if society changes following the Para Olympics. Would the blind, deaf, infirm, wheelchair users be in or out of the mainstream of Brazilian society, perhaps continuing to overcome prejudice in each and every effort of everyday life?

Somewhat away from expensive 'Rio' property, some 800 metres from the centre to a practitioner of body repairing, human, not cars. Entering the sliding double door into an atmosphere of clinically clean air conditioning, everywhere smelt clean. Behind a tall reception counter sat a young man, perhaps no more than 23 years old. A firm greeting with a request to take a seat, help yourself to a cool drink. A polite notice stating 'Never Be Late', that was a warning on how quickly appointments could be lost to the elite physiotherapist of the city.

On the dot of time, a young lady appeared in pristine clean medical white, including the shoes and tights? Stockings perhaps? At a casual glance the same age as the young man in reception. On the left, entering an unusually large treatment room, a large cubicle for patients who needed to change. All the time the young lady entered into constant medical chatter about the aches and pains she was expected to cure with her often referred to 'magic hands'.

Within a few minutes the patient lying in the correct position, awaiting those 'magic hands'. A regular patient, of whom most of her clients were, knew the routine worked to the clock.

Appointments ran for 45 minutes, 30 minutes of treatments, 15 minutes of dressing/undressing. The young lady always taking a 15-minute break between clients. Regular clients knew, new clients could not guess, the young lady was blind. On closer examination all around the room a discreet hand rail, colour matched to blend in with the tasteful room decorations. Unless you knew, you did not even notice that one hand held the rail at all times until treatment started.

The young man had in-bedded brail signs along the full length of the treatment bed (couch) on both sides. She knew to a centimetre where she was standing. Her feel, her touch, gave no indication of her so-called disability, she forever always stating she cured by feeling. If she could see her treatment would be less effective. Payment made to the young man before a client dare exit, never get onto the 'black list' of her none-payers.

Any regular knew the young man used a wheelchair as a result of an accident when little more than a teenager. He always claimed to have had a 'lucky accident', a Western Embassy diplomatic registered car had been shot at, the driver swerved catching both legs of Inacio embedded under the front wheels. Without exception, he received the most advantaged treatment available in 'Rio', notwithstanding the use of both legs was lost. Inacio still receiving treatment when the first of the ambulance chasing lawyers arrived.

Word spread fast in legal circles, minutes, not the usual days a client waits when once in the firm's client system. Big fees. Diplomatic car, plenty of witnesses, young boy with life changing injuries, Western Embassy. The massive fee that lawyers can only dream of. For the 'wet behind the ears' Inacio, the luck of a passenger in the car being the embassy legal representative. She took absolute control. No one knew who were the other passengers in the car, who the shot had been intended to hit. Lilianna, the Embassy legal head, had matters under control in moments.

The following car had the other two passengers out of the accident vehicle well before any police or medical staff arrived. The unhurt driver himself administered emergency treatment, obviously not a simple driver, his first aid equipment not available in 'Rio'. Lilianna set up the cordon, the driver directing the first of the ambulance crew. As to which hospital would accept the injured teenager. (Acceptance not an issue as it was that hospital that treated all diplomatic people and, of course, the elite politicians of Brazil.) Lilianna sent the baying pack of lawyers away, some making dark mutterings about 'the lad's human rights.'

The television crews pushing one and all aside to get the best of bloodied pictures. Reporters (as bad or worse than lawyers) desperate to be the first to discover who was being shot at, who was the shooter? Gangland, drugs, diplomatic, spies, all there to be discussed as possibilities. How news reporters delight in uncertainty, meaning a story can be kept alive for that little longer period than rolling 24-hour news allows. Lilianna and Inacio in hospital, he undergoing surgery, before the distraught parents arrived in a police vehicle, with her brilliant language skills, the benefit of a private room, the imminent arrival of the Ambassador, she expressed sympathy intermingled with ideas for the lad's future.

Thoughts of compensation, would they allow him to be operated on in her country if the need arose? Yes, of course, the parents would be with him. Much having been discussed by the time the Ambassador arrived. He pleased to enter the calmness of compensation talking, keen to understand from Lilianna if any questions had arisen about the other occupants of the crashed vehicle. None was the quiet response.

Ignacio spent 12 weeks in the hospital, never recovering the ability to walk. Part of the settlement from the Embassy meant he had a small, regular income for life, to him the most important part, a University education in Computer Sciences. He developed great aptitude as a programme designer, now earning enough money to be self-sufficient without his 'accident settlement money'. It was at University he met Bededita, which he exclaimed would never have taken place without the car accident.

From the first days of the first year, he had set his eyes upon her, eventually meeting in a disability group set up by a progressive Senior Lecturer out of normal hours. Disability remaining a sign of a second rate citizen. He knew she had total blindness, from when or how he had no idea. With the meeting dissolving, somehow she caught her foot on a chair leg, falling backwards she landed on the lap of someone still sitting down. Shocked, embarrassed, she could only imagine what Ignacio looks like. Now. She knows every last millimetre of his body to touch, the length of his hair, his useless legs. Now they are inseparable. More than one of their relatives stating with conviction that they are a couple made in heaven.

Concluding a working day, as usual, they set-off, she pushing the wheelchair, his directions quietly given. All the neighbours knew them; many spoke on the ten-minute push through downtown towards the beach area. They had a normal spot where he described the comings and goings of the beach crowd. The regulars calling out 'hello' to the couple. To see a shooting star in daylight is a privilege of the wonders of nature. Their concerned families raised the alarm when no one could contact them later that evening. Many beachgoers came forward to say they had seen nothing, their attention taken up by that rare shooting star.

Turkmenistan, in Central Asia, with its capital of Ashgabat, is the home of the Turkmen, until recent times part of the 'Soviet Block', now recovering from the death of the long-time president. Hubter (a girl's name meaning very beautiful, the most beautiful) and Munis (boy's name), last year students at an Ashgabat University spending their long vacation on the never ending dig/excavation at the 'Jurassic Park' (local name) Plateau of the Dinosaurs. The area is the location of one of the most magnificent collections of fossilised dinosaur tracks anywhere on planet Earth, which only became known to paleontologists in the 1950's. The two were staying in the local village of Khooja

Pil at the foot of the plateau.

On the plateau, some 2500 dinosaur tracks have been discovered. Some are 40 centimetres long and 30 centimetres wide, others even bigger, measuring 70 by 60. A dinosaur five to six metres (16-26 feet) tall could take a stride of up to two metres. The Plateau is renowned for having the longest trackways – continuous lines of footprints made as a dinosaur walked or ran – anywhere in the world. In places, they reach up to 200 metres. 150 million years ago, when dinosaurs ruled the world, the area was not an arid plateau but an area of lakes, marshes, river banks and herds of dinosaurs, both vegetarian and carnivorous. Herds, what an under-descriptive name for these groupings, perhaps humanites exist in herds.

'The sandy marshland quickly silted up so these prehistoric tracks left their mark forever and a day' said Anatoly Bushmakin, a Turkmen scientist specialising in the plateau. The plateau is located deep in Turkmenistan's Eastern corner on the border with Afghanistan and Uzbekistan.

For Hubter and Munis to travel from Ashgabat meant an aeroplane from Ashgabat (on the far Western side of the country) to Turkmenabat. Then travelling by road some 450 kilometres (280 miles), a bumpy eight-hour journey.

The village, Khooja Pil, where they were staying means 'miracle of the elephants' in Turkmen. Hubter knew elephants had never existed in Turkmenistan, from her earliest days she had been fascinated by the legends that the 'tracks' were left by elephants taken by Alexander the Great on his campaigns. History shows Alexander never passed through the area, for the locals who knew nothing of dinosaurs, but could follow the footprint tracks, elephants had been the obvious explanation. Elephants the largest animal they could imagine. Hubter had a dream of proving the elephant story to be true. Munis, with his more scientific approach, of finding new footprints.

This year the intrepid university group totaled ten plus a professor, with a keep your eye on the students, burly male assistant, ex-military, not to be messed about and all the students knew that. Mornings started early, rest period during the heat of the day, then into late afternoon. University administrators had always insisted travel from Khooja Pil and back from the plateau had to be undertaken during 'daylight hours'. Accommodation in Khooja Pil a small 'complex' financed by the University, basic, with the strict requirement of keeping male/female students apart. Out of University use the 'complex' much sought after by those sparse tourist groups. The day on the plateau accommodation consisted of four permanent large Soviet army tents; they also provided respite for the tourists. In the middle of the day, the tents inside were warm enough to bake bread; water had to come up from Khooja Pil with any food required. Again, one tent for female, one tent for male, the kitchen/eating tent, lastly the sample tent permanently occupied by the Professor, his laptop (battery of course), excavated items for examination, dating, recording.

Oh yes! Those toilets behind the tents also needing water from the village even though they were only portable toilets. Young ladies rather hold in all day long, uncomfortable but better than that poignant stink of heat attacked portables. Add to that the smell of the rotting living tents which had a Word War II leftover look, best Soviet Union construction, made to last a lifetime. Hubter enjoyed the work at the same time hating the smells. Easy to forget deodorants are a new addition to smelling nice. For her the delight of getting back to the campus and that clean refreshing shower, changing into light, airy clothes for that evening meal treat. Wholesome describes evening meals, prepared by two 'babushkar' (possibly each 100 years old) producing delicious meals from the very basic of basics. They knew how to skimp, how to save, how to prepare meals in the days of near starvation during and after World War II. All students agreed that meals were good and plentiful. Soup, salad, main course, local fruit, local fruit juices to drink, and the conversation meandered through every topic under the moonlit velvet coloured night sky, then bed. Early to bed, early to rise, the watchword for the group. With the exception of Hubter and

Munis, always the last to turn into bed taking the opportunities to sit under that velvet coloured night sky. Munis pointed to the brightness of a shooting star racing across the sky.

Morning came early, that they were absent not apparent until breakfast time. Family connections had a military presence looking for the missing within a few hours. That vast unpopulated plateau a vast area to search.

CHAPTER TWO - HUMANITY

Humanity exists within a very small range of temperatures, fully clothed perhaps zero for a limited period, naked perhaps at plus 40 degrees Celsius for a short period, then there is that humidity. Hot, humid, very uncomfortable. To keep comfortable in Florida 'Disney' air conditioning everywhere. To keep comfortable in Paris 'Disney,' central heating needed. In autumn/winter/spring, warm-blooded, intolerant to small temperature movements, need to eat (then defecate) regularly during a twenty-four hour day, then the need for daily sleep of perhaps eight hours each day. If this happened to be the description of some new engineering discovery, the discovery would be ineffective, too much downtime, not enough production time. A poor investment for the capital outlay.

Humanity, this poor investment destroys most of the world around it. 'The swat a fly,' 'tread on an ant,' 'runover anything in front of the all-important motor car.' Are you a killer of something that was alive until 'you' became a murderer? (No I am not a murderer, they are only birds, animals, insects, I am more superior. I am a human.) Strange how the Earth existed for so long without humanity. What is it they say? If the life of the earth is a football field, (pitch) humanity arrived 1 (one inch or 2.5

centimetres) in front of the other end goal line. In other words, no time at all of the 4.54 billion years Earth has existed. Humanity has been around about 200,000 years? Within the last period, perhaps 300 years, since the start of the Industrial Revolution, humanity specialising in life (for itself) as the fantastic destroyer. Fantastic destroyer of anything, everything if money can be made. What is wrong with the brain of the fantastic destroyer? Self first, 'me' only matters. A society where a positive judgment is made for the creation of individual wealth. How many people exist as worker ants for the creation of another's wealth, the Queen Bee of commercial activity? As they say 'money makes money', a society where the worker ants keep their money in bank accounts, who makes money from this borrowed money, the Queen Bees of the banks. Has a bank ever owned up to giving back any profit they make on this free money in bank accounts? They act as a cartel giving nothing, keeping the lot, until they lose your money and sorry nothing left, that is nothing left except for those professionals (other bankers, lawyers, accountants) who will charge fancy fees to deal with the corpse. Amazing how quickly those Queen Bee's find more worker ants to continue their wealth, they know how to protect themselves when the ship starts to sink, not the morality of a 'sea captain', the last to leave the sinking ship, no, the morality of the 'rat' off first clinging onto as much wreckage as possible. Captains of 'industry', that collective of the self-interested who look after each other, secret-society, freemasonry like. Examine those none executive directors of companies quoted on any stock market anywhere, see how many names keep reappearing. Remember they are called 'captains of industry'. (It is fortunate that 'captains of industry' is a none-gender word.) How do they communicate together, probably in those corporate 'boxes' at the best sporting events? Yes! if it is a bank, your account money may be paying for the event.

A captain of industry conversation. Bill asks Peter if he is <u>free</u> (that word most important) to go to the tennis in Paris. Peter responds 'yes' then continues to ask Bill if he is <u>free</u> to attend an international rugby match in Rome. They both agree to travel together in each other's corporate jet. Business will be discussed to justify the 'time off'. Sometimes corporate jets crash. Sometimes Queen Bees are swatted dead.

Ilisaguik College is a public community college located in Barrow, Alaska, on the shore of the Artic Ocean. It is the only tribally controlled college in Alaska and is the northernmost accredited community college in the United States. Final year students Anik and Anernerk (a girl's name meaning Angel) continued their studies during the long vacation, eager to get summertime readings for their study into Earth temperature change. The fact that summertime temperatures had increased could not be disputed, they were interested in the effect, not the cause. If changes were manmade or climate made remained a contentious issue, their interest only in the loss of the ice mass, the change in habitat for wildlife. Anik, when feeling on the lazy size, would suggest to Anernerk that all they needed to do to convince others was to take footage from that television programme 'Ice Road Truckers' taking footage from the first series and comparing with the latest series, where the ice roads were disappearing earlier than in the past. The ice roads only exist in the middle to late winter period as the lakes freeze over, allowing the large trucks to drive across the frozen surface, not a haphazard experience, well organised, well-defined roadways professionally made for the safest way across a lake. Truck owners can make big money, truck drivers taking risks every day of the season. Even the most experienced drivers dislike that loud sound of the cracking ice, a crack to many, frozen death in the frozen depths. The driver of little value when the vehicle might cost US $100,000, not a career for the fainthearted. Then again a good winter season means holiday for the rest of the year. Anernerk had recently read 'Always Never, Global Warming', and like the author, she found it difficult to comprehend that human brains cannot understand the damage CO_2

gases continue to do to the protective layer of the atmosphere of Mother Earth. Although the college had only existed since the 1990's detailed measurements had been meticulously kept of the ice caps, of hour by hour daylight temperatures, hours of sunlight, nighttime temperature, that more difficult with students needing to sleep. Other figures existed, going back a hundred years for annual snowfalls. (<u>Old timers</u> now saying that even the snow is different now from how it used to be.)

Anik had learnt the ways of the dog sledge from his grandfather eventually inheriting the team of dogs with sledge when grandfather died fifteen months past. Anik was fortunate his grandfather had left a sum of money in trust for the dog team, the trust fund being large enough for all expenses to keep the dog team intact for a ten year period. As is often the case, Anernerk accused Anik of thinking more of the dog team than of her; she knew it not to be the truth. Quietly telling herself that when they travelled they were not polluters and that travel was much safer than those polluting motorised sledges, when the lead dog always had that sense of 'underpaw danger'. She had found the sledge exhilarating in the summer months of near permanent daylight, in the early hours of the morning rushing onwards snuggled up under animal skins, she accepted the criticism of inconsistency of carbon emissions versus killing animals, her response, 'animal skins keep me naturally warm, no need to burn fossil fuels for warmth'. Travelling in that near twenty-four-hour daylight, to the current site of measurements, she shouted to Anik to look at that fantastic shooting star.

Lead dogs know the way home, even when the sledge is empty. The team were waiting at the college for the working day to begin. An instant extensive search found no bodies, always difficult to bury the dead without a body, in the wild wilderness meat is food no matter if it is animal or human.

Within the last thirty years, the transformation of China from an agricultural economy into a major industrial nation has been phenomenal, Communist China and Commercial China, two C's, one China, millionaires by the thousands. Still education a fundamental concern of the family, many families still only one child (boys required more than girls). Those rich enough now sending children to those elite schools around the world where money buys 'unrivalled education'. With the unwritten guarantee of entry into a top university, perhaps the best of military academies, perhaps premature death from 'drugs', the super rich always with plentiful extra cash for the newly designed drug producing the best of 'highs'. Enough money to use only the best of first class on the best (safest of international airlines) a good time not to fly the beginning or end of term. Imagine the only adult on a plane full of over excited children, over excited on coke (drink). The older ones boozed up on free alcohol after the inevitable argument with the Chief Steward as to their age. Can you imagine 300 children being locked up for eleven continuous hours, flying to Hong Kong, with as much drink (alcohol or not) that they can consume? Then, of course, that lack of adequate toilets quickly finding themselves blocked up to overflowing. Again, at least one teenage couple taking advantage of joining the '7-mile high club' (if you're not sure, it's having sex at 7 miles high). Cabin crew certainly know if they are in favour with management as these flights are those that cabin crew avoid like a plague. 'First class high jinks' can get very upsetting for the cabin crew who are not allowed to answer back.

Such were the recollections of Jiang (girl) and Dong of their school days in England, as they continued their observations into the Urban Wild Life in a residential suburb of Beijing (Peking). As the junior members of the research team, they were given the night shift. Not just a suburb, only that suburb that the communists created to hide the Politburo nuclear shelters from where the elite would continue to govern in the event of a nuclear war. As with most of these cold war nuclear bunkers spread all over the world, the main occupants were now rats. Not the 'elite rat's who were going to save their skins in those 'bunkers/shelters', such secrets for the elite who were the chosen few, in a male dominated society husbands not telling wives, not telling parents, not telling children, 'if I tell you, I will lose my place.' Only the administrators of the life-saving invitations knowing there would be ample young, attractive females to help preserve life after nuclear attack. With an expected population of 10,000 plenty of openings for young ladies, officially employed as bookkeepers, cooks, nurses, cleaners, amazing how many jobs could be designated female-only, to the Politburo (who would be saved) the continuation of the population equally as important as the initial group of self important politicians.

Jiang and Dong were part of the study group looking into the life of the bats that now inhabited the mile upon mile of tunnels and side rooms. Jiang was extremely happy not to be on the day shift where studying went on within the complex. She did not like bats into the face, or the poo they deposited everywhere. With some excitement, Dong pointed out the brightest of shooting stars.

An extensive search of the underground complex by soldiers in protective clothing failed to find any trace of Jiang or Dong, generally assumed they had found a secret passage then getting themselves lost. More 'lurid' of all, having fallen into a nest of vipers.

Governments, health experts, constantly talk about addictions to drugs, by which they mean cocaine, marijuana as examples. To be an addict is not good for health, obviously tobacco and smoking, but some countries base their economy on the production of such addictive products. Pain-killing medications are addictive, as is alcohol (witness Alcoholics Anonymous). Some foods are addictive, creating obesity. How many consumers of such items consider themselves an addict? Is driving a car addictive? The human brain is told an item is addictive, then needs more of that addiction. In more recent time a new addiction, 'the mobile telephone' more specifically the social media sites, the free access to pornography, now so addictive that increasingly newly married men have to receive counseling after they are unable to achieve an erection in a normal relationships having spent so many nights playing with themselves whilst watching 'porno pictures'. That is one extreme, another extreme the overwhelmingly need to look at the mobile every minute or two, that feeling of 'no one wanting me', then another extreme with 'vehicle drivers' incapable of not using the mobile while driving (driving a killing machine like a car or a lorry). Again, the addiction to meaningless games played on the mobile, so easy for a young teenager not wanting to communicate with parents to disappear into the world of make-believe, or text to friends about nothing of important other than to 'slag off' (be nasty about) other people. From 'Google' (American based) very easy to start to use American word spelling, no thought just an addiction to the self-correcting word spell. Why write original work when it is so easy to copy something off the 'net'? Who would want to be a marker of exam papers knowing what is written comes directly from the internet. That good for mankind, the internet that has quickly turned to evil.

Addictions, the old fashioned one of sitting in front of the goggle box (television) without moving other than to exercise the mouth with food, then express disbelief when the body gets fatter. How many diabetes sufferers watch the goggle box for hours?

Is property ownership an addiction? Is drinking too many fizzy drinks an addiction? That's what dentists think (the future looks very bright for technicians who make dentures). Flying to holiday destinations can that be called an addiction? Saving up all year for two weeks in the sun, all that pollution that those cheap holiday flights pump into the atmosphere, then later on in life complaining about $CO2$ emissions. Amazing how that human brain always blames the others with no responsibility taken for personal actions. Is shopping an addiction? Perhaps for necessities, no! For many shopping has taken over as the new Sunday religion. No longer a saving society, now the card payment machine, only praying for sufficient money to be in the account to pay for the none needed item purchased. Is there a fundamental conflict between Christianity, or religion of any denomination, and capitalism? How quickly capitalism took over communism. Communism as practised almost as a religion, until it started to disintegrate, then it became a smash and grab for those who had the largest muscles or who were prepared to have blood on their hands, is an oligarch in fact a bloodedgarch? The addiction wanting, wanting to be the super rich (the oligarch) who is the oligarch subservient to? Such people having the addiction of the pretty, young, tall, slim, trophies (ladies) keep the toy for a year, then find a new one. The addiction of the beautiful young ladies 'money', not difficult to be an actress faking whatever the money man wanted to hear! Rumour has it that at the other superpower of the Cold War one famous man would pay his extremely beautiful wife US $250,000 for every child the marriage produced (she produced three) before being replaced by a younger model, rather like the automobile these men preferred a new car, new female. Now a growing addiction for the very rich 'hoping to live forever' the body not disposed of at death, no preserved not by pickling or mummified, no 'cryogenics' freezing the corpse then waking it up at some time in a future time when medicines are created for longer life and curing today's incurable diseases. What immense trust is placed in the providers of cryogenics that they will keep the machine working? What happens if they go bankrupt? That would cure the addiction to ever-lasting life.

In reality, this period of the early 2000's will be recorded in history for that addiction to pornography, where with mobile phones in particular (but also the desktop computers) a click of the switch opened up the pornographic world to the very youngest. No longer romance, extreme sex, to make even the best inadequate. From future people looking back into this period of history, astonishment that those search engines only paid lip-service to control the abnormality. Why pay lip-service, obviously, there is money to be made! A more pertinent question, why don't the political class place controls, legislate, do something about the search engines? Could the political elite have a vested interest in ensuring only the lightest of legislation makes progress into law? Are the so-called political elite addicted to politics, in the sense that politics give them power, an addiction to power, the ability to rule over the Plebs, the underlings, they are the Queen Bees, sent by divine right to rule? The Greek Gods of the twenty-second century. Your life in the hands of the cryogenics God.

It might be suggested that authors are addicts, addicted to the belief that others have an interest in the author's thoughts.

Some universities of the world are known for excellence; some are so good in their field that their very name means profound excellence. One such name is MIT. People may not know where MIT is, but know it means the very profound thinking on a subject matter. Karren met William (don't call me Bill) during the last month of their first year studying 'Space propulsion'. Now graduated, now spending a further three years, research funded by one of those pioneering companies attempting to make space flight a reality. It was the prospectus that had attracted Karren to the course which stated 'this course covers the fundamentals of rocket propulsion and discusses advanced concepts in space propulsion ranging from chemical to electrical engineering of micro thrusters, solid propelled rockets, electrothermal, electrostatic, and electromagnetics schemes for accelerating propellants/ Additionally satellite power systems and their relation to propulsion systems are discussed, the course included laboratory work emphasising the design and characterization of electric propulsion engines.'

William, from as young as he could remember, wanted to be involved in/with space travel. Growing up he had been surrounded by his mother's interest in science fiction, films of Star Wars, Star Trek; his interest totally focused on speed of travel, introduced to the concept of 'warp drive' spacecraft propulsion at speed faster-than-light. A spacecraft equipped with a warp drive may travel at speeds greater than that of light by many orders of magnitude. Spacecraft at warp velocity theoretically continue to interact with objects in normal space. John W Campbell in his 1931 'Islands of Space' introduced the general concept of 'warp drive'. From an early age, William knew that Einstein's theory of Spatial Relativity stated that energy and mass are interchangeable, thus, speed of light travel and warp drive is impossible for material objects that weigh more than photons. That is where technology has arrived to date. A new forward nudge now proposed by Karren and William, neither of them can remember which one made the initial thought, thought developed over a period then jointly agreed. Now they worked on the theory together, for them future travel would be by capturing neutrinos as the new generation of propulsion.

Many days had been spent by their group of first-year students looking for an explanation as to why space travel had almost ceased to exist. Since the pioneering days of the 1960's, there had been a continuous decline in scientific advancement as if getting to the moon had been human's greatest space travel achievement. Of course, within the group, there were several who attached validity to that conspiracy theory which believed the Americans never went to the moon and that the whole event actually took place in one of those immense underground caverns in the American Western Deserts. For a time the group split between those believing in conspiracy and the others. Conspiracy believers also had an explanation as to the reason space travel had made so little progress since the 'none moon landings', according to the conspirators the film 'Close Encounters of the Third Kind' recorded an event that actually did take place. This event so petrified the leaders of the two Super-Powers (America-Russia) that they decided jointly to keep their feet firmly on the ground. Better to be a Super-Power on Earth than a nobody out there in space. Conspiracy or not, why had space travel disappeared into thin air? It cannot just be a case of no money being invested. Conspirators say again that a warning was given that 'microbes' should not be allowed to enter space causing contamination, which, regardless of conspiracy theories, how can you clean a space vehicle to ensure no Earth-made microbes do not enter the great Cosmos. Eventually, the group took it upon itself to engage the course director as to whether there existed any purpose in the degree course taking into account the near collapse of any government funding into 'space propulsion'. A number of students then changed courses, Karren with William continued for the challenge as William said, "going where no one has gone before'. Original thought, original ideas, the answer into 'space propulsion' has to exist. He would always pontificate that the alternative would be that humanity existed as in a prison cell called Earth with no opportunity to escape.

MIT allowed their minds to think freely, impressed with their ability to think outside the 'box'. Of course, when they suggested that the way forward would be to harness that power that already exists in the atmosphere, many a professor was surprised that they had not thought of the idea themselves. Great efforts were then made to provide patent/copyright protections for the intellectual property rights. Influential journalists published articles from which came the funding for the research to continue. MIT providing necessary research facilities. Notwithstanding the interest in their fundamental ideas, Karren expressed surprise that 'nuclear' powered space travel never entered the discussions, perplexed the expression that best described their reaction (then they laughed at using the word 'reaction' in a nuclear context).

Mystery surrounded their sudden absence from the study place, the conspiracy enthusiasts working overtime. Only one common fact had general agreement, that very bright shooting star. Those American security agencies were quickly on the scene worried sick that competitor countries (notably China) had abducted the special two. No doubt Forty years ago the Soviet Union would be the expected culprit, now it is China that is

Michael Cooke

hungry for advanced technology.

Aleppo has been the centre of a modern day urban battle undertaken by proxy armies representing either the United States or Russia, the protagonists of the 'Cold War', and Iran. The University students have asked for their names, university, study course, to be kept secret as no one has been safe in this conflict. Weapons are supplied through complex webs of middle persons, all taking a profit. Obviously, the manufacturers could easily prevent the arms trade if they wanted to. They don't. Weapons Kill Children. If the various outside countries wanted the war to cease, it is easily within their power to stop the proxy armies. With universities closed the two students (male and female) gave their medical knowledge 'freely'. At all times they wore identity vests, white metal helmets, not much protection in a war zone.

At the start of the war, Aleppo had a population of over two million. The divided city remains with a population much the same with residents having to live in bombed out properties. Media of the world reports on divided lives with different stories (not facts) provided as directed by government publicity teams of taking opposite sides, the truth would damage the reputation of the 'Presidents'.

The two students were used to the horrors. Each had been physically sick when acting as stretcher bearers, as with all the population of Aleppo, the haunting questions on why all these foreign troops were destroying their city, destroying innocent lives. World media may call it a proxy war between U.S.A and Russia, do they not care about the devastation they cause safe in their capital's thousands of miles away from this hell-like nightmare. All day long they had been stretcher bearers, running from one casualty to another. It was the maimed children, scared for life, screaming in pain, that they attempted to help first. No time to wash the blood from hands before dodging bullets racing off to the next victim, splattered blood across the face stuck on as if designed into a pattern of death. Blood encrusted clothes ripped off at the end of the day into the communal wash, ready for the next day.

Even in the middle of the night, the noise of skirmishes filled the air. Sitting around warmth from the night fire, exhausted voices in despair, pleading to the none listening ears of Presidents of the warring factions, one of them pointed to a shooting star racing across the night sky.

Only in the last moment of a second did they hear the incoming missile, body parts exploded into death. Never too young for the innocent to die. Two stretcher bearers less for tomorrow.

Television depicting a world of the overweight, fat, obese, anger of the group of women turned into sobbing tears of despair. The small group of malnourished women had near to death children clinging onto life. This group of starving to death were awaiting that minute delivery of life saving milk provided by a humanity charity. All around the 'Horn of Africa' starvation is a normality. Man's abuse of each other in a world of eat or die.

Within this world of human skeletons, Mary and Joseph, converted their religious beliefs into practical assistance. They themselves came from another area of South Africa where life remained an everyday struggle. They had both qualified as doctors, after qualification deciding to spend two years giving a 'tithe' of their years of education. Now twelve months into those two years they had learned to deal with the hollow eyes, the bloated stomachs of children born into premature death. Always and forever they knew their lives would be haunted looking onto those faces of the living dead. Why, why, why is affluent, greedy, fat society in other countries unable to help? Why have such people no morality, no consciousness, self-centered bigots, I'm alright Jack. Mary, with Joseph, arrived at the sprawling village heading immediately for the three little tents that made up the village hospital; the queue spilling out into the baking, red-hot, sunshine. (That baking, hot, blue sky sunshine that affluent tourists flock to for sun-tanned skin. White skinned, hoping to turn brown skins but only for the holiday period.) Not here in stinking deprivation, no five star hotels with multiple swimming pools, purified drinking water, specially prepared meals, local dancers to provide evening entertainment. With the essential, must have air-conditioning.

First patient not a patient, the first patient the village elder to collect his bribe (gift) of enough 'Viagra pills' to last until their next visit. With reluctance he accepted a similar number of condoms. Mary and Joseph knew he had tested positive for H.I.V. In this area H.I.V. more common than a cold. 'First right' continued to be claimed by this 'elder' as girls moved from childhood to womanhood. Mary often wondered what he did with the condoms. The constant flow of young pregnancies he obviously did not use them. Without the gifts, Mary knew their visits would be terminated. Quite a problematic ethical dilemma. Following the Elder, the pecking order for the village women determined the order for treatment. Babies sunken eyes, no sparkle, lifeless, balloon bloated bellies bursting full of nothingness. Joseph referred often to the 'stare of the living dead'. He knew without the food they had brought more than one of today's babies would not survive through to the next week's visit. Mary wondered at the natural beauty possessed within these near skeleton bodies, the village teenage girls, 'waif' like fairy models, strikingly beautiful. Yet within ten years reduced to figures like that of the 'Hunchback of Notre Dame'. To be 39 in the village is to be old. Money that a family of 4 would spend on a Sunday main meal would keep a family of 4 in the village in food for a month. Some say life is a lottery. What they should really say is that the place of birth is the starting point of the lottery of life. How would those expecting to be born into affluence cope if by some act of time-shift they ended up born in this village? What would be their skin colour? Every day Joseph and Mary prayed that the village children would be less hungry, less thirsty. After each visit the journey home existed in near silence. Joseph made a comparison comment on every return journey to the base hospital some 22 miles away that if they had flown up into space they would have just passed through the troposphere, which is some 11 miles high, onwards into the stratosphere. This day the start of the journey home had been very late, the black night sky peppered with stars. Mary pointed out a large shooting star.

No trace of their bodies, the vehicle found with no sign of damage.

Afghanistan, home to Ruqaya (girl) and Kaamod (boy) existed in a state of war for most of their lives, their town some 160 miles from Kabul had experienced much violence notwithstanding which they had qualified as pharmacists now working for a distant relative who had made very substantial wealth during that time of American military presence, distant relative no longer living in Afghanistan, much too dangerous. Now in Switzerland close to the Bank in Geneva where he kept his ill-gotten fortune. That fortune arriving very quickly between 2004 and 2009, a shared, equally split with a government minister who had no connection with the provision of water and sewerage infrastructure which is how the distant relative amassed his multi-million fortune. For normal people, in the affluent West it is impossible to imagine a life without running water to flush away human waste. Great areas of population had no comprehension of clean, clear, instant drinking water. Such populations not believing that precious life giving clear water is extraordinarily thrown away when flushing the toilet.

One flush of the toilet will keep another human alive for one whole day. Think which child without water you will condemn to childhood pain with death every time you flush.

To flush or not to flush, literally to be or not to be (to be alive, to be dead).

Would it be such an engineering challenge to separate clean

drinking water from a 'fluid' to flush a toilet? How is it possible for the 'with running water at home population' to inhabit their world of selfish, self first, I've got it and I will waste it, water use extravagance. Cover the conscious with a small donation to a charity providing water to some African town, unheard of, in the middle of nowhere. Consciousness, pure, cleansed, a good deed done, but I must go to the loo.

Think of flushing in context of a household of 4 with one flush each less on a 365 day a year basis.

365 x 4 = 1460 saved flushes.
A village of 200 people.
365 x 200 = 73,000 saved flushes.
A small town of 2000 people.
365 x 2000 = 730,000 saved flushes.
A large town of 20,000 people.
365 x 20,000 = 7,300,000 saved flushes.
A small city of 200,000 people.
365 x 200,000 = 73,000,000 saved flushed.
A city of 1 million people.
365 x 1,000,000 = Work it out – frighten yourself.
A city of 8 million people.
365 x 8,000,000 = Work it out – frighten yourself.

Water, a precious life giving natural resource. For almost no personal cost affluent world could provide life-giving water to the thirsty, build water pipelines as well as those for gas and oil. Divide the pipeline inside. But that would mean capital investment with no profit. Mind you it could be a good project to create another capital earning scam financed by some International Agency.

Amazing the capital that can be made within a warzone, by the time the visiting military bean counters look at the 'Books of Account' they will have little paper trail to support the extra 'outside' of contract payments, often greater than the contract itself.

Switzerland, the distant relative discovered, proved to be a gold mine for testing pharmaceutical products. No! No! No!

never test a new drug on your own population, no, send it off to Afghanistan. That distant relative quickly established a profitable formula for testing the products on a willing Afghan population, that secret, to offer the 'testing' as a solution to illness, a privilege to take part. Enough military trained medics to conduct any trial could be enlisted with minimum cost. That distant relative extricated from those pharmaceutical companies, requiring the tests, those profitable extras at none or negligible cost. Antibiotics, long superseded in the affluent countries, were the best – the word antibiotics enough for any Afghan family to drain the family money for life giving/life saving antibiotics.

Kaamod and Ruqaya were responsible for taking the mobile pharmacy out to those villages where no permanent pharmacy existed that also required them to provide basic medical care. It was on the last of those visits that they disappeared, the village Elder where they had last been was heard to tell the investigating police that he knew the shooting star was a bad omen.

CHAPTER THREE - SHOOTING STARS

During that time of the shooting star the world media quickly established that a male and a female from every country of the world had disappeared in mysterious circumstances. Every county of the world? How many countries are there, as crazy as it is the various world organisations cannot agree how many countries there are. A starting point of agreement is at least 190, then it cannot be agreed how many more there are.

When politicians remain unable to decide how many countries there are it can hardly be a surprise that the world is in such a mess. When humanity sits in front of the brain numbing television set the thought of how many countries there are in the world is of no interest. So who decides what a country is? Who decided who is admitted to the collective family of nations (is it decided by money, or politics, bribery or the old boys network, a democracy or a dictatorship) or decided by language, not a common language but a diversity of different languages so that one cannot understand what the other says without an interpreter. Without any doubt more languages exist than countries of the world (estimate of 8500 languages), and then within a language there are different dialects, therefore more languages are recognized than countries are recognized.

Is the United Kingdom one country or are England, Scotland, Wales, Northern Ireland, counted separately as under F.I.F.A (Football Ruling Body) or one country as for the Olympics (Team G.B.). Is Taiwan a separate country or is it part of China, or in 'no-mans-land', or has the status changed since World War II? as it is no longer needed as a military base for a Western power. Mind you, if you are visiting Taiwan, the International Airport does have nuclear fallout shelters if Mainland China decides to be aggressive, the flight for life.

Will it be decided in the future that the E.E.C. (European Economic Community) is only one country made up of constituent parts (countries by any other name), that would mean the United Nations smaller, and the Football World and the Olympics? Is the Arctic or Antarctic accepted as an individual country, if not, why not, they are very enormous, but, the big but, they are not politically strong.

Currently the United Nations has 193 members (2016) and two U.N observer states, Vatican City (Holy See) and Palestine. In addition six states with partial recognition, Taiwan, Western Sahara, Kosova, South Ossetia, Abhazia and Northern Cyprus. Let's make it more complicated, there are then six unrecognized *de-facto* sovereign states, Nagorno – Karabakh, Transnistria, Somaliland, Islamic State, Donetsk People's Republic and Lugansk People's Republic. Because these last three are located in active war zones and have only limited government structures, some do not accept them as even defacto countries.

Confused?? There are 206 Olympic Nations, starting with 193 United Nations members, United Nations Observer nations, 1 only Palestine (Vatican City not interested, though the popularity of the Roman Catholic Church would be enhanced, how would the clergy dress?). Olympic States that are partially recognized by the U.N., Kosova, Taiwan, plus ten Olympic nations that are independent states (not United Nations members) Puerto Rico, Bermuda, Cook Islands, Aruba, British Virgin Islands, Cayman Islands, Virgin Islands, Hong Kong, American Samoa, Guam.

Confused?? There are 211 F.I.F.A. (football) countries eligible for the Football World cup, arrived at with the following members. Teams of United Nation Member States (186 out of 193), Teams of U.N. Observer States 1, Teams of Partially Recognised States 2, Teams of United Kingdom Constituent Countries (England, Scotland, Wales, Northern Ireland) 4, Teams of Dependent Territories 18. Total 211.

Confused?? The I.S.O has 249 county codes in the ISO Standard List. Why so many? The code is officially called ISO 3166-1, most people use it when filling out internet forms and having to choose from a very long list of countries. The standard includes convenient two letter codes for each country, like these examples; United States (US), Germany (DE), Japan (JP), Antarctica (AQ).

The ISO standard is based on an official list kept by the United Nations.... Why are there so many, many more than the total number of U.N. member and Observer Countries? There are country codes not only for actual countries but also for nearly every independent state, overseas territories, uninhabited islands and Antarctica. This is because organisations might need an option for every place that any person can be located and dependent territories often are not technically part of the countries they belong to. So 249 is made up as follows:

U.N. Members	193
U.N. Observer States	2
States with Partial Recognition	2
Inhabited Dependent Territories	45
Uninhabited Territories	6
Antarctica	1
Total	249

THE MEDIA HAD A WONDERFUL TIME CALCULATING THE TOTAL NUMBER OF THE DISAPPEARED.

How to explain that moment in life when death is less than a breath away. How can the brain explain that last moment when all of the previous knowingness ends. How the futility of a lifetime surrounds the mind having lived for a period of time without the knowledge of what is an existence following the last breath, to have been, to be no more, forever now a memory, fading as those remaining in turn enter the final breath. Will that fleeting moment remember into eternity, the gone beforeers? Mothers, fathers, grandparents, husbands, wives, grandchildren, are they assembled to welcome your spirit into the continued existence? For as much as we remember nothing before the first breath, a lifetime, briefly interrupting the eternity time of before, of after, a time with no scientific explanation. "I was, what I was." The grain of sand in the desert of the unremembered, the forgotten, the has been's. Why is it that an existence, once departed causes so much distress to those remaining. An imperfect emotion of eternal separation, a none existence of a present past. An ability to shed tears, the outward expression for that no longer existence. We say the only certainty of life is death, that certainty without an expectation of the last breath, unprepared to be switched off, of the next moment of which we have no knowledge. "I was what I am no more." That last breath welcomes in the unknown tomorrow. What did I forget to do before I am no more?

When will a scientific experiment study those last messages passing into the brain? Would it be the same for a pauper, for a president, for female, for male, for the newborn dying at moments after birth? For the religious fanatic blowing themselves up with a body bomb, bits, pieces, scattered everywhere, those poor humans remaining with body parts stuck into the face, the smell. Think of a war, many splattered body parts from one explosion, who was whom now stuck onto the face of the remainers. Enemies in life forever stuck together in death.

Death? How many can say "I have died?".

The word 'death' is a very undramatic expression to explain that critical path into unknown eternity, cremated, fired into ashes of nothingness, buried into blackness to slowly decompose' not a very attractive choice. Has anyone heard complaints? Yes different religions have different outcomes for that 'eternity time', immoral (or inhuman) their inability to agree an outcome for 'eternity time'. A before 'birth time' can they agree where or what humanity was/is at that moment prior to conception, or agree when that growing bundle of cells arrives at individuality. Somehow before individuality that growing bundle of cells is available to be killed (terminated) then after a given number of days 'murder' enters the equation.

They say I was not, then they say I am, did anyone ask me 'a growing number of cells' if I wanted to be terminated (killed)? No! It is those clever medical humans who determined that time at which I can be lawfully killed. My growing cells experience that pain of terminality, an inglorious disposal of my growing cells (please do not flush me down the toilet) into that water blackness cascading into those sewerage beds, US CELLS deserve better than that. How cruel can humanity be, destroying that unable to protect itself, cells, no different from the birds, fishes, animals, easily destroyed into extinction.

How will humanity manage without a mobile telephone upon death, play safe have it in the coffin. How fragile human life is; the life now gone, the mobile lives on.

Doris, not her first name, which she did not like, by general consensus the brightest pupil for a generation at one of the two best Universities in England. Privileged background not even touching the surface of the wealthy Christian family she was born into. One of those pioneering early Victorian food families, where a religious belief required adequate provision for the employees (note not 'workforce'). Her great, great, great grandfather made full provision for any family member that followed. He acquired large areas of land around the factory to keep a 'park like' landscape, then at the furthest end of the south park a 2000 acre residential estate for the family. A fine mansion house with, for that time of male domination, a provision that the mansion house passed to the eldest child, male or female. Then as the need arose, more and more large independent family homes for the every growing family, a large church, planting a near forest (wood inadequate description) which he intended to provide fresh air into the expanding factories. Now it provided a barrier between the 'now factories' and the mansion house. Employee houses now backing onto the 'forest' which if they were not 'employee housing' would cost an absolute fortune to purchase.

Growing up, Doris, the fourth child in the family had learnt that the Christian ethic now out of vogue and favour remained the back bone of the family business. Fortune that now stretched into what in past times would be called the British Empire. She knew tragedy, the second child of the family, her brother, Sebastian, killed when she had just had her twelfth birthday. That day always in her mind. Five o'clock in the morning a call from the very expensive private school Sebastian attended, a coach crash on the return home from the school Easter skiing trip. Sebastian a good skier, particularly those long, long runs at speed. Initial news very limited. There were at least sixteen fatalities, but as yet no identification. From school the offer of transport, from grandfather an instant hired plane for any parent who wanted to travel, speed of the essence, it would leave within 90 minutes from a nearby airport. It would make one journey, return and be back for a second journey. Money buying privilege or a human act of kindness?

Within moments Doris remembered grandmother arrived, parents gone. She had never seen her father unshaven in her life. As if in no time the other members of the family arrived, she remembered those hushed voices of adults, every parent's nightmare, a precious child injured on an excitable school trip. Twenty-four hour rolling news mumbling through an unexciting early morning lack of interest, the story broke, British school children killed in coach crash in France returning from a skiing holiday. As with all these true events, the initial news is so limited that speculation takes over from hard fact, then the frantic race by News Teams to get to the accident for those heart bleeding stories of young able athletic teenagers killed before adulthood. In a foreign country the local news team arrive at the accident first, usually with only a sparse spattering of foreign language, they quickly reported the coach in-bedded in a motorway bridge, little remaining of the front, little remaining of the back with a heavy goods vehicle nearly slicing the back into two, then tipping over onto at least one passing car. Spanish tomatoes everywhere across both sides of the motorway. Now the death toll had increased with the comment at least twenty children now encased in the nearly destroyed vehicle. Fire a very real concern; rescuers removed to a safe distance, fire services trying to prevent fuel igniting. Moments after the plane had landed, two coaches full of parents expecting the worse, hoping for a miracles, sped under police escort to the first of the hospitals where casualties had been taken by those blue light flashing, screaming, ambulances. Only when arriving at the first hospital did parents understand that this would be the first of four where casualties had been rushed into. A troop of tearful, starting in the morgue, into accident/emergency, then a ward, already a Roman Catholic priest at the entrance to the mortuary. No one from the school in the room of the dead, four families left at the first, onward under police escort. On 20 kilometres to hospital two. Now two way radio contact between a police officer on each of the coaches with an unseen member of the rescue teams. Grim news emerging regarding those trapped within part of the coach rear, cutting equipment now in use, medics administered oxygen, pain killers to the trapped. Second hospital, first of the school children dead. Distraught parents no longer on the departing coach, not really enough room in Accident/Emergency for parents to sit with a maimed child, compromise one at a time, distraught discussions on limb amputation. After the third hospital the group now reduced with only one coach needed. Desperation setting in. If not in hospital 4, reality of a dead child, ice cold, still unrecorded within the tangled tomb of that chamber of death once a coach of happy teenagers.

Grandfather constantly remaining positive for those hanging onto the modern curse of mankind (mobile telephone) at home only wanting to hear positive positives. Running down battery, back home literally praying for Sebastian to be well and alive. He wasn't in the fourth hospital, only three families left to find their children. For the authorities, that agonizing decision, what to do with the three grieving families?

It had been the mayor of the local large town that had organized the coaches, the police escort, he followed the coaches around in a police car. Grandad's P.A. (personal assistant) who had achieved all the organizing while the group were preparing to travel, while they were flying. Miss Hazelwood came from the old school, unmarried, worked for Grandfather since leaving a red brick university some 37 years ago. Her ability always to anticipate grandfather. She did not have to wake the mayor, he had been involved in the accident within minutes of the tragic event happening. He would say after the event he did nothing special for the important man (Grandad), untrue, it was he who against all advise from the emergency services instructed that all three families should be allowed onto the crash site. He himself a grandfather, a father. Along the closed motorway the distraught group of 11, 3 x 2 parents and three grandparents, the mayor, the Chief of Police. Ahead the area of the accident illuminated as if daytime, a shout from the driver as they approach the baying pack of media. Out went the interior coach lights, windows previously having their blinds closed. Paparazzi only interested in that scoop (valuable) picture of the preferably dead children/teenagers. Rumour already rife of the importance of a grandchild of a world famous businessman. Pulling over, blocking the view of the media, some 100 metres from the scenes, medics produced hard hats, visible jackets, which the group must wear. Ears listening between the tears. "There are three boys together, two in seats, one in the aisle. They are alive, critical, now on life support equipment. It is as if they are cocooned together in a nest of tangled metalwork, lengths of metal work sticking into their bodies, limbs mainly, one with metal work through the right side of the chest, therefore missing the heart, compounding the problem. Time is against them. You are aware how long it has been since the crash. There are still dead bodies in other vehicles. None are of the children from the school." One of the brave father's choked out a question, "What are their chances of survival?" The answer, with compassion, "prepare for the very worst."

Sebastian arrived at a specialist teaching hospital twenty-seven days later. One of the three died at the scene, the other boy also in intensive care, his prognosis better than Sebastian who remained in a coma. He died with the family around him never having recovered, when a religious family (Christian for Sebastian) has that belief in faith tested to the ultimate. A life changing happening for Doris. She could no longer believe how a 'God' could be so cruel, but and a big but, for the sake of the family, she continued to keep up an outward appearance of religious conformity.

Over the years, grandfather died, the generation following (her father, his brother and sister) lost grandfather's ability to see the next opportunity for business. Still a strong global player which the stock market quickly judged as a takeover potential (translating that means potential large fee income plus, the big plus, of using insider knowledge to make capital from buying shares at the most advantageous time, not of course in ones own name. No! In some investment fund with nominee directors, nominee shareholders, in one of those tax havens of the world.) Eventually the ruling family relented; pushed somewhat by the trustee of the Charitable Trust that held a 20% stake in the business from those philanthropic days of the Victorian generation. Having cashed in the family fortune, yes a cash transaction. Even Doris received a few million short of eighty million pounds, a fortune to a University student, an unbelievable fortune to 99.999% of the adult population.

Directly resulting from her concern of the Christian God, she had from not long after Sebastian had been taken from her, studied in great depth World religions. In schooling academic matters she studied science, by Sixth Form, those two years before University she specialized nearly as an expert in Chemistry, Space Science (Astro Physics), Space Travel History as an extra new type of subject. Fairly well undefined as space travel as such seemed to have stalled almost as soon as it started. In addition to a more normal subject of Human Biology.

After securing her University place a year out was taken to spend time at both NASA America and Baikonur, the old centre of the Soviet Union space programme. Regardless of what these 'space travel people' thought her primary objective to discover 'why' had space exploration made no meaningful progress since the International Space Station established itself those not many miles above the sea level of the Earth.

She remembered all too well what her grandfather used to say. "If Super Powers (at the time the Soviet Union, the United States of America) need information they will point the International Space Station at 'an interest'", then he would say that it is not International anyway. He was really quite passionate about it saying what do they really do up there in their separate sections? Forget about those cover story experiments their public relations people give them to play with. Super Powers jointly spying on the world, he believed.

Doris had a long term relationship with a lady of similar age who lived in one of the houses provided by the 'factory'. Gwen (Gwendaline) had parents who were both middle management at the 'factory'. Father one of those production managers, mother in customer (homeland) relations. To Doris the relationship had just been a natural progression since Sebastian died, she responded with venom to anyone who called her 'gay', 'lesbian'. Yes they held hands/arms in public, kissed in public. Her life, her decision.

In the beginning Gwen's parents feared the relationship would result in them losing their jobs and therefore the home. Christianity wears a badge of tolerance, yes people talked, Doris constantly saying people will always gossip even if I had a boyfriend who might be King of England. Then she would remind everyone that the factory had pioneered employment of staff from the then 'British Commonwealth'. Colour or creed not the concern, 'ability, hardworking' that to be the judgement.

During the long summer break after the first year at the famous University, Doris rented a house near the beach, at Sea Paling (Norfolk) to complete an academic paper on the finding about 'The Far Side of the Moon'. Gwen contributed by 'typing up' the manuscript that Doris insisted should not be seen or read by anyone else. They were not alone, Edward employed as a security protection for Doris, had been one of a group of security personnel employed by the family, concerned for the possible kidnap for ransom of any of the wealthy family members.

Now Doris had very particular concerns as her soon to be published paper would come as a bombshell to those so-called Super Powers. By diligent research, she had discovered about 'the dark side of the moon'.

Edward had gone to the toilet, upon returning 'his girls' as he always called them, were gone, the shooting star he later commented the brightest he had ever seen.

Over those first few days of the 'disappeared' the full extent of the missing entered that 24 hour media. News reporters now so stretched that the most junior found themselves in places they had only dreamt of visiting. Speculation rife as to what had really taken place. Why two people from every country? Why young people? Why this? Why that? Why the other? Speculation at fever pitch when a copy of what Doris had been writing found it's way into the public domain.

Doris had given Edward this task. He laughed when she had, some weeks before, told him if anything happened to her it was his duty to take whatever she had written to the London Times. When they disappeared he spent the first four minutes doing exactly what she had instructed. She had provided two copies of the updated writings the night before, afterwards he thought, "did she know a terrible event would take place?" Edward always carried a walking stick as his first line of attack/defence. Doris gave him a strong, thick, branch like walking stick but partly hollow, as if it had been a sword stick.

Many security guards have a bulletproof vest. Edward had one that incorporated a back support strap, a medical belt, within that support strap he hid the second copy. Doris could not have made her instructions any clearer. Edward would take the one copy to a long-time journalist friend at the London Times, the second to her mother.

In her paper Doris suggested that the Big Bang Theory represented nothing other than exactly the same event as happened with the creation of a human life form. Putting it simply other mature Universe created a new Universe, her Universe, that now continues to expand, itself to create another Universe in time to come. Can the human brain understand that two mature Universe would produce a new baby Universe.

CHAPTER FOUR - FIVE EYES

Betty, with Philip, was on secondment to the 'Five Eyes' site of the New Zealand Security Service (GCSB) at the Waihopai Intercept Station on South Island, New Zealand. Yes, New Zealand has spies!

'Five Eyes' is the name of a group of countries that work together as a group agreeing not to spy on each other. They are United States of America, Canada, Australia, New Zealand, United Kingdom. Since an upgrade in 2009, Waihopai had the capability of 'full take' collection of satellite intercepts. Collected information is fed into XKeyscore database operated by the United States National Security Agency. At that moment the information is available to all members of the 'Five Eyes Group'. Surveillance from Waihopai is targeted at Tuvalu Naura, Kiribati, Vanuata and the Soloman Islands, New Caledonia, and French Polynesia, Samoa, Fiji, Tonga. An impressive list of South Sea tourist destinations. Betty and Philip had been an item since second year students when their computing ability had been assessed as the finest of their generation, one professor as 'paranormal' as so called 'boffins', they only enjoyed each other's company. They lived together, two 'boffins' in a world comprised of an intellectual underclass. Money of no meaning, they always having to be reminded to have 'money in their pockets/purse'. Happily they would have worked for nothing other than board and lodging and clothes. None computing activities did not exist in their world. Philip just about knew that New Zealanders were rugby fanatics as more than once at school his inability at rugby was ridiculed Now he could destroy any of these mere mortals credit rating for ever, in less time than it takes to say rugby.

Betty achieved the distinction at school of the last of her year to achieve womanhood, even today it took more than one stare to see if she had breasts, her fine feminine structured face gave her away as a women. Their final year dissertation only understood by each other, eventually the University authorities requested an expect from Waihopai to assess if they were in a world of computing fantasy.

Waihopai answered by employing them instantly on the most top secret work currently in operation. Could Waihopai computing security be compromised? Could an outsider at the touch of a switch obtain whatever they wanted? They were on Operation Snowdon. Management decided to leave them alone with a review after four weeks to explain, what, if any progress they had made directly to the five members of senior management. Around mid-afternoon of the Thursday of the first week they asked for an immediate meeting with the Head of Station who by agreed convention was a New Zealander. The purpose of a New Zealander Head of Station in order that he (it had always been a he) could answer to the New Zealand parliament. At that immediate time a meeting scheduled with 'visitors' from the other 'Five Eyes' countries found itself interrupted by Betty and Philip who would not be put off by those security guards stationed outside the meeting room. As normal Betty spoke first, words that no one present at the meeting would ever forget. "The system 'Escalon" had been compromised." Acute fear engraved on long time experienced security chief faces.

From the instant official fear those present were later congratulated on the break neck speed of their response. John (whatever his real name might have been) the New Zealand

Chief looked them squarely in the eye saying, "Are you sure?" Without an instant of hesitation they both replied "Yes." From John, the then obvious second question, "Which government?" to which Philip replied, "too early to say but not Russia. We believe China."

Now the other four members of 'Five Eyes" were onto their Station Chiefs, only Australia existed in the state of awakeness. America, Canada, United Kingdom needed to be woken up. John again to the two, "How long do you need to find out which Government?" Betty this time, with as much emotion as if she had just cracked her 'always' breakfast boiled eggs, then, "Perhaps three more days." John again, "for how long have we been compromised?" That produced a very positive answer from Philip. "Since your 2009 upgrade." Profanities hit the air, as if there would be no tomorrow. Betty making matters worse with again words that no one would forget, "Your systems are naive."

Heads of Government, Presidents, Prime Ministers, do not like a middle of the night, 'get up call' this news warranted more than a 'get up now' call. One question. Has our systems been compromised or only that within New Zealand? Immediate plans were made to fly out the two 'boffins' to America early the next morning. Hours had gone by, the 'boffins' eventually instructed to return home to pack, be ready for a very early morning pick up for the military plane flight to America. On exiting the base they ran quickly with heads bowed in a frightful thunderstorm through sky split from side to side by rolling lightning, that lightning with no end, constantly appearing from one end of the night sky to another.

No one could recall the shooting star through the lightning, they were gone, disappeared, the brightest stars of the computing world. Where were Betty and Philip, Mainland China?

When did humanity lose the ability to live in harmony with the planet home humanity received as a gift? Humanity conditioned on the third rock from an unimportant star lost in the

Milky Way of an estimates 100 to 400 billion stars, humanity so clever it can only gestimate, there is a huge difference between 100 to 400 billion stars. Of course, that is stars, how many planets? Humanity has no provable calculation.

Humanity contented to be alone in the Universe, contented in a belief of supreme self-importance. Imagine, from out there 'another' appearing to turn the status quo upside down, the overweight rich become the starving poor.

Before the start of World War II, in 1939, before he became Prime Minister, Winston Churchill wrote,

'I am not sufficiently conceited to think that my Sun is the only one with a family of planets.'

'I for one am not so immensely impressed by the success we are making of our civilization here that I am prepared to think we are the only spot in the immense Universe which contains living thinking creatures.'

More than 70 years on in time would he say the same? What in the science of this great Universe would have changed his fundamental thinking of 'I for one am not so immensely impressed that I am prepared to think we are the only spot in this immense Universe which contains living thinking creatures or that we are the highest type of mental and physical development which has ever appeared in the vast compass of space and time?'

Arrogance of humanity will conclude, yes, we are the only 'living, thinking creatures.'

Consider what degree of change would prevent 'humanity' standing up straight, not becoming a 'dollop' of squashed humanity or what degree of change to prevent feet touching the ground, humanity turn into 'floating humanity?' What little change would be needed for the journey of the Earth around its Sun to alter? Could the weight of humanity have a 'pull and push' effect on that delicate balance existing for billions of years? Humanity is a very elaborate way to describe those that take out or destroy that which existed before humanity first planted its oversized boots into the purity of 'before human time' (BHT). Humanity is deliberately negligent of that only place in the Universe it has found to plunder. Swat a fly, tread on an ant, that community from which they exist will not miss them, 'humanity' the self-appointed executioner.

Let humanity feed the animal kingdom, then execute the fed animals then eat the animal flesh. Wrap the flesh in a nice presentable package. Do not show any blood. Mass media tells us that in some cities of the world, 'children' do not understand that milk comes from 'cows' or do not know what a cow is. Milk comes from the supermarket shelf, next they might think apples grow on trees. (Ha ha).

In some countries of the world 'wildlife' only exists to be hunted, killed, eaten. Look at the vast areas of flat land in Russia, in the Ukraine. Perhaps some birds but forget about rabbits. What do the inevitable rats eat, dirt?

That vast expanse of European flat lands that provided ease for those conquering military to advance with consummate ease. Humanity easily, repeatedly, taking that one small step to killing other humanity. What mechanism is missing from humanity brain that allows the idea of 'killing humanity' to be acceptable? History allowing more and more technologically advanced methods of humanity killing, maiming each other, without even the excuse of killing for food. No! Human meat not to be eaten by other humanity, that same brain showing revulsion at eating other humanity flesh.

At this time in history, two potential mass destruction weapons exist, germ warfare and the nuclear bomb. History suggests that all weapons are used at some time. It is not difficult that home (the World) would be a better place without humanity, some species losers, e.g. who would milk the cows, but most gainers in a humanity free world, or should humanity be given another chance to be a better humanity? In the short term, labeling food as is compulsory for cigarettes? A label on, say a chicken, saying when it was born, when it died, how it died, then as technology advances, a picture of the chicken alive.

Where fossil fuels are consumed, a recognition of the age, perhaps Sat Nat providing information on a car journey, telling how many miles are provided for every one hundred millions year old fossil fuel used. As usual for humanity, no recognition of vital resources plundered for short-term benefits, as definite as death, fossil fuels will be exhausted. Will humanity have to walk and use those legs again? Or will some seismic event cause the Earth crust to cascade into those voluminous areas of extraction precipitated by fossil fuel extraction? Not so sure footed then, experts who predict no long-term effects to the subterranean. Don't mention the word 'cancer' in case those fossil fuel extractors might be proven responsible, more than one expert commented 'where was cancer?' before the combustion engine? A note of danger, two 'C's,' cancer, combustion.

For how much longer will the authorities keep secret that information as to where the cancer originated, a chemical warfare experiment that went wrong when 'cancer' escaped from the research facility? No doubt not so dramatic as that, no doubt an everyday chemical of the modern industrial world. It is perhaps a surprise that some religious group/cult have not promoted that it is a 'curse on none believers.'

Fear in the air as the hundreds of the 'Disappeared' awoke together, instantly as if a light switch went 'on' for all at the same time. Within the same instant a voice, no one speaking; no one could see anyone speaking, obviously a simultaneous explosion into the brain. They say in early humanity life 'telepathic' was the norm.

In the minds of The Disappeared, who am I, you will immediately think of words, like Gods, Founders, Protectors, it is not important, we are what we are. You will be asking where are they; we cannot see them, I will only believe if I can touch and feel?' Thoughts continuing, 'your Universe is part of another whole, think of a string of 'D.N.A.. Your Universe is only a minute D.N.A. sequence of the whole. You will not understand, there is no beginning, there is no end, to 'Life of the Whole' is infinite. We sense you are all troubled (all non-telepathy) at such a dynamic thought of your Universe, we use a different word, existing with others are part of; interconnected; perhaps think another way.'

'What do your scientists believe exists beyond that place called Universe, nothingness, emptiness as a vacuum? Naive thinking of mankind humanity. You are permanently afraid if you cannot touch, cannot see, cannot smell, cannot hear. We will give you no new education at this time until you have understood about your 'Universe.' Restored to you all the original way humanity communicated through the mind with no need to talk, as it was in your beginning.'

That light, having encompassed all their surroundings, now dimmed, a burst of talking, not about the information of an infinite of 'Another Whole.' No, typical of humanity, 'where are we?' 'How did we get here?' 'What are we doing here?' A hubbub of the self-interested, self-concerned thinking. Will I see family again? What about the money in my bank account? Are the car keys safe? Having been given the answer to the ultimate question of 'The Universe' small minds concentrate on the mankind inhibitions to a free thinking mind.

Concern for food, water, toilets; those basics that show mankind as an inefficient user of the gifts of the planet Earth's resources. How many individuals are employed in nothing other than producing/providing food to keep that inefficient human body ticking over? Many more than in that banking industry that actually produces nothing, but very highly paid for doing it.

Doris sat on a stone. 'That hurts,' a powerful electrical type shock through her brain, automatically Doris jumped up, looking down anxiously at the stone. Brushing her long calf length solid royal blue skirt to remove any dust/dirt. That electrical type pain through her brain. 'I am not dirty, Doris.' A face as white as a sheet contrasted with that royal blue skirt, a credit to

Doris with her spoken reply. 'So what is your name?' Again, pain in the brain, less strong. 'I am a Computron.' Doris, still talking, 'Is that a collective name or your own personal/private name?' Can you get a hint of humour in another brain thought? 'That's very forward of you, young lady.' Now a group were looking at Doris talking to herself. Doris continued. 'Come on, what is your name? I have never, ever met a talking stone called Computron. Anyway, how do you know my name?' 'I can tell you all the names of the 'humanits' here; we Computrons absorb all knowledge exactly like a sponge. Would you like to know about your 'humanits' from your beginning of time? My name is Betty.'

Now cross, with a cross voice, Doris demanded. 'Where are we?' Doris is very bright, however, this thought transfer is a wee bit strange, she thought, receiving a response from Betty. 'No it is not.' Doris with more confidence. 'Betty, where are we? Where am I?' Betty, 'What a basic question. You are on the dark side of the Moon attached to Earth.'

Everyone had, by some miracle (telepathy?) heard Betty say, 'You are on the dark side of the moon attached to Earth.' Not a sound, no screaming, no shouting, no crying. More of 'we are all in the same ship together.' Doris, who had often watched a television programme with her grandfather called 'Dad's Army' kept thinking, 'We're doomed, we're doomed.' (A catchphrase of one of the characters). Now experiencing the greatest event in her life, her mind over-run with 'We're doomed, we're doomed.'

Doris to Betty, but everyone conscious of the conversation. Afterward, Doris thinking, 'what a stupid question.' 'Have you arrived at the same time as us?' Betty replied, 'In your method of counting time 127234 years, six months, three hours, twenty-six minutes, is that precise enough?' Almost dismissive Doris asked, 'Are you alone here, do you have family here?' Scathing, Betty replies, 'What a parochial, short sighted question.' Saying 127234 years, six months, three hours (now twenty-seven minutes) brought no response, not even a blink of the eye. 'To be straight forward,' Doris replied, 'It is nonsense, you can't be that old. Anyway, how do you know English?' From somewhere in the crowd Anna from St Petersburg volunteered 'And do you speak Russian?' Not to be outdone, Anastasia from Ukraine, 'And do you speak Ukrainian?' Can a stone get angry? 'We are not speaking, we are communicating through our minds. I can speak any language. Now Doris, Anna, Anastasia communicate together in the Welsh language." Embarrassment all round. Without speaking a word, the three were exchanging thoughts in Spanish. Now the stone (Computron) continued. 'You are all going to communicate with Doris in your own native language, and we will find out how many languages Doris has learned.' Without exception, everyone received a reply specific to the question. Very difficult to decide who was the most surprised, the least surprised was Betty the Computron, who nearly suggested everyone sit down to receive a lecture on their newfound ability. Betty realized that the brightest and best of their generation were now thirsty for knowledge, that light that had dimmed returned, brighter, more intense, mind words again. 'Betty, you might as well continue. However, the basic fact will be repeated. Earth humanity must remember 'your universe is part of another whole, think of a string of D.N.A., sequence of the whole. You will not understand there is no beginning; there is no end. That is very impossible for your minds to begin to understand as your Earth-crust humanity has the opinion that it is an important, an all consuming, without equal, without competition for supremacy of the Earth. Arrogant stupidity, poisoning themselves, destroying the very fabric of what you call Earth at an alarming rate. A humanity that is willfully destroying what it had been given, so self-important with no realization that the Earth could cease in any moment of time. Nature exists in equilibrium, your universe exists in equilibrium. That example again, explained as D.N.A., exists in equilibrium. From the beginning to the end of all that is known, all that is unknown, to think that a 'neutrino' has a greater knowledge of the Universe than you do, greater knowledge of the planets around your Earth than any of your scientists. If only you could stop a neutrino asking for 'spatial' information, what a mammoth amount Astro-physicists could learn. Would a neutrino scream and shout if caught/trapped, or perhaps change shape to escape? Your scientists have not the faintest knowledge. No longer think of them as traveling through the Universe, they travel through the D.N.A. of never ending 'Universe'. In a motion from the beginning of time to the end of time, perhaps an end is a humanity concept, there is no end a 'continuum' for which your humanity has no adequate language. Your humanity is afraid to admit to the unknown, a humanity giving nonsense names to galaxy, stars, and planets. Your humanity would not have enough names to name galaxies in your Universe, forget about naming stars and planets.'

'Futility to name, to number. Your scientists with their limited knowledge calculate/estimate that the number of galaxy in this Universe (your home Universe) is 2 billion (a new estimate at the end of 2016 calculates the Universe contains 200 billion galaxies, 10, yes ten times more). Your feeble, fragile brain is unable to produce an image of the number 200 billion. Think another way; how long would it take to count to 200 billion?'

'Counting to 200 billion, they calculate that at counting at 1 second a number it will take 999,999,999 seconds to reach 1 billion. Yes, you can argue for another second, or thirty-one years, two hundred and fifty-one days, seven hours, forty-six minutes and thirty-nine seconds. Now multiply by 200, say 6200 years (100 lifetimes) it then sounds beyond belief, continuous counting from about 4200 BC, no sleep, no food, no water. All those family members that will be born and die during the counting, at least 100 generations.'

'Thinking beyond 200 billion galaxies, how many stars in a galaxy? How many planets to each star? The human brain with 'no earthly' possibilities of comprehending the numbers. Poor person of humanity too busy watching a television programme to think about anything other than what to eat and drink, an in-between programme snack. In the greatness of the Universe, many television addicts have calculated how much water to put into a kettle so that a hot drink can be made during the commercial break. Enjoyment of a programme interrupted to entice the watching addict to make a purchase of that mostly unnecessary of capitalist production, national broadcasters looking down into that all self-importance, tell the populace how to think.'

Greater intensity of the light. 'Karren' thought 'is the light getting angry?' 'Your humanity in a belief of self-importance, none destructibility, did those dinosaurs that existed for a 100 million years have the same mindset of indestructibility. According to your humanity, you rule the Earth; everything is subordinate to humanity wants. Are movements in the earth crust (earthquakes) more frequent as resources for humanity are removed from within the Earth? So you take out 'oil', what fills the space left behind? To be honest, your humanity has no interest in any bad outcome. How many of you have driven around as a single person in a motor vehicle using up precious resources of your Earth? Worst offenders, those commuters who could live closer to their workplace and then walk to work.'

'What in or on the Earth can halt the progress of mankind? Flood, pestilence, disease; humanity survives everything it believes. What are they saying? Most of humanity will have cancer at some time in their lives. Cancer cells that now replicate antibiotics.'

'That new sleep illness with sleep loss due to having that mobile phone on all night, phones and tablets producing a generation of sleep deprivation. The human body at any age unable to function without adequate sleep time. Reports of young teenagers trying to live with only two or three hours sleep, an illness caused by continuous texting, playing games, watching the unsuitable. Parental controls non-existent, 'Oh leave them alone, they are quiet, causing no trouble, hurting no-one.' Ignorant parents opting for the soft, easy option not thinking of children falling asleep during class/lesson time, unable to concentrate. Irrational, bad-tempered, unreliable; what will happen when adulthood is reached? A mobile, a tablet, now like a drug user always needing more of the same, more thrills, a compulsion to disregard reality, the desire to spread tittle tattle, to project personal harm to another, to humiliate another member of humanity about any visible imperfection. Those mass following of 'tweets'; how many followers do you have to read your self-important thoughts, have a race to release that important thought before anyone else.' Is it only so few letters to a 'tweet' to save the illiterate the problem of constructing a sentence.'

Betty Computron gave an appearance of fidgeting, obviously annoyed, waiting to address these pathetically equipped human things. Betty started again. 'We Computrons, inhabit everywhere, retaining all knowledge, knowledge to answer most questions. In no way do Computrons fit into your accepted view of what 'life' in the Universe is like. Somehow life is 'bipeds', is as far as your feeble minds can think, the total preoccupation that 'life' as a prerequisite needing 'water' needing 'oxygen'. You always depict alien bipeds as aggressive, then the extremes, very beautiful, very aggressive, very ugly, very stupid/unintelligent. Your preoccupation with 'are we (humanity) alone in the Universe?' it is such a brainless, self-centered, self-importance, ignorance of a Universe beyond the feeble knowledge exhibited by your humanity. Your humanity (whatever you think that means) dictated by a belief in money, that worthless paper or overvalued metals of gold/silver, the so called valuable rare stones e.g. diamonds.'

A thought entered the minds of the group from Bededita, the young physiotherapist from Rio De Janeiro (Brazil), directed at Betty Computron. 'I am blind therefore I cannot see, why should I be blind when nearly all the Earth population can have a visual experience?' Bededita did express an opinion of 'this is unfair' and 'I am disadvantaged'. Emotionless, Betty replied, 'It is not a technical difficulty to restore your sight, to the greater Universe it is impossible to understand as to why so much of your resources have been used by your political elite (as they think of themselves) to cause death, destruction, disease, despair.'

(Continuing), 'Chhab (Indian doctor) is sitting on a Computron named Alfred. If Chhab takes Bededita to Computron Alfred, he will explain the very simple technique (not surgery) to restore sight.' Blank looks on two faces, Chhab worried about what she would be expected to do, Bededita thinking 'how can I trust my health to these Computron?' Alfred, with indignation, 'up to you Bededita, if you want to see. It will not hurt.' Bedidita in reply, 'it is difficult, everything I am taking on trust, will I still be alive in 2 minutes?' Computron Alfred undisturbed and well aware he had a captive audience now watching just sent out the thought, 'this is not a miracle. Your human brain controls you. When you discovered D.N.A. sequencing, it should have been followed by a full understanding of the 'wiring' in the humanity brain. All are interconnected, interactive, interdependent.' Interdependent still hanging in the air (so to speak) when a yelp from Bededita, a very thunderous yell. 'I can see.' Ignacio only had one thought, 'what will she think when she sees me?' The air sucked out of his body with Bededita squeezing, hugging, kissing every last breath, both were ecstatic. Stunned silence from all around. 'It was a miracle', the generalized thought only for Alfred to administer the strongest of rebukes with, 'it is not difficult as long as you understand the brain.' Chad had moved closer. Chhab, who went pale, weak at the knees, short of breath, then asked, 'what happened?' Talking, not thinking. Chhab was talking. 'I had this diagram in my mind exactly like a London Underground map. Clearly, I could see where the interconnected problem existed. It is so simple.' Continuing, 'it is as if D.N.A. had only been developed as a tool for police crime investigations and there existed no need to progress a further step into the wiring of the brain.' At which point Computron Alfred thought, 'to many vested interests is the money to be made from those who cannot see, speak, hear!!' D.N.A. more difficult to sequence than the interrelated activities of the brain. Forgetting their ability to communicate without speaking a general hub-bub of excited talking reverberated around the humanits, the word miracle constantly in use.

Mary, the doctor from Eritrea, looked at Computron Alfred talking, asking if a similar 'cure' (she couldn't think of a better word) for those children dying from starvation that she worked with. Alfred gave a stark, abrupt answer, 'No, starvation is an effect of humanities own actions, this is a matter that your humanity can correct itself. It is a self-inflicted medical condition by your humanity on itself; all your humanity has to do is to share with some equality the fruits of your home 'rock'.' The immediate outcry over the word 'rock' from the humanits who requested the word, 'Earth.' Both Computrons joined in, 'You are only a lump of rock, not very large with no particular value to your solar system or the Milky Way or your so called Universe.' Stunned silence, humanity put in its place, of no value, no consequence, if the 'Earth rock' were not there it would not be missed.

Self-conceited humanity more than alarmed at the thoughts of precious Earth being no more than a rock, then someone tried to remember that television comedy, what was it called? Third Rock from The Sun? Very prophetic. It is a salutary thought for Earth crust humanity to be relegated to 'a rock of no consequence in the Universe'. Oh dear! Self-importance Earth Crust humanity no longer in control of the home solar system, the Milky Way, the Universe. In as much as a Computron has an amused personality, both Betty and Alfred were much amused. It is a long story told in another 'Always Never' book confirming that Computrons also exist on that 'rock' called 'Earth'.

For all the young humanits gathered in this place, a lifetime of understanding of the importance of humanity, the importance of the Earth, ingrained into the fabric of thinking. That general belief that for other intelligence to exist it must have water, it must have breathing air, that it would have two legs. Humanity is supreme, any other life/intelligence could only be subordinate. An early BBC radio programme of the 1950's summed up this attitude in Journey Into Space 'The Red Planet'. As the spacecraft entered orbit around 'Mars' one crew member says to the crew Doctor 'that at this very moment two men of Mars are sitting on Mars looking at Earth, one smiling to the other saying that place would have too much oxygen for us to breathe'.

What Earth humanity uses as a template for life in the Universe is only that in which Earth humanity stays alive. The ultimate fear of Earth humanity that something out there will be more intelligent. Yes! Must be the answer, just remember those neutrinos (or whatever they call themselves). Of course, that question 'why would you want to visit that rock of an insignificant sun (star) with all its inherent humanity made problems?'

In St Petersburg, the office of 'Isvestia' continued with the story of the Disappeared on a regular, irregular basis. Aza (female name) who first broke the story, now had a researcher who compiled a library of each and every one of the Disappeared, without a doubt national security services kept the same information. Aza, after a few weeks, published another dramatic headline, 'The Disappeared, The Cream of a Generation,' that produced worldwide syndication, more fame for Aza.

By one method or another, she had contacted all of the hundreds of families who had lost a loved one, more than one bogus claim had been exposed, all the families had her email address in case of any new information. Aza found one couple in Switzerland who did not fit the mold of 'the cream of the generation.' They were a few years older than the established age range of 20 to 25, they were the only couple actually married, neither had attended a university, neither showed any ability at original thinking. No other words could describe them any better than 'Mr. and Mrs. Ordinary.' Both employed by an internationally known bank in the Geneva office, aspiring to nothing higher than lesser middle banking clerks, in fact, that type of employee required by every organization to do the ordinary, tedious daily/weekly routine where thinking would be a handicap. Gretta, along with Alfonso, had left school as soon as possible, both joining the bank as junior clerks (or in military language 'canon fodder'). They lived in a flat with Gretta's mother, her father having been killed in a bizarre military accident when she was fifteen. In Switzerland, men attend voluntarily military exercises often up to the age of 49 keeping their equipment (not ammunition) at home. Conscription is at 18 when all receive basic training. Gretta's father had risen through the volunteer ranks of the first armoured brigade based at Lake Geneva. He had the rank of Major for his specialist communication skills. It is often forgotten that the Swiss Military regularly provide troops to N.A.T.O. (North Atlantic Treaty Organisation). It was on such a mission that he was killed in a bomb explosion. Gretta, as an only child, knew she would inherit the family home on the death of her mother. Their two incomes, with no rent or mortgage to pay, provided a comfortable way of life. Children were not in the mind of Gretta (Alfonso did not have a say), she was a career girl. Her ambition to fill dead men's (ladies) shoes in the many years to come, ending up as Principal Clerk in the 'Numbered Accounts Department', specifically, the 'None Active' numbered accounts. Some of these 'None Active' accounts go back hundreds of year, many with huge balances belonging to persons the bank knew were dead, e.g. German military from the two Great Wars, members of the Romanov dynasty who did not survive the 1917 Revolution. This is what Gretta liked, names behind the numbers, some were very exotic like American gangsters from the Prohibition Period, members of Soviet Politburos, of those far flung Asian republics now awash with oil. Banks like deposits that no-one can collect the money from, increased capital base for lending purposes, capital that costs nothing, a bankers dream. The 'clerks' skill in the 'None Active Numbered Accounts Department' – firstly to inform the investment department when individual funds needed to be reinvested. Once a year activity would take place on an account as if to prove to regulators that the account continued to receive instructions. Secondly (and here the skill), to deal with any inquiry from an outside source as to the ownership of an account, even worse a party trying to claim funds for repatriation. None of these account records were kept other than handwritten in large leather bound ledgers, each ledger with five locks. Keys to the hundreds of ledgers under the control of another department kept/stored, within the underground vaults, which contained the numerous safes and safety deposit boxes. With numerous safes within the eighteen vaults, it would be a burglar/thief with mind reading skills to discover that one that glistened with gold bars, coins, jewelry. Banks practice required Senior Management to inspect each airtight safe once a week always on a Monday starting at 10.45am, a thief with knowledge would have seven (7) clear days to effect a removal of valuables. More than one attempt had been made by management to reduce the costs of the security staff which had to be employed 24 hours a day, 365 (366) days a year.

Alfonso worked in that department that kept records of who the numbered bank accounts actually belonged to; each numbered account had a code name (e.g. horse) or code number. This had always been the system since the beginning, again, lockable ledgers, hand written, only accessed in the vault when authorized. To the casual observer, the two sets of ledgers ((1) transactions of numbered accounts and (2) ownership of numbered accounts) were identical, to the banking employees the fundamental difference on the leather spine where gold embossed letters indicated the difference. 'A' for transactions, 'Z' for account ownership, the only other numbers on the spine were the ledger numbers.

Alfonso had undertaken his military service, after what happened to Gretta's father, he did not intend doing any more than the absolute minimum. Sport never provided an interest, all his spare time and money went into his 'Star Wars' memorabilia collection. His most valuable item to date a boxed vinyl cafe jawa for which he had paid $1000. He often counted up his collection, always wearing white museum gloves, now nearly worth $100,000. Gretta supported him; her mother thought they were both quite mad. In her opinion they should be producing grandchildren for her, not acting like children themselves. In that respect it was a good job she was unaware (as was Alfonso) of a surprise birthday holiday to Florida that Gretta had purchased. Alfonso would be able to visit those 'Star Wars' themed parks.

In any business it sometimes happens that illness coupled with holidays means that the rules get broken as to 'key holders' so it was that at the time of the shooting stars both Gretta and Alfonso were left as the main key holders, they, with the keys disappeared. Not the next weekend, but the one after that, parents of the Disappeared received $250,000 into their bank account as if from nowhere. Directors of the bank assumed that money taken was from the 'None Active' deposits, especially since they knew the depositors were dead. It had to be Gretta and Alfonso working out a sophisticated fraud. Who would complain of deposits of the dead disappearing? Who would believe Gretta and Alfonso could be so untrustworthy? Directors more than confident these funds would never be claimed decided to keep the whole theft secret within the bank. Colleagues of Gretta knew about the intended visit to 'Star Wars' theme park in Florida, informed a director, the director then sending their most senior compliance officer to America to start digging for any information about the Disappeared.

Graham from Sydney looked at his watch, which showed the same date as it was in Sydney with time only having advanced 49 minutes. Disbelief. Betty Computron understanding his perplexed thoughts confirmed his watch continued to work, continued to display the correct Earth time. Needless to say, Graham expressed greater disbelief, 'how could he have arrived here within a time span of 49 Earth minutes?' Continuing with his thinking, he had little doubt that most of that forty-nine minutes had been spent 'here,' impossible if he/the group really were on the dark side of the Moon attached to the third rock of a fairly inferior star. No doubt the reality more like the supposed none visits of Americans to the Moon, he must be involved in a conspiracy story of his own, probably in those vast expanses of North-East California exclusively existing for the American military, particularly the 'Black Operations' that involved all sections. Financed with funds from the American government, never itemized, in the interests of National Security. A few billion dollars here or there easily lost in the vastness of American military spend. Most politicians are eager for 'Life After Politics' with a few directorships within the great expanse of the American military machine, the reward for not asking too many questions.

Without hesitation, Betty Computron made sure Graham from Sydney understood that he really had a presence on the dark side of the moon, as did all the others from Earth. Graham thinking, 'safe, secure in some type of building with Earth life supporting oxygen, no funny space suit, what a disappointment, childhood dreams of walking in space in a space suit dashed in a moment.'

Without exception, all the Earth people now had the same pressing question. 'How did we all arrive here with no recollection of any form of transportation?' Betty knew the answer; somehow her mind sealed that information, the Earth people having no knowledge of her then thoughts. Computrons had developed 'a mind in compartments', for them easy to block-off the feeble minds of Earth Crust humanity, who had managed to lose the gift of communicating without speech/talking. (Imagine Earth with no language barriers, no misunderstanding in a translation, no excuse for conflict, how was such an ability lost?)

Betty Computron thought now would be a good time to give information about the 'Dark Side of the Moon,' without extolling any conspiracy theories as to why Earth Crust ceased traveling to the Moon. 'There are some buildings similar to this one spread over the Dark Side of the Moon if you think of Earth Crust humanity only, then you are inhabited. If you can open your minds that other 'life' exists besides us Computrons. Many

Computrons are here, many Computrons can be found on your homeland called Earth, perhaps when you get back, they will introduce themselves to you.' An audible relief, did those few words let the cat out of the bag? 'When you get back.' With one accord, one thought, 'when and how do we get back to Earth?' No response from either of the Computrons or any other Computrons that were around. Those Computrons knew the answer, why would they communicate the answer? 'What were they hiding?' as Vladimere whispered to Anna. 'They didn't say 'when' we would get back, only that we would go back. We might be here until we are old and gray.' Anna whispered back, 'Could we have children while we are here?' To which Betty replied, 'You will not be here that long.' To which Anna thought, 'thank heavens', without ever thinking what does that mean? Without thinking, I am on another 'rock' in those heavens. So why are those long sticky sweets from the seaside called 'rock?' Why is the rock we live on called Earth?

Another Computron, more like a male voice in the mind, 'you are all supposed to be the brightest of your generation. What do you know about Apollo 10 (American space programme) crew reporting they had heard 'music' when passing over the dark side of this moon rock (an earthling group responding two fold, 'heard nothing about that and are you joking?'). Tony (Computron) went on.

CHAPTER FIVE - APOLLO 10 MOON MUSIC

'While orbiting the moon in 1969, the Apollo 10 team heard weird music. They were on the far side of the moon, so it could not have come from Earth. The team debated whether to tell NASA command team back on Earth. Recordings of the event were declassified in 2008 and can now be heard on Science Channel's NASA's unexplained files. The Apollo 10 team were Eugene Cernan, Tom Stafford, and John Young. The sound began once the Apollo 10 capsule began an hour-long trip around the far side of the moon, out of the range of any Earth (third rock from the sun) broadcast. At one point the baffled astronauts can be heard discussing whether they should tell NASA command or not (actual recording). 'You hear that? That whistling sound? Whooooo,' one of them says. Another astronaut says he can, 'it sounds like, you know, outer space type music.' The sound lasted for almost an hour and was recorded on tape but was not released by NASA until 2008 when it was declassified, but probably abridged. The moon has no magnetic field and not enough atmosphere to cause these sounds.'

'Michael Collins, the pilot of Apollo 11, says he also heard the noises when flying around the Dark Side of the Moon.' The far side of the Moon is sometimes known as the 'Dark' side of the moon although both sides have two weeks of sunlight followed by two weeks of night.

Tony Computron continued, 'you may not have the information about Apollo 10 and 11, however, you are now on the 'Dark Side' in a building/surroundings that do not require you to wear a space suit. You are now going to be taken to another building. You might call it sightseeing.' 'A buzz of excitement into the unknown,' Helga whispered to Thomas. 'If only those Astro-physicists from University could see us now. What would they give to be here with feet on the Moon.' Thomas, in stoic Germanic mode, replied, 'they would claim it is an illusion, not a reality.' Helga thinking, 'well Thomas has accepted that this is a reality, where we are. What we are doing is real, true, current.'

One of those strange thoughts kept circulating around the group. 'A breath of fresh air'. Each had a small extension on the nail of the thumb on the left hand, then into the brains a message saying that all breathing, atmospheric pressure now controlled through the 'nail extension'. (No one questioned! No one laughed!) William from M.I.T. looked at his left thumb nail in total scientific disbelief thinking 'I can go anywhere on the dark side of the moon with this little item of nano-engineering magic providing life support'. Inquisitive mind thinking 'how can so much be built into here?' to which Tony Computron communicated. 'Is it manufactured, or is it a 'living' of which even with your great intellect you have no comprehension? The answer is 'a living'. To give a name that you Earthlings might use instead of 'a living' the name Ursa.' (William immediately thought Ursa Major, the third largest constellation in the night sky and is readily distinguished by a cluster of seven bright stars in the Northern heavens known by a variety of names, 'the plough,' 'the frying pan,' 'the dipper.' The whole, perhaps 12 million light years away. William received an Earth splitting sound as he thought, 'Could I deconstruct Ursa?' Here the feeble human brain not comprehending that this 'living Ursa' would provide sufficient oxygen to breath, somehow creating a gravitation field to keep feet on the ground. William now unable to remove either his eyes or his attention from that small extension to the nail on his thumb on his left hand, a 'living' like me, his thoughts, 'talk about wonders of the Moon!' Tony Computron seizing the moment to explain, 'eating unnecessary with so many minerals constantly hitting those frail human bones, water (the Earth humanity obsession with water) available from these places indicating to a stone like fire hydrant structure; but you will rarely feel thirsty, sorry Thomas, no beer here.' (Thomas from Munich more than enjoyed his German brew, as witnessed by that expanding 'tum tum.')

As if Tony Computron had been waiting for that moment, he made sure all the Earth people were listening, it sounded like an angry referee whistle, 'your humanity is so ignorant, so self-centred, so ignorant, somehow you have no ability to think about the big picture. We Computrons, have very often thought your say 50000 years of existence, this self-first reaction to all that exists on your third rock from your inferior sun/star. We have said to your humanity before, we will say it again 'your Earth planet would exist in harmony if your humanity ceased to exist. Species would cease to be exterminated, species would not be killed to provide food, mothers would not have their young removed for humanity food. Of course to you, all animal life has no emotion, no feelings, no family life existence. Chop down a five hundred year old tree, no pain felt by a tree, give it a good spring axing.'

Intense increasing light, without exception the Earth visitors covered their eyes for protection, even with such protection the brightness pierced through the hand. The community of young Earth humanity simultaneously receiving mind messages.

'Your observable Universe exists in harmony, even stars/suns come and go. There is now nothing to prevent Earth Crust humanity from destroying itself. Your contribution is out of harmony with the whole, the arrogance is destroying. Your contribution to any life form existence is negative, the third rock from an inferior sun is no longer fit for humanity, or rather, Earth Crust humanity is no longer in harmony with itself or with all the others that exist on that rock. You have all been selected as a last effort to bring compassion to Earth Crust humanity, (a terrified gasp from the young mass). You will act as a group that will run all political institutions.' 'Impossible,' came back an incredulous reply. Perhaps even more an expression of 'I do not want to spend a lifetime in politics, dealing, wheeling, a lifetime of exaggerating the truth or whatever the party line story might be, spinning out the untrue, creating none existing facts to prove a point.' General mind agreement, no one interested in such a life of deceitfulness.

'Impossible,' that word flying through the air. 'Impossible, impossible, impossible.' To which the reply came back, 'nothing is impossible. You will have advantages that any competitor against you will not have. The thumb nail extension will now be permanently embedded, a permanent life support system. The same device will enable you to communicate together in whatever language is natural to your land.' Repeating, 'will enable you all to communicate together.'

'As you practice you will be able to speak as normal and communicate together without speaking, if you like, as if you were a television newsreader, receiving instructions and reading the news simultaneously. Most of it will be a protection for any danger than might befall you (it must be obvious that you will receive opposition).'

'Within your own fields of excellence you will each (pair of you) receive new knowledge not yet available or been discovered, to be used exclusively for the benefit of humanity, not for personal profit.'

'You will each be returned to the place you left. Without a doubt you will be interviewed extensively, after that, for a time, you will be kept under surveillance, everything you do will be monitored by suspicious humanity. Your refuge will be in your new ability to communicate together as a whole, if you like, a collective of minds. From the very start of your return where necessary, you will have the ability to forecast events, that again will bring you to the attention of those who will be unfriendly, they will fear you.'

'Strength happens with you individuals acting as a whole, in uniform unison, as a whole acting as one you are invincible to the remainder of Earth Crust humanity. You are the new normal. The rest of Earth Crust humanity is the abnormal with a brain polluted by self-conviction of self-importance. No longer does the Earth require the polluted, every part of the natural world with enhanced life when the polluters understand their mortality.'

'The fate of humanities next generation is in your hands. Earth Crust humanity stands on that precipice of self-annihilation. The finger on that button of self-destruction only one possibility. A major epidemic, that rotten core of religious fanatics destroying the apathetic majority of none-believers. That movement from the Third World spreading as a flood consuming all standing in front of the flood tide.'

Heightened tension within the Security Services worldwide created the need to communicate instantly together. 'Five Eyes,' grouping having first been affected took the early instant decisions. Common interest, intensified with a comprehensive list of the Disappeared. Speculation constant within the Security World, within the political world, within the media.

Three 'W's' instituted themselves as a common interest: why, when, where?

Within the 'Five Eyes' grouping existed an underground facility in North Yorkshire, which already had in residence senior staff of each constituent member of 'Five Eyes,' plus the European agencies plus 'Mossad,' short for *Hamossad leModi'in ule*

Tafkidim Meyuhadim, formed on December 13 1949, headquarter, Tel Aviv, Israel.

The North Yorkshire facility although on United Kingdom land had been bequeathed to the United States of America security agencies. For good order the name of the facility started with R.A.F. (Royal Air Force), then the actual name. For ease of aircraft access there were international airfields at Manchester and Leeds/Bradford, more importantly a real Royal Air Force airfield facility ideal for those small jets much enjoyed by the wealthy elite (and military).

Even the smallest of military airfields has an embodied group of ardent plane spotters, more than one having ended up with Military Police in those far flung airfields of the world where photography is against the law. The most prized photographs arising from some elicit act when landing or taking off at some airfields where military and commercial share runways.

Messages soon passing within the group of intensive aircraft movements, running rampant explanations, involving dark military secrets. Excitedly, out went the message, 'planes are coming from everywhere, everywhere in the world.' With each plane arrival no disembarking in public 'binocular' view, no taxiing into the open doors of a large aircraft hangar. Most of the executive jets would have passengers of eight, perhaps ten, some up to sixteen, with each arrival a number of blacked out four by fours would exit through a little used none public military road. Aircraft spotters knew every inch of the 'opposition' airfield, to them military were the opposition. The 'spotters' were prepared, pairs of high performance motorbikes stationed at each possible exit to give chase. Heightened excitement, fuel tanks full to overflowing, they had played the chase game before, cat and mouse, would military police cause problems? Reports already received about high numbers of 'police cars' out on major roads. 'A good chase in prospect.' Mark and Luke, two of the more ancient 'spotters' were ready (their finest achievement the first pictures of a USA airforce stealth bomber on British soil at RAF Fairford). Better than sex to them, that first, early

74

hours of the morning photography.

They knew the game well, they had positioned themselves at the end of a 'no access farm track,' they had seen twenty feet of hedgerow slide away (enough hedgerow to convince the unknown observer that no exit from the airfield existed onto the unusually tarmacked farm track, must be a very wealthy farmer, were all his farm tracks covered in tarmac?)

John, the third member of the Mark and Luke team, had been positioned behind the far side hedge directly opposite where the 20 foot hedge would slide away, his only responsibility to photograph the exiting vehicle number plates.

That sliding hedge barely open as the blacked out Range Rovers exited, as predicted, that large pool of oil spread thickly across the tarmac caused enough lack of tyre friction for John to get good photographs of the number plates. Mark and Luke set off in pursuit at a respectable distance, drivers of the Range Rovers would see they were being followed, to the drivers, to Mark and Luke, all part of the spying game.

Exiting the airfield roads brings the group onto the A1 (one) that never ending trunk road from London to Berwick upon Tweed, still very limited overtaking even in the world of heavy vehicle travelling endlessly North to South and vice versa, but not as bad as the A14 from the East Coast ports to the Midlands. As a generality why is it that most motorways are North/South not East/West, that is of course with the exception of the M25, but of course, that is London Commuter Territory?

With the Range Rovers now exiting the A1, Mark and Luke could now guess where they were heading. Luke, at speed, overtook the Range Rovers, causing the inevitable comments of 'mad bikers' from the Range Rover drivers. Just over a mile ahead, he pulled into a layby, watched the Range Rovers speed passed, Mark waved as he passed. Luke telephoned John, John telephoned the emergency police service, reported a hit and run accident with the driver not stopping. Yes, he had the vehicle registration number. Within moments the emergency police service had instigated a 'stop' instruction to police in the local area.

Some 18 miles passed Luke, now in a ditch covered in blood, a very diligent police officer on his usual round of the villages, 'showing the flag' as requested by his sergeant, could see a Range Rover shooting passed a 30 miles per hour sign, his moment of glory almost upon him, blue light flashing, he caught up with the Range Rover (plus another one leading) after a three mile, cops and robbers, chase. Bingo! The hit and run vehicle. He, P.C. Ian Trepid had called in for backup, and having managed to block off further progress along the 'not much wider than a country lane,' locked himself into the car awaiting back-up. Quickly he called in to state he was under attack from very large thugs demanding he pull out of the way. At the station, the duty sergeant could well hear the commotion and banging of windows, continued to instruct P.C. Ian Trepid not to move out of the car. 'Back-up' arrived six minutes later blocking the country lane from the rear, fortunately the only other vehicle in front was a motorbike. Out of the second police vehicle emerged the local rugby team prop forwards, but also full time policemen, and the station detective sergeant. 'No one gets away with crime on my patch.'

The motorcyclist captured the events on film (well a top of the range mobile named after that fruit that helped 'Newton' define gravity) some how only managing to record the valiant attempts of the police to calm the aggressors. The incident was not even over as footage appeared on the World Wide Web. Much pushing and shoving, swearing, flashing of identity cards in one another's faces produced a volcanic calm in assessing who had senior authority at the incident. Ugly inter-service rivalry boiling away under a skin-deep surface, agreeing that the group would continue on its journey escorted by the two police vehicles then at the now whispered destination, each party would take advice from more senior officers. That motorcyclist was instructed to follow to provide evidence.

All the vehicles parked and passengers escorted into the guardroom at the American base, Menworth Hill, in Yorkshire,

Michael Cooke

England.

At about the same time a long-time businessman waited outside the Russian Trade Delegation in Highgate, North London. Waiting outside a permanent obligation for any visitor, large sliding metal gates (large 30 feet long, 10 feet high) prevented access for all. While waiting the businessman named George looked at the trees in front to each side of the gated entrance at the only red squirrels left in London. The Russians with red squirrels! George Atha knew these red squirrels were of long living age well beyond the normal life expectancy, a family of six or just friends of red squirrel land. The London 'reds' if a British political part must be labour, although the colour 'red' associated with the old Soviet Union Communist Party.

In fact, George knew from his many visits that the red squirrels were, in fact, camouflage for the surveillance cameras. Experience gained over the years knew best to switch off the car engine as several minutes always elapsed before he crossed the threshold of 'another way of life', knowing the Russian 'spy' cameras he assumed the British Security Services and their own 'spy' cameras somewhere close.

Slowly, more slowly, opened that gate, the dividing line existing as if the Cold War still continued, entering in front of an abrupt sign, 'keep right,' looking in his rear mirror the 'slowly, more slowly' gate moved much more quickly preventing any immediate escape. Caught as if an insect by a 'flycatcher' plant, George knew the imposing austere entrance façade, knew the visitor parking, locked the car after pulling out his briefcase, walked the twenty or so paces to the entrance doors. Normality as his current contact stood waiting with his assistant, four paces inside the very dimly lit entrance lobby. A little over thirty years had elapsed since his first visit. Then butterflies in his stomach, as he crossed from the freedom of The West, into dim-lit Soviet Union Communist World, as president Ronald Reagan said, "the evil empire.' The flag, the brightest of reds. At this time naughty children were threatened with 'a red under the bed' so easy to instil into a generation a 'fear' of the Communists. All that was evil attributed to Communism, those allies that joined together in World War II to defeat 'Hitler' now the enemy superpowers of the Cold War. In Moscow many a question asked (when the State Security was not listening), why 'Stalin' prevented the Soviet Military Machine going beyond Berlin. In the uninhibited early morning drinking gossip many a General lamenting the decision not to proceed through Germany into France then down into Italy with an already existing strong Communist Party.

Handshaking all round, the two members of the Russian Trade Delegation determined to speak in English, identical pronunciation a sign of the Moscow University with that language school where all 'civil servants' received language skills, in this context 'civil servants' equates to those spies of the FSB (came after the KGB) and GRU (Military). A president of the Russian Federation called 'Putin' started life as a spy, they say with German his other language.

With the formality of handshaking completed, George Atha proceeded to the lift and staircase, with usual normality he received the instruction, 'the lift is not working. We will use the stairs.' In all the years George had visited, the lift had never worked. Over the visits he had learned that this lift had permanent mechanical problems, in reality, he knew no lift had existed from the opening of the delegation buildings. Many conversations within the British Intelligence Community had concluded that the lift shaft had been lined in lead, with atomic number 82, a barrier that absorbs sound vibration and radiation. British Security had well-informed information that the lift shaft consisted of a basement area to be used as a nuclear fallout shelter, then on each of the three floors, lead proofed rooms behind the lift doors which were also lead lined, then on entry, an additional lead curtain would be drawn across the lift entry doors. Each of these rooms could be used for secret discussions, that great fear of the Cold War that somehow listening devices were everywhere within a building, in the grounds, even in a driveway.

George sat down opposite (always opposite, never side by side, Vladimer, his contact, spoke to him in Russian, Victor the Interpreter translated into English, then after George spoke, translated into Russian. No doubt in the mind of George that Vladimer could speak excellent English, but that was not the way the game was played. Victor, the interpreter, explained that the factory of which George occupied the position of Managing Director would be offered a three-year contract to provide 'men's suits' to the appropriate Russian buying organisation called 'SovExport."

Terms of the contract would be to provide 50,000 items of three-piece suits (men) each year at a suggested ex-factory price of £90 each suit. George had difficulty in containing a smile. This was a very, very generous price, too generous. What were they expecting in return? That came next. A condition of the contract required 'SovExport' to have two inspectors on site throughout the length of the contract, that the factory workers would provide the necessary invitations to the British Embassy in Moscow, stating the factory would provide and meet all expenses, accommodation, motor vehicle, air tickets, living money, but not salary. SovExport would pay the salary themselves. George knew this remained too generous. What else did they want?

George had the customary cup of tea, no milk provided, sugar, yes, plus a very sweet Russian cake. Polite comment on how tasty, then a working copy for him of the proposed contract. Next meeting for a week's time at his office, would he remember to inform the Home Office so that the Russian group would receive permission to travel outside of the London M25 circle? Almost not listening, George preoccupied with calculating the potential profit for the three years from this unexpected 'windfall'. He knew his costings down to the last millimetre of cloth, £40 per three-piece suit, well established as a price in the trade for such a supply. The Russians surely had a reasonable idea of a realistic price, what did they expect as compensation?

Goodbye's completed, that entrance/exit gate moved slower than ever, then out, released, back into normality. The custom existed that upon leaving he would make a telephone call to his MI5 contact arranging to meet sometime later that afternoon in Central London. Not today, the potential contract information needed to be communicated with the other Directors, a phone call back to Yorkshire, his, secretary instructed that his Directors, Line Managers to remain at work. He expected to be back by 19.00 hours, instruct the canteen to prepare enough sandwiches for late night meals, 'we have a new big contract.'

Tedious described the drive back, his mind constantly preoccupied with that fundamental of all business, 'money'. How could the finance be obtained for such a large value contract? Smash!! So preoccupied he failed to notice the stationary traffic in front, double smash as something ran into the back of his car, just after the Nottingham junction the motorway closed for six hours. George flown by helicopter to emergency and accident at Nottingham Queen's Hospital Specialist unit. Nearly life or death, unaware of the accident staff at the factory cursing his later arrival. Didn't he realise they had home lives?

George Atha would never know how close he had been to death. It was an unmarked special branch car (Police) that had been first on the scene. The members of the Security Service MI5 as always suspicious when a prearranged meeting is cancelled by a regular long-time informer/contact. Knowing he drove to London (cameras picked him up close to the Russian Trade delegation) those everywhere surveillance cameras picked him upon entering Junction 1 of the M1 (motorway). From not far away, (parked up at the first service station) two Special Branch Officers firstly overtook George to see if he remained alone in the car, then eased back to follow his movements, checking if he made any deviation from that route which was expected. His briefcase found its way back to the Security Service in London. Following a careful examination, taking a copy of the proposed Russian contract, a grateful wife received the briefcase 24 hours later while she waited for George to have a life-saving operation.

No branch of the British Security Services should be underestimated. Within hours of looking through the contract, they were ensuring that the contract would be continued by the factory with or without George. First step easy, contact the friendly none-executive Director sitting on the board of the Bank which the factory used, let's called him Sir Ted, to ensure that confidentiality remained intact. Sir Ted informed the District Bank Manager that George Atha had contacted him very briefly about a new contract and as the District Manager had no doubt heard, 'George' had been involved in a life-threatening motorway accident. Did he (the District Manager) know anyone at the factory to assure the 'factory' that the Bank would assist the 'factory' if the new contract George had briefly mentioned to Sir Ted went forward. Sir Ted already knew that the District Manager played golf more than once with the Factory Finance Director without any real effort the Security service was now in control of the new Russian Contract.

At about that time of the motorway accident near Nottingham, England, two bodies were found in Alaska exactly where the local guides had expected to find Anik and Anernerk. They were not dead but almost as if in hibernation, just alive, emergency helicopter took them to the nearest major hospital. Within record time they were placed in isolation as if from nowhere, the armed military already present when the two bodies arrived. A news media blackout imposed before Anik and Anernerk arrived. To a casual observer, a well-rehearsed plan instituted.

At about the time of the motorway accident near Nottingham, England, two bodies were found in St Petersburg, Russia in the house, really a palace set in enormous grounds surrounded by walls with a gated entrance. The 'Palace', the official home of the Admiral of the Northern Fleet, the back of the grounds bordered with the open seas providing ample area for mooring of the so-called 'Admiral's Barge'; not a barge, rather the best of motorized small ships to get the Admiral in and out if whichever vessel of the Naval Fleet he wanted to visit. Within the 'palace' the bodies were found lying on top of the oversized Snooker table. In relation to where they disappeared they were literally on the opposite side of the Little Neva. Not dead, almost as though in hibernation, just alive. Emergency helicopter had them in Yuri Gagarin Hospital No 1 within minutes. Yuri Gagarin Hospital No 1 well known for a large isolation unit. From nowhere armed military already in position as the helicopter landed. Under protective cover, two bodies were carried into isolation and confirmed to be Vladimere and Anna. A nurse telephoned her favourite 'Pravda' (newspaper) reporter to give the information. That Pravda reporter at the hospital within seven minutes, that nurse waiting for her at the reception, with the official badge of management.

At about the same time of the motorway accident near Nottingham, England, two bodies were found on the River Inhul river bank on the opposite side of where they were last seen. Nikoliev Emergency Services arrived instantly only to be placed at a distance by those grey-suited, leather coat wearing, sunglass wearing, members of the Ukrainian Secret Service (once upon a time the KGB). Anastasia and Peter were pronounced as being in a deep coma sleep. No one knew where the helicopter had been waiting, in it swooped, two bodies stretchered in, the helicopter gone as if never actually landing. Nikoliev awash with conflicting stories, only one question, 'where had the bodies gone to?"

On route to an undisclosed destination the helicopter crashed with official reports stating all on board, six people had died in the crash, goodbye to Anastasia and Peter, consternation in the worldwide 'spying' community with two pieces of the 'disappeared' jigsaw puzzle now dead.

Early in the 'spying community' meetings at Menworth Hill various scenarios were discussed, one of which concerned the 'finding' of any of 'the disappeared', all of 'the disappeared', or any number returning over a protracted period of time, where, how to imprison/interrogate, which agency would take the lead position. Fierce competition, calling in of favours, plenty of backstabbing, all agencies wanting first information from 'the disappeared'. Then the ability to adjust the information received prior to sharing to that interested worldwide security community, competition rife, much could be gained; very little could be lost. Presidents, Prime Ministers, Country Leaders, all brought into the discussion, everyone after first rights. Primary consideration, accommodation if a large number returned.

After a passage of time an inevitable compromise, use the United Nations Security Council permanent members as a basis. Each permanent member to establish a facility with all interviews conducted with a representative of each permanent member present. Now the critical matter, how would the 'returning' be allocated, many suggestions.

1) Fill up one facility, then move on to another, but what would be the order? Which facility would be first? Which facility last? Every group wanted to be first or second.

2) A facility to specialise in a language so Chinese, English, Slavonic, Spanish as examples. Fierce competition, rivalry, with both American and British convinced English should be their own prerogative.

3) Each member be allocated a continent obviously the Americans to the North and South America, then a concern over the disproportionate population numbers in the Asian continent. Poor little numbers in Australasia.

4) What about a division based on 'Types of Employment', that dismissed as soon as it had been suggested.

5) By age a further suggestion, impractical with less than ten years separating the youngest to the oldest of the 'Disappeared', also 'Couples' needed to be kept together regardless of age differentials.

6) In some frustration, a lady from the British Security Service (with tongue in cheek), what about by height? In some disbelief, she could hear the suggestion being taken seriously, on a roll she threw out what about waist size or shoe size?

Always Never The Disappeared

Even those nationalities known for not having a sense of humour realized the stupidity of some of the suggestions. Commonsense eventually prevailed with the obvious solution of allocating in the order of returning. But! But! Who would receive the first, how humanity can argue over nothingness, self-importance, nationalities better than others, and of course, the unspoken, 'white more important than black', 'men more important than women.' Who are the permanent members of the United Nations Security Council? When did they achieve permanent status? Why did they achieve permanent status?

A history of the politics of the United Nations would fill many hundreds of volumes, effectively starting at the end of World War II, the permanent members made up of those nations considered as the victorious nations of World War II, United States of America, United Kingdom, China (not mainland, but Taiwan), France, Soviet Union. How the world has changed with Taiwan replaced by the Republic of China, so our infamous '5' still the same World War II victorious nations now with additions. Agreement eventually that these 5 would each set up the centres with representatives of 'the 5' in situ at each of the centres, of course it would not be Security Services if the centres did not have a code name, each, which became George, Henry, Duck, Frog, Hockey, now which was which your clue, frog is not France.

Of the initial meeting group at Menworth Hill much self-congratulation that foresight had prevailed as to the possible return of 'the disappeared'. Members to polite as to accept that the decision actually involves one person (member of Mossad) not the group as a whole.

It became a matter of fact that within 24 hours of Anik with Anernerk bodies recovery in Alaska, the remainder of 'the disappeared' were found at or within a short distance of the place they were last seen. Notwithstanding the initial planning with all appearing within a 24 hour time period the logistics were stretched, without doubt, the strict order of whom went where disappeared into practicality, roughly an equal number residing as prisoners in each 'centre'. Well not everyone. In one of the five centres, Peter with Anastasia were not. Those who died never identified, none of them mourned by grieving family. In fact, no bodies found in or near that crash. Access denied to the crash site by one of those independent militia controlling land during the Russian/Ukraine conflict/war/killing. Did any national government really have no influence in the conflict zone?

Medical teams were stretched beyond limits with all of 'the disappeared' requiring extensive medical check-ups, a permanent area of hold up around the MRI scanning machines (note, another British invention gobbled up by American capitalism). Within reason, other than for drinking water, no food allowed until basic tests completed. Part of the protocol established by the original Menworth Hill Group required all human discharge of pooh to be examined for clues as to where 'the disappeared' had been. Would food remnants indicate an area or country that had been providing food. In-house laboratories given brakeneck timetables to get results quicker than 'as soon as possible'. Initial results were profoundly worrying, retest, something is more than inaccurate. Are clean rooms, clean? Have they become contaminated? Are the tests deliberately encountering fraudulent change? Has someone infiltrated the medical teams? How could that be, from each of the five centres, the anomalies exactly the same, results made no biological sense. Having little regard for the individuals, each centre received instructions to operate on one male, one female, at the centre to take samples directly out of the 'gut', results replicated, exactly the same.

Peter with Anastasia awoke in St Petersburg, Russia, in exactly the same 'palace' belonging to the Admiral of the Northern Fleet where Vladimere with Anna had been discovered now the Russians had their own 'disappeared' with no need to share any information with the other members of the United Nations Security Council. This medical team reported exactly the same medical anomalies.

Up there, somewhere, perhaps still on the Dark Side of Earth's Moon, Tony Computron with the medical Computrons, were in Computron hilarious laughter, so simple to fool those feeble 'humanit' minds. How long would it take to discover what the Computron medics had done to 'the disappeared'? Certainly, they had felt nothing when the change had been made. How could the Computrons know what Earth medics were doing? Think the other way around. Why would they not know? Humanite is a little less than primitive! Time for greater Computron fun, deciding to turn their attention to the Earth centre secretly named FROG (not in France). They started with an easy one. Wherever staff at FROG were, whatever they were doing, everyone 'froze', unable to move, or speak. Frozen lasted exactly (in Earth time) 2 minutes and forty-eight seconds. A degree of panic set in at the other centres when for that period of time all forms of communication ceased. Frozen panic. Tony Computron proved correct with the cause of the 'frozen panic' taking over completely all activity as to what was the cause, the obvious question, 'did 'the disappeared' have any input into the frozenness?' For the Computron's, this could be a game of endless fun, they left matters for an hour, at that time that centre named DUCK near Peking in China lost all electricity, again no communications with the other four centres, with one communal thought of the Computrons, 'how primitive are humanits without electricity?' Followed immediately by 'how primitive are humanits?' Then the in-joke. Humanits once upon a time visited their moon, now they cannot get there, humanits stuck on their little rocky planet (on that little rocky planet, those Security Services in panic). Computrons with their unimaginable memory intelligence decided on a little more excitement. That centre named HOCKEY instantly flooded up to a height of sixty centimetres, not fifty-nine, not sixty-one, exactly sixty. Look at those floating papers with the red 'top secret', Computrons did not need to read to know what the contents were. Wading waist high in water collecting back together sodden pieces of 'top secret' paper the overriding concern, 'the disappeared' forgotten about. Those 'prison-like doors' that kept them in living quarters opened themselves, without exception they decided to have a walk around. Seeing more of the prison/facility/centre. Managing to collect together some of those 'top security' papers, now able to read that information already collated which then produced a topic for conversation. 'Did you know we are a danger to humanity?' Consternation from those responsible for keeping them locked in, who opened the cages? How did they get out? The water will contaminate their bodies affecting medical tests already in progress. They will be washed clean, any trace of 'where before' gone. As always suspicious, those security minds convinced themselves that this was not an accident. Inevitable a committee established to investigate the cause. Tony Computron, with the Computron gang, could foresee endless amusement with the pathetic humanits. Lets spread the disruption, came the thoughts from inside the Computron gang, let's 'bully off' hockey in Russia, ice or grass. That word 'ice' conjured up immediate thoughts of trouble making. "Fire and Ice,' another thought, agreement on 'ice', the outcome. Even Computrons have to develop their skills. Accordingly one of the young Computrons received the simple task of ensuring all the heating and air conditioners operated on minus fifty Fahrenheit. 'HOCKEY' centre quickly entered the realms of an ice-box. How did the cell-like doors open? Congratulations all around for that young Computron. A Computron chest puffed out in pride. Russia, not a good place to be if you are the person in charge. Those so-called prison camps in Siberia can feel very close at hand. Within moments those crystalline molecules of ice form a film over everything, everyone, men quickly with white beads, ladies not pleased with their new style white eyebrows. How have 'the disappeared' got outside of the buildings, keep them together under armed guard, too late, Thomas from Munich already off into the surrounding forest, when chaos reigns those first few minutes ideal for a quick exit, not that Thomas from Munich made quick movement, more of a man taking his dog for a walk. No more than ten minutes into the forest, he came upon one of those ancient tree trunks almost hollow inside, somehow, by a miracle of nature that tree still fully alive. Somewhat low for tall Thomas, a seat carved out of the tree. In sitting down, to his left were some bottles of beer with a note in German saying, 'help yourself, weary traveller.' Fortunately the bottles were screw top, as instructed he helped himself, it tasted very good. Thinking would he have time for another one prior to them finding him, his foot kicked a stone. (Not deliberate), to be greeted with 'ouch be careful'. He had not had enough for drunkenness, from his visit to the Dark Side of the Moon, Thomas knew, another Computron!! Are they everywhere? 'Yes,' the positive reply. Thomas could now hear the baying of dogs in the near distance. 'Kick me hard,' Thomas received a message, he did as instructed, before his kicking foot returned to normal, Thomas found himself safely returned to his cell, not freezing, temperature in his cell normal. 'Sit still and wait,' the message he received, chaos all around waiting to be found exactly where authority did not expect him to be in residence.

Outside fully armed troops determined not to lose anyone of these weird people, keep them together, let the medical experts sort out the mystery. For that Commander of the establishment, his hand literally burning as a string of Russian language profanities roared through the ether. At the crescendo of words he froze (literally froze) unable to speak, move, at the other end of the phone astonishment at the lack of response. The phone call continued longer and longer, how long can a one-sided conversation go on? That area around 'HOCKEY' camp had to be seen to be believed. 'The Disappeared' (minus Thomas) were standing around as a group surrounded by a cloud of warm air, still, in the clothes, they were wearing when inside. All around them in numerous posses of movement the frozen statue like military. 'The Disappeared' could with ease disappear again. Frozen military, unfrozen 'disappeared', animals with birds happily proceeding as if all existed in normality. Those dogs with handlers, outside of the frozen area, were racing around the now empty tree trunk, every time they ran over a volcanic like stone they yelped in pain, jumping in the air. Having amused themselves the Computrons 'up there' allowed normality to return, the frozen, unfrozen, those military reports would make unbelievable, literally unbelievable, reading.

News spreads quickly through the 'centres', the three so far unaffected wondering if or when their turn would come. Those on the Dark Side of the Moon would ensure they were 'not left out in the cold.' Back to a Computron think-in, at the five centres immediate increase in fanatical type security. FROG, they decided upon as next. FROG, of course, turned out to be England, frog in the secret minds of the secret world had to be England (which was conquered by the French in 1066) where had they hidden the FROG centre in England? Possibly Wales. The obvious place, Menworth Hill, with all the existing infrastructure. Another Computron think-in, 'fire and ice.' A fire at Menworth Hill. Not in the underground areas, let's have the mushroom-like listening devices explode in sequence (the front cover of this book is of those 'things' at Menworth Hill which the Computrons are planning against). In doing that those naughty Computrons would knockout all listening capability of (? That's a real secret). It is not a secret that those working there are American.

CHAPTER SIX - MUSHROOM FIRE

Fire alarms screamed with the first of the mushrooms setting alight, within moments the in-house fire brigade burst into action thirty seconds after the first, the second, third and fourth ignited. In theory a well rehearsed evacuation of the underground facility would commence, however, 'the disappeared' hidden away had not yet received any form of instruction. Humanity instinct had them joining in the long exodus of shuffling, worried, verging on scared, employees heading for their appointed fire exit route. Would they exit in time? Perhaps panic of the last thought, that smell of 'their own' flesh burning as death came with agonising acute pain, 'please let me die instantly, no more pain please.' A life ended unexpectedly with no goodbyes.

Doris and Gwen, the students from England who studied at one of the two best universities, managed to detach themselves from whatever exit group they were following. Almost as if directed like migrating birds they set off down another of the myriad of underground passages, with three thousand people working permanently twenty-four hours a day, 365 days a year, many passages, many routes. Hand in hand, Doris leading they moved military like from one passage to the next, from one room to the next. Gwen commented 'pity that they could not stop and study all that secret information.' Within ten minutes all, repeat all, the mushroom domes were on fire, the need for outside fire services obvious. Harrogate Fire Brigade was the first 'public' funded to arrive with extremely sophisticated equipment for a large county town. Specialist beyond a firefighters dream arrived from that airfield constantly surveyed by those motorcyclists who made sure a group were travelling behind the equipment. They soon had the call out on their social media pages for any one who could make the journey to attempt access to that place. Sometimes a vetting procedure fails to take account of the obvious, another small town in the immediate call out area only had one fire engine manned by 'part-time' firemen. No doubt in one of those past time saving money exercises that station had lost permanent firefighters to be replaced by 'only paid on a call out basis,' this fire station now manned by four of the airfield motorbike friends. Beyond easy into the complex they had planned to enter for years, directed at speed to one of the 'listening' burning mushrooms. Plans quickly thrust into eager hands, instructions to keep the fire away from certain areas on the plan which has cable entry from the 'listening' mushrooms into underground, at all costs the fire to be prevented from entering underground. With Christmas coming early for them, one instantly had photographs of the documents marked 'secret', not 'top secret'. Christmas moments later had better gifts with two receiving verbal instructions into going through a nearby 'exit manhole' looking for anyone not yet evacuated. Over the years they had talked about getting underground, they had dreamt of getting underground, now in reality, now underground would it produce any 'secret information' worth knowing about

Doris, holding hands with Gwen, were encountering no-one. They assumed they were on security cameras if anyone continued to monitor, with so many alarms sounding at the same time it was difficult to know if the security alarm had been activated. With passageways continuing in all directions they entered a nondescript door marked 'strictly no entry' pushing gently, still holding hands, they entered the room, bigger than the centre of Christianity in Rome, so not a room an area also with a large domed ceiling, no paintings on this ceiling, more of a planetarium with the near Milky Way vividly displayed. All around the room what must be at least one thousand terminal screens, all around the vastness of a middle empty. Doris had seen a similar but much smaller dome at the planetarium (next to Madam Tussauds) in London. She looked for a lighting control panel. She turned the dimmer switch, out went the lights, out came the near Milky Way. In the dim light, it was all around; they walked through the vast space touching unknown, unnamed stars within the Milky Way.

It happened to be Gwen who commented about some stars looking red, not many; she counted eleven, scattered in no uniform pattern. Meanwhile, Doris attempted to understand what projection the near Universe had as an axis. In that instant evacuation order, computer screens were without exception still switched on. Rather like Goldilocks of the three bears fame, the two of them started moving methodically looking at each of the live screens; they again accepted somewhere a surveillance camera was watching their every move, when will the guard arrive?

Those motorcyclist part-time firefighters found themselves unsupervised wandering around the underground complex. For effect they decided to carry a fire extinguisher, in turn, the other carrying a high performance 'torch light' powerful enough to see many hundreds of metres and pierce a certain thickness of smoke. They soon worked out the colour coding of the ceiling height cables running along every passageway. Their immediate concern was for the battery life of the assorted mobile phones in use to video all they were seeing. This now turning into many Christmas days all in one, now a preoccupation in making those arrangements to smuggle out the illicit information, dynamite of information in their pockets. It turned out fortunate that they found six people appearing as lost in a corridor so decided to use them as an excuse for being where they should not have been. Motorbike firefighters surprised at the lack of English these young people spoke, they were absolutely not American. With one motorcycle fireman leading the way, following the exit signs, the group of six behind, with the second motor cycle fireman at the rear. Out of the ground, they huddled into a deluge of smoke, bits of things still alight, downfalls of piping hot water. Obviously, some part of the organisation had been looking for this group which were quickly moved away from the white-hot inferno. The motorcycle firemen were thanked profusely, had they seen any more staff underground? People remained missing!! If they had seen others, nothing would have been reported with their primary concern to get mobile phones stored, hidden for their departure which now could not come quickly enough. Cunning, one of the two tried to explain where the six had been found, however without a detailed underground map he could only describe the area, not now being too helpful in case a suggestion he should go back underground. With fortunate timing one of the two motorbike clad firemen shouted for help, the other that had gone underground in the fire engine cab hiding the now priceless mobile phones in one of those many nooks and crannies that exist in an older Denis fire engine. The look between the four said it all. 'Praise be to local government money saving amongst the local fire service.' Otherwise, we would not be here! With fires raging all over the 'site' no quick exit would happen unless, of course, they received a call back to their fire station to deal with a local emergency.

Having established the approximate area that the six were found within, discussion had 'Carruthers', the Station Commander, dispatching two members of the in-house firefighting team specifically to look for those 'disappeared' still not accounted for.

Doris, wandering at ground level through a 3D effect of the near Universe wondered where the 'back-up' system had been located that kept this wonderful Universe alive? What are those red dots for?

On-site security professionals were frantic. They could see nothing, everything on the screens was blank. Someone in planning had not taken into account this eventuality. Poor person in for the obscure position in the middle of nowhere. Every large organisation has such positions signifying the end of future promotion. Security professional frantic needs to make unwelcome decisions to protect the highly sensitive establishment, cost not a deciding factor, initially call in a drone with a camera. Ask for a surveillance satellite to be repositioned, either would take time, all need to be sanctioned through the British, European, American chains of command. No sensitive site like this can operate effectively without surveillance; effectively they were blind. Blind, the site in mayhem, all of the mushroom domes now blazing, not one unaffected, set on high moorland that at the height of the inferno people fifty kilometres away could see with ease the intensity of the fire destruction. How the media pack can arrive at a disaster is only known to the media, the first group arriving following the Harrogate fire station equipment. Do they have informers who live by fire stations, ambulance depots, police stations? Whose reward is thirty seconds of fame when interviewed by a television reporter? With media arriving this would be a big story with the American networks wanting live feeds of the happenings.

It may or may not be generally known that the largest of American Military bases have a branch of the American Embassy on site. Normal every day business concentrating on dealing with Visa's as military staff travel around the world. Today no different, that training in dealing with a major incident that all hope will never be needed now a reality. First priority, establish three-way links, the American Embassy in London, the Pentagon, everyone needing the same information, 'casualties,' those professional media who provide the news briefings anxious for every crumb of bad news, need to be ahead of the inevitable media, the priority. Remembering that the American media delight to ask those awkward, embarrassing questions whenever possible.

Still wandering through the near Universe, Doris noticed that Gwen had settled down in a comfortable swivel chair in front of an array of screens. In her own mind, Gwen could see red dots/marks on the screens resembling those in the three-dimensional world that surrounded herself, surrounded Gwen. If not a pointless action Doris appeared to try catching those red dots, Gwen knew she would not be stupid enough to try that so what could she be thinking about? Doris, deep in thought, thinking about her visit to Baikonur Cosmodrome, the former Soviet Union and current Russian Space Centre. She remembered catching a glimpse of an area with identical twin-like appearance, the glimpse instantly moved on by staff, enough for a thought to germinate. To Gwen, an out of the deep blue instruction, 'see if you can find any screens connected to Baikonur Cosmodrome.'

Within the cab of the four motorcyclists' Dennis fire engine, the all-important two-way messaging system had an urgent voice calling the engine back for an emergency 999 call. Now it takes time to place all the equipment back into place before leaving the scene of any action, the 999 control voice not happy with the reply of when they would arrive at the new incident. What the 999 controllers had no idea about concerned the urgency with which the fire crew wanted to leave for their own illicit reasons. All fire crews have a senior office on board to take immediate decisions; this senior officer gave instructions 'just get it all on board, let's get out of this place as quickly as possible.' That left a jumbled up mess thrown into the engine; the emergency blue lights switched on. They were inevitably stopped at the manned-in-desperation security gate, seeing the emergency blue light flashing, security waved the engine immediately through. With a collective sigh of relief, enough breath to inflate a small balloon, they were outside in the free world.

Departing, the crew was astonished at the scene of devastation, even more, amazed that they had not dealt with any casualties. With that blue light flashing, the crew had every excuse to extricate every drop of speed the ageing Denis fire engine could be capable of, problem; this moorland continued up and down with the normal slowness of up-hills only picking up speed on the down-hill stretches. Glowing intensity of the fire followed them as they passed through small hamlets, not really villages, groups of residents standing around looking towards that intense glow in the distance. Within three miles of their home fire station, the driver noticed another blue light in his wing mirror and travelling much faster than the old Denis engine. 'Put your foot down,' a voice barked, 'take no chances, get back to base.' The reply from the driver not what the crew wanted to hear. 'It is travelling too fast. It will reach us, overtake within two minutes at most. Make sure all the incriminating evidence is well hidden. Let's be prepared for a search of the vehicle.' Paranoid or sensible? Knowing the road well, the driver told the crew a straight road would come round an approaching corner; he would deliberately slow down, either to be overtaken or whatever. Without any doubt, the now overtaking 'blue flashing light' vehicle indicated that the fire engine must come to a stop.

Security back at the flaming inferno concerned at the missing, not only some of 'the disappeared' prisoners also some of the on-base family members, a considerable number of family homes existed near that area of shops, restaurants, bowling ally, church, junior school. Several of the fire meeting points were abandoned as being too close to burning buildings, then information about the changed meeting points being difficult to communicate to the missing. American media pressing hard for information, already they had deduced that base personnel were missing, they at the moment had no knowledge of the group called 'the Disappeared'. Media all over the world searching for any of 'the Disappeared', unusually not anyone anywhere would leak information, for any lucky reporter the scoop of all scoops waiting out there, if only the baying media pack knew how close they were to that story of a lifetime. Humanity (American in this instance) has a natural instinct to look after its own kind, the pressure coming from security organisations all over the world that 'the disappeared' were more important, fundamentally more important, if during this catastrophe a choice existed of who to save it must be 'the disappeared', lives more important than American including American children, infants, babies. Yet officially no Menworth Hill staff knew about 'the disappeared', officially, only a handful of people in the world knew of their location.

Denis fire engines of a certain age take longer to come to a halt than those of a more modern vintage. The overtaking blue lights, having come to a halt at a reasonable distance in front, found itself having to move extremely smartish or be shunted along in front of the fire engine, two vehicles came to a stop.

Not one, but two burley 'Menworth' security guards jumped smartly out of their military jeep, adjusted hats, padded down ruffled military uniform, walked with deliberate intent to either side of the now very dirty-red Denis fire engine. New York American accents are different from many other Amercian accents as if as children to be heard it is necessary to shout over the noise of the mass, that continued into adulthood, perhaps it is to be heard over the New York traffic noise. Approaching the driver side of, the New York-born sergeant barked, 'please get out.' Not what the occupants wanted to hear, were those telephones safely hidden away, they really did not want these two searching around inside the home from home passenger cab. Spread the firefighting equipment, helmets, breathing equipment all around. One slipped his arm into a ready-made sling, having to be helped out of the cab, the four naughty 'school boys' stood in front of the headmaster (sergeant) awaiting their fate.

Within the fire-ridden camp, that search intensified for the missing 'residents'. Now, much more intense concern as military parents had reported children missing, that select group hunting for 'the disappeared', those already discovered now under guard within the community church, all of the three doorways locked, guarded, still twelve unaccounted for. Large military bases, this one three thousand employees, plus families, have both a small hospital and the hospital again by necessity having a mortuary. A stretcher with a covered over body arrived at the hospital entrance, dead, relief all around as the identity badge, welded from heat onto the uniform of the now dead, showed the deceased to be neither a member of the base or one of 'the disappeared' just a member of the outside caterers staff catering service which had been contracted out some years ago in the inevitable cost saving (not cost cutting) exercises. Decision to release the information to the baying press, give them a morsel of information to keep their news producers back in the studio happy. Now plenty to speculate on. No name given (next of kin would be informed first) the statement, 'a foreign worker employed by a contractor has died in the fire. The foreign worker was not from America.' Researchers back at studios now looking for any information about outside contractors at the base.

Doris, with Gwen, continued uninterrupted wandering through the three dimensional near Universe with those irregular red dots, Doris thinking, 'why did I not ask more questions about the Baikonur Cosmodrone red dots.' In truth, she thought, 'I have never thought about that incident until today.' Red dots (not red planets) of the near Universe and the two arch enemies of the Cold War apparently showing the same information. Gwen continued going around the computer screens that were along the walls of the great dome. Not particularly sure what she needed to find other than 'red dots' or any information about the red dots. She came upon a little cluster of three screens rather shielded in the furthest point away from the door of entry. Difficult to make out any meaningful information so she called, well in a hushed call in case anyone could be listening out, to Doris. Gwen, again in a whisper, 'look at these screens with red dots. They make no sense to me.'

Standing outside the dirty red Denis Fire Engine the four part-time fire men were waiting for the worst for the New York broad accent of the American military sergeant talking, the question,

'You four have been fighting the fire,' (without awaiting an answer), he continued. 'Flight Commander Carruthers sends his compliments, in the chaos no-one took down the name of the fire station you came from. He wants to write a thank you letter, and he has sent eight bottles of bourbon (sorry, not whiskey) as a personal thank you, and for finding those people underground.' With that two sets of blue lights set back off in their opposite directions. For the firemen, their mobile phone secret hiding places remain intact. The New Yorker sergeant, anxious to get back to base, stupid idea about bourbon, he thought it could have been delivered at a later date, they were only doing their paid work.

Underground at Menworth Hill, the death rate went up with another body found. Sad. Thank goodness the dead adult did not belong to the base. Strangely still unable to recognise clothing. The security at the 'ingate' had no record of a courier visiting that day. Searching commenced for a courier delivery.

In far off North Korea, the fire received prominence on the news bulletins. News stations stating a fact that the fire started as a result of funds now diverted to finance a build up of American armed forces on the border zone between North and South Korea. Facts, or no facts, twisted to meet a political objective. What hope for North Korea in a military encounter with American might? The main sufferers the South Koreans, no doubt the pre-conceived plan of North Korea's Supreme Leader.

Gwen held the hand of Doris, asking, 'What do you think it means?' and then continuing, 'we are so insignificant in the Universe. We are so insignificant within our own little solar system; we have almost no knowledge of 'out there'. Somehow we think we are in the middle of the Universe with the Universe circling around 'us'. As a human being I am less than nothing. I do not even feel those wonderful things that speed through my body ('you mean neutrinos', interrupted Doris.) What is wrong with us, we believe we control all, in reality, we control nothing!!' Doris squeezed her hand tightly. Changing the subject Doris commented, 'it is so quiet in this vast space, we could almost be alone in a world of our own.' It then occurred to her that in the middle of the room a small fountain bubbled away surrounded by stones making a circle around itself. It made little sound. It bubbled, a natural spring, she decided, they will not die of thirst. Immediately, feeling a thirst come upon her, Gwen moved over to the fountain, cupped her hands, kneeling on a couple of stones, no small boulders by size. 'That's not comfortable, Gwen,' who jolted back, hearing this Doris burst out laughing, shouting, 'Computron?' 'Yes' the small boulder replied, not quite a meeting of old friends until the Computron started, 'hello Doris, hello Gwen. My name is Trevor, Trev to you. You met some of us on what you call the Dark Side of the Moon.' 'Yes,' replied Doris, 'that's why I burst out laughing, remembering what a strange encounter that was in the beginning.' Continuing, but not really thinking about what she said, 'Trev, what are you doing here?' 'Might ask you the same,' he replied. 'But of course, I know about you with the other 'disappeared'. For myself, with the other Computrons here, a long, long tale. Some of those California Americans decided when this place started construction that the sound of bubbling water conveyed calmness in this area of intense hyperactivity.' Both ladies thought together at the same time, 'why won't he say more?' To which they both received the same thought, 'it is too early'. They looked at each other with a most perplexed expression. Trev appeared to clamp up, saying nothing else. They returned to the screens with the red dots in the near Milky Way. They both had the same thought about Trev. 'What did he mean? It is too early?' 'I hope he hasn't died (Trev)?' To prove the contrary again, both having the same thought, 'all have a time, even this living, growing universe will have a time.' Then almost mocking, 'it might expand so much it breaks in the middle, that would cause the 'big bang' of new beginnings proportions.' Silence, more silence, Trev had done whatever Computrons do when they have had enough, just like a man going off to the garden shed.

It would be too obvious saying that Doris began to recognize those red dots of the near Milky Way, always, forever, afterwards, she became convinced that it had been Trev directing her thoughts. Sirius A the first, then as she recognised more and more (the Light Year distances she added later that day).

Sirius A 8.6 Light Years from Earth (sixty trillion miles)
Canopus 320 Light Years from Earth
Procyon A 11.4 Light Years from Earth
Castor 49 Light Years from Earth
Formalhaut 25 Light Years from Earth
Barnards Star 6 Light Years from Earth
Regulus 69 Light Years from Earth
Altair 16 Light Years from Earth
Arctusus 34 Light Years from Earth
Luyten 8.4 Light Years from Earth
Ross 248 10.4 Light Years from Earth
Achernar 69 Light Years from Earth

What a random, cross-section of the millions of stars that could have been included, only these with the red dots. Gwen trying to remember school lessons about what a Light Year measured, she could never get her head around such an enormous number. Doris prompted her. '9,500,000,000,000 kilometres or 5.9 trillion miles'. Numbers that the humanit brain cannot comprehend. Gwen, thinking again, trying to remember how long to get to the nearest star, a figure of 70,000 (seventy thousand years) she remembered, that was using the fastest form of space travel that humanity can technically manufacture. Ask the question, 'how long has humanity like us existed on Earth?' Not long, only tens of thousands of years, perhaps 70,000 years.

Mosquito time in St Petersburg can result in many a nasty bite if they like the smell of the blood, or are genuinely hungry. With the beauty of St Petersburg buildings, it is very easy to forget what type of wetlands the city had been deliberately built upon, protection from the enemy. In the deep waterside palace of the Admiral of the Russian Northern Fleet, matters were not progressing as demanded by the Head of the Russian Security Services (the F.S.B) KGB to give it some old Cold War initials). The interrogators, trying to obtain the truth, had specific instructions to use no physical force, otherwise, proceed as required. Peter with Anastasia, were isolated from the world, no communication in, no communication out. No access to news, television, radio, no mobile phones, living in a 'cut off' world. Interrogators were required to obtain information as to where they had disappeared to, what they did wherever they had gone. For a professional interrogator to make no progress with a client is not good. They had become incredulous, constantly receiving the same recurring answer from both Peter and Anastasia, 'we were on the Dark Side of the moon'. Question, 'what did you eat?', the answer, 'water.' Question, 'how did you get there?" answer, 'I was asleep, no memory.' Question, 'who was with you?' the answer, 'hundreds of young people.' Question, 'who did you see or meet in addition to the hundreds of young people?' the answer, 'a Computron and a very bright light.' Question, 'what is a Computron?' the answer, 'like a large stone that communicated and is full of knowledge, like a sponge.'

Whatever the interrogators attempted to bend their minds the answers were repeated with monotonous regularity as if Peter and Anastasia had been programmed or brainwashed.

The top floor of the 'Admiral's Palace' remained as the living area for 'the disappeared' two, an enormous main bedroom with a bed of enormous proportions, certainly enough to sleep a family of ten, or according to local legend, the Admiral sometime before the Soviet Union was born, slept with many friends. No modern development for an en-suite bathroom, rather across the coldest of marble floors into even colder marble floor into a bathroom large enough for that family of ten to shower separately, then plunge into a deep (perhaps three metres) ice cold plunge pool. From there into a sauna which by the state of the pine wooden sitting area, not currently in use. More bedrooms, now occupied by security staff, another bedroom for the cook, cleaner, then a dining room, kitchen, laundry room, all now a self-contained unit. One of the two staircases now blocked off, the second with a twenty-four hour permanent armed guard, many parts of the ground floor area fitted out as a high dependency hospital ward, the extensive basement wine cellars (yes plural) empty of wine, full of sleeping quarters for the special forces ground troops. Those large exterior parkland grounds full of military equipment, missile launchers, tanks, two missile carrying helicopters, artillery. Electric fencing of the strongest most 'shocking' construction. How serious were 'the Disappeared' taken that armed troops marched around the inside of the log perimeter fence, then along the Neva. So serious the protection/imprisonment taken that on each circuit the first ten troops were changed, water front providing a logistic problem of greater proportions. A series of barges moored the full length, not in singles, in this instance three wide, underneath just installed electric fencing, again frogmen in the water twenty-four hours a day. One hundred metres out into the waterway very serious naval vessels, guns, missiles primed and charged. Further out into the channel an interconnected barrage. From way up there a satellite had been manoeuvred into a position to view all.

Anastasia attempted to look through the now blacked out windows only to be pulled back by a member of the 'medical team'. She and Peter conscious of a military presence with no real understanding of really how imprisoned they were. Military authorities with a concern they might attempt to escape of more fundamental concern that an attempt from the outside world or a world outside of this world, to give them freedom highly expected.

Papers circulating at the very highest levels of Russian Government these two the most precious asset the State had, those officials sent to those other centres where all the other 'disappeared' were variously imprisoned having no knowledge of the two 'Disappeared' and 'Disappeared again.' A decision made at the highest levels that they were not to be trusted with this most secret of secrets, with no knowledge then it could not be extracted, spoke of in a drunken moment, spat out in a moment of rage. Leave then uninformed, left in the dark.

Within the 'prison palace' the ground floor was almost completely separate from the first floor prison of Anastasia and Peter with the exception of the well head with a bucket, with a winding wheel. Still in use for fresh water, even in the modern world, fresh water an ongoing St Petersburg infrastructure problem, Peter not long after their arrival had looked to see if the well provided a means of escape. He soon shocked himself on an electrified well cover just wide enough for the water bucket to pass through. In a moment of dark depression with the circumstances he had joked with Anastasia that even she, with her thinnest of thin bodies, would not pass through the space for the bucket. Poor Peter, his so-called joke only made matters worse, Anastasia did not like her enforced isolation, she felt as a caged zoo animal, made significantly worse with the piercing eyes of the military looking at her 'male dream like figure'. She knew exactly what these coarse soldiers were saying, were thinking, were wishing a sexual act with her. Her perception quickly giving her an itemized list of the depraved preferences, breasts, bums, legs, eventually she insisted on loose-fitting clothes with nothing showing to excite the bored (funny word with sexual connotations) military. During the first few days Anastasia insisted they should be allowed to use the well to have fresh drinking water. Great concern expressed by the medical team at the lack of food the two prisoners consumed, yet their digestive systems continued to function with as normal regularity. Medically strange, unexplained, now a concern to study, more medical people brought in, now all 'poo' and 'wee' under the microscope, baffled medical. In the cleverness of the Russian Security Services their representatives at the 'disappeared' prisons were asked to compile reports and circulate to all interested parties (in other words not a specific area of concern).

1) Eating habits of the 'Disappeared.'
2) Weight increase or loss of the 'Disappeared.'
3) Sleeping habits of the 'Disappeared.'
4) Hygiene habits of the 'disappeared'
Then to be mixed in (areas of no interest)
5) Sporting activities
6) Reading habits
7) Writing habits
8) Particularly female grooming habits (?were hairstylists, manicurists provided?)

Those eight areas mixed up so as to avoid anyone realizing the purpose of the report. For Anastasia and Peter every day consisted of the same routine, identical questions, the same replies as truthful as always, no variation, monotonous boredom, not a life for these super intelligent students.

Boredom relieved with permission to operate the well-wheel, empty the contents into drinking receptacles, lower the bucket into the well. They discovered if they bang the bucket against the well walling on the upward or downward movement small pieces of stone brickwork came up in the bucket. Anastasia, for want of nothing better to occupy her time, collected those fragments using them to make a mosaic pattern. For the military guards with her occupied presented less of a worry/concern, they could relax a little, once started she would play with the mosaic for long periods of time. Peter looked at the various colours wishing he could get into the well shaft to examine how the shaft had been constructed. No chance of that, he thought.

Clean, fresh drinking water a much desired commodity within St Petersburg, for those who have drunk tap water in that beautiful city, the experience most unpleasant. A captive population for spring bottled water from wherever it could be obtained. Many a stomach disorder blamed on the water. In past time referred to as Leningrad gut ache, in current time called Leningrad gut ache, so clearly blaming the days of the Soviet Union, tourists constantly reminded to boil water before drinking. Over time locals are immune, not those hard currency bringing tourists. St Petersburg, like the other world tourist destinations, now plagued by those Chinese tourist gangs with those relentless mobile phone cameras constantly at work, making the daily video. Whatever is happening, they will need a picture.

Peter constantly thinking how he could enter the well-shaft, Anastasia deliberately lowering the water bucket to add to her collection of little-coloured stones. Within each bucket of water always a very dark blue, Anastasia started a separate little selection for the very dark blue.

Medical reports came in from those other centres, of the other 'disappeared', they all ate, defecated as expected nowhere else this living on water as did Anastasia and Peter. An obvious conclusion that somehow the well water needed to be tested for potential abnormalities. No! The tests came back as normal water, that made the questions more persistent. What food could keep them alive, could there be something in the atmosphere that their bodies absorbed? An alteration made to them during 'the disappeared' period? One scientist made the comparison they had a tree like feeding system, converting carbon dioxide into oxygen. Special report to the super spies in Moscow, the impact of a population not needing any food production in Russia, producing all food for export; all that foreign currency, more important a political tool for negotiations. Imagine the concept of an army without the long supply lines of food to feed the troops. One of the groups of 'the disappeared' held in a Russian prison under the code name of HOCKEY, to experiment with their telepathic powers.

HOCKEY prison had not been built specifically for the present occupants; it had been established during the days of the Great Patriotic War, World War II 1939-45, or earlier for some European nations. Complex 'S' (S for Stalin) a small town excavated out of the high mountain slopes on the eastern side of the Urals that dividing mountain rage where Western Russian (white-man Russia) rubs shoulders with Eastern Russian (Asiatic non-White Russians). Complex 'S' created as the area would be difficult for Germany to stretch supply lines the thousands of kilometres from Berlin. The complex still the Russian centre to deal with dissidents, these they quickly removed to create space for the hundreds of 'the disappeared'. How now to create an experiment on living only on water, real water group, standard food group, Urals well-water group, separate out those from the same country to ensure they are in separate control groups. Conclusion after the first week proved nothing, Urals well water group were permanently hungry with significant weight loss, exactly the same result for those given tap water. For those left as normal, the control group, eating, drinking as before, no change in any foods or drinks a severe case of dysentery for all groups.

Although no admission the experiment a total failure, meanwhile in St Petersbury, Anna and Vladimere blossomed on their water only diet, that collection of dark blue stones continued to grow in number.

Gunfire from the riverbank of the Neva had the military on instant alert, more intense than frantic an appropriate description. Communication chatter at heightened intensity, why is it always two or three in the morning when these events commence? Events were simultaneous, attacks of various parts of the electrified fence, attacks also from the river and the sea. Peter escorted, with Anastasia, into the newly created emergency shelter, Anastasia detoured to collect her now precious blue stones, squeezing them tight, a thought flashed through her mind, 'you're squeezing too hard.' Peter stopped dead in his tracks looking intensely at his right hand, his left hand holding tightly to the right hand of Anastasia, again, 'you're squeezing too hard.' Now they were looking at each other with more than a perplexed expression. 'Anastasia, you're left hand, you're squeezing me!!' Bizarre one-sided conversation with the military pushing them into that newly created emergency shelter. Those military not messing around, they were responsible for getting the precious two into safety more quickly than quick. Anastasia loosened her hand slightly, 'thank you' that voice came again. Intense white bright flashed all around, intensity of x-ray, they could see inside bodies. That deep, very deep flashing, in their eyes, descending hand in hand, descending the well-shaft. Supported as if thousands of hands protected a slow descent. Their feet now flat on the ground, why are we not standing in the water of the well? Peter felt a tap on the shoulder, in turning he instantly recognised Samuel from Nigeria. Welcome to 'HOCKEY', come and see some of the others. Anna remained clutching, not allowed to squeeze, her very, very dark blue stones. She thought (not how did I get here) rather where are we now? As if the moving around without any known form of transport had become the new normal. Her left hand with those stones gave the answer. 'Look', (the stones) communicated, 'can you find a container to keep us in? We have been separated in that well-shaft for a long time, once we were one, then we were broken into lots of little pieces, we Computrons can function at any size, however, the larger we are, the more information can be absorbed, one humanit once described as being like a sponge, continually taking in.' Anastasia quickly found a container for her precious, very dark blue Computrons. 'Did they, him, her, want to be in water?' 'No! No! No!'

At Menworth Hill in North Yorkshire, England, fire damage continued to be assessed, now a fundamental question, 'should the site be abandoned completely? What were the cost benefits of rebuilding on the existing site?' A secondary problem, four of 'the disappeared' were remaining unaccounted for. Doris, with Gwen, had been joined by Philip and Betty the New Zealand computer boffins, who inhabited a computer programming world of their own. When they first found the sort of planetarium already occupied by Doris, Gwen, they expressed a little professional admiration for the complexity of that array of computers, computer screens, after some thirty minutes they concluded most sophisticated firewalls, access codes, were under their control. Of greater interest to their brilliant minds that they did not have to east, a drink of water more than enough to keep them on top form. Disappointing that sleep remained a necessity. With never ceasing computer beyond brains they showed no interest in that chemical composition of the water, once drinking had commenced no second thought given as to how that feeble, frail futile human body no longer needed food. In the past, a very serious discussion on could they function only with a head/brain. That idea fell flat, somehow convinced they needed hands for keyboards. Gwen, by a contradiction, extremely interested in cracking the 'water' chemical composition. Three finest brains of their generation focused on those stars with the red dots, professionally they organized a schedule for 24 X 7 X 365 days a year, yes, they were planning to be underground permanently. For all those who may wonder, yes, the complex had toilets, showers, most important, hospital type gowns in abundance, within the very many lockers, which had been locked until Gwen decided to use her secret talent of lock picking, a fine assortment of top clothing, footwear, even undergarments for ladies. Gwen took it upon herself to be mother hen. Practicals involved ensuring the entrance door could be secure with plenty of obstacle desks and chairs, making a barrier. She did not know that on the other side a landslide blocked everything. Sleep quarters, private quarters presented more of a challenge not as a result of space, no the need to create a dark black-out area. Then a much-desired issue, power for their new home. She started with the thought it had to be self-sufficient. All this down here had to have a separate independent existence. One obvious source of information, 'Trev' the local Computron. Once she asked he gave the impression of wanting to help, he took Gwen under his Computron wings, informing her of all that he knew, she suspected he knew it all. Obvious to begin, water, sewerage, heating, lighting, air conditioner all now under Gwen's finger tip control. Now back to sleeping, living quarters.

The three boffins consumed in those red dots, all knew that 'red stars and blue stars' have been in accepted knowledge for years. This establishment would not have been set up to study 'red stars' many a university did that, no this had to have greater significance, the set up easily costing hundreds of billions of American taxpayer dollars. Gwen wondered if Trev the Computron knew the answer. Is he here by accident or design? How much knowledge existed in the apparent stone? Or perhaps, not a stone, looks like a stone, feels like a stone, no doubt a 'superman stone'. As Gwen continued to contemplate 'red stars and blue stars', the three computer boffins decided to investigate the computer power within their hands, they decided it would create international turmoil without, in theory, causing the loss of human lives. For maximum effect, a closure of some international airports, not the airports themselves only the control towers, take them all offline but only where a close alternative existed for in-air night flights. Throughout the world, airports normally have a closed night period, then an early restart of flights the next morning. With control towers inoperative no aeroplanes could land or take-off. Betty, with Philip, took less than thirty minutes to have a 'computer virus' ready. Sydney airport to be first to go off line at 5.00am that morning, there is a mandated curfew from 11.00pm to 6.00am. They felt closing down an hour before flights had permission to land gave ample time for alternative landing arrangements. Sydney airport completely closed for landings, take-offs. Local news instantly becoming international news. They planned for twenty-four-hour closedowns. World airports panicking, who would be next, the question. How could it be possible, computer programmers wanted instantly to rectify the 'glitch'. 'Glitch' the word given to P.R. people(the truth is a moveable moment of information adjusted to represent the required explanation of a news story.)

Next, in fact, Singapore, there the Menworth Hill boffins, advised the airport control tower that they would close the airport down in eight hours time. Now they were getting bored.

This all too easy, no challenge in this. So a decision to finish on London Heathrow (leaving the other London airports free to take on the excess capacity) and New York (J.F.K.) also leaving the other New York airports unaffected. Their little game caused endless days of coverage for the 24 hours rolling news channels on who could really undertake such a world-wide disruption, had to be either China or Russia with none of their airports affected. Deflated, three boffins with it having been so easy to cause the world airlines such difficulty. Doris thought the thought they all had, 'it may be necessary to inflict loss of life for a more spectacular event. Loss of life is expected by the military, let us cause naval ships to run out of control, run into each other, get marooned in shallow water, leave docks with no crew other than the always skeleton crew, vessels in the Panama canal, to lose engine power, have their own Mary Celeste naval vessels. Betty suggested they would also need to make naval helicopters grounded, for planes not to take off from aircraft carriers. They set themselves the task of all these events happening at the same moment in time, day or night, the same instant of time.

That next instant exhibited for the first time their new seventh sense created to give them a group communal thought. Whichever location they were placed, with no respect for time of day or night the intelligence of all focused on this one momentous activity, naval shipping in disarray in all the oceans, seas, waterways of the third rock from that insignificant sun.

Those guards/minders, medical personnel, were all to comment soon afterwards of the eerie quietness descending on those under their watch, various described the quietness as an event never encountered before, they felt compelled to be stony silent so as not to disturb whatever 'the disappeared' were experiencing, perhaps an out of body experience. Computer programmes exist as man-made, only secure until the group of brains unlock even the greatest sophistications. Most common event of the naval destruction were collisions at sea, out of control naval vessels of every size and description rudderless in the choking sea lanes of a marine world unable to explain mass failings. Less common, more spectacular, almost crewless vessels leaving naval dockyards. Someone/somehow under control until that time of entering shipping lanes then becoming random in movement. Spectacular those that acted like homing pigeons somehow forgetting they need water underneath to operate, very impressive stuck deep into shorelines listing with crazy angles. Naval tug vessels of no help, they themselves running out of control. Nuclear submarines only one safe place, on the surface of the deep oceans somehow American submarines, Russian submarines, not quite within hailing distance, certainly within the same horizon visibility, getting closer to one another. Submarine captains sensibly ordering as many on deck as possible with basic weaponry, this would a conventional attack/defend encounter using AK47 made in Russia, against the new American made AK47. In 2015 the then President of the United Nations banned the import of Russian made AK47 resulting from Russian aggression in or against Ukraine. Now a possible sea skirmish to see which AK47 performed the most accurately. (Not the outcome the then American president could have predicted.) Floating towards each other the newest class of Russian submarines, the Borei-Class SSBN (SS denoted submarine, B denotes ballistic, and the N denoted nuclear-powered). Borei-Class, a giant of the seas measuring 170 metres or 557 feet 9inches with an unlimited range, the endurance time at sea only limited by the food that can be stored. The Americans would like to capture a Borei-Class, number 1 on the list of desirable captures. Also floating an Amercian Ohio-Class SSBN, also 170 metres long, this would make a fine capture for the Russians. Ohio Class submarines also capable of unlimited range and endurance although normally at sea for seventy-seven days, then thirty-five days in port for restocking. Each Ohio-Class had two different crews sometimes referred to as 'Gold' for one, and 'Blue' for the other.

Two command officers each receiving instructions from military high command to capture the other causing as little damage as possible. Two humanmade giants of the military world bobbing up and done in benign sea conditions, drifting closer. Tension, the Cold War back in operation, some thirty years after the Soviet Union broke up with member nations getting governmental democracy back. Yes, the Soviet Union almost penniless (broke) most of the submariners on both submarines were under thirty, therefore, their own knowledge of the 'Cold War' obtained from military academy lectures which were slanted, reinventing history. Under thirty, one crew expecting to be killed, perhaps captured, which side 'blinking' first. Message, instruction flow intense on both sides, both sides manoeuvring satellites for the best view. What were they thinking up there on the International Space Station? Now the only way of getting on or off by using Russian rockets, the Americans no longer with equipment to get there. International politics confined to small rooms not very far above the Earth. Will the two groups, up there, talk about the submarines over that next meal out of a packet?

Much involved within the disappeared group thinking process were the two from Nikoliev (Ukraine) who had connections with that military shipyard in the city. Peter, as part of his university course, seen detailed plans of a Borei-Class submarine. In fact, his group were given a task of finding storage space for conventional weapons like the AK47. Naive, young brains produced the simplest of answers, replacing internal fittings with gun parts, e.g. bunk beds made from gun barrels, lengths of bullets dividing inside of rooms, gun butts a very effective creator of storage lockers. With ease Peter's group hid 2000 AK47, ready to be assembled within seconds. What astonished Almaz submarine builders, all these weapons resulted in no overall increase in the vessels weight. 'Almaz' incorporated these ideas very quickly, an unexpected consequence upon crew behaviour, that thought of so many easy to hand weapons had a very positive outcome for crew morale. Incessantly drifting closer together, more tension.

CHAPTER SEVEN - URALS IN RUSSIA

Having joined some of the others in the Urals in Russia, Peter with Anastasia recounted their experiences in St Petersburg, however without an explanation as to how they had left St Petersburg, arriving into the Urals at the secret base named HOCKEY, Anastasia reluctantly placed the container with those very dark blue little stones, which called themselves Computrons, on a corner stool leaning against a wall. Security guards were not interested assuming that the St Petersburg security group would have examined them at some time in the past. From St Petersburg that medical team arrived within twelve hours, their instructions to carry on as before with medical testing, not (repeat not) to enter into any dialogue regarding the miraculous move. Any comment, question, explanation from the 'two' to be recorded. Russian security on heightened security, they the only part of the international community with the knowledge that they evaporated then reappeared instantly. (More than one of the Russian medical team insisted on saying 'beam me up Scotty' a reference to the fictional means of personal travel in the television series Star Trek).

With their newfound communication skills, Peter in particular, to a lesser extent Anastasia from the shipyard in Nikoliev, managed communication with Gwen, Doris, Philip, Betty within Menworth Hill on the various naval vessels that Peter had knowledge of. Naval vessels all over the world were now leading crazy lives uninhibited by human control happily heading in whatever direction winds, tides, shipping lanes dictated. An exception, any shipment destined for humanitarian aid, a good will gesture which backfired within hours of the worlds money men discovering that these vessels continued to operate. Cargoes now trading, buying and selling, making a profit, forget humanitarian aid, a profit could be made in seconds. These vessels themselves now going around in circles.

How easily international trade can be affected when all shipping is affected. Populations afraid to fly just in case they could not land, those cruise ships like prisons, perishable cargoes going nowhere other than rotten. Fortunately for humanits, 'the disappeared' having established their newly found ability decided the exercise did not serve their longer-term interests, normality returned to shipping, to aircraft, abnormality for all those institutions trying to comprehend how the events had overtaken the third rock from the sun. Security services everywhere at wit's end, what could be happening? Who does responsibility ultimately rest with? Each major security service convinced another security service had full responsibility for the happenings.

With their new found ability to understand each other regardless of distance 'the disappeared' now knew where every one of the group had been imprisoned, Australia, Unites States of America, China, England, Russia, then the four at Menworth Hill. Everyone now accounted for. Quickly they exchanged experiences of living conditions, various styles of treatment, regardless of the hardships the group now a whole, a completeness of individuals, a ring not to be broken, the naive thinking from the young not yet understanding how interlocking international conglomerates really rule the world, not politicians, absolutely not the United Nations where the defeated political class is put out into grass. Ideology from the young, vested interests of the old creating a world of self-promotion, self-interest, self-protections, self-styled democracy, self-indulgence, self-gratification. How quickly the young absorb themselves into the first-self-interest world of make-believe. Religion has failed to create an antidote to 'self', in reality creating a self-interest of the so created politically correct world of dumbing down.

In exchanging experiences those at the centre/prison within China referred to by the name DUCK were catered for most luxuriously, accepting the existence of prisons guards, they actually had servants, one female servant to a group of six people. Couples were not separated, having their own private accommodation. For the group sports facilities Olympic sized swimming pool, cinema, their own hospital. Food prepared to individual culinary tastes, a daily menu, snacks in a variety of coffee shop type establishments. A comment of fattening up guinea pigs mentioned variously in conversations. Medical testing as regular as the other groups, somehow less intense. In contrast those members of the international community were in much more basic living conditions, a daily menu, communal washing, communal toilets, exactly the picture world media creates about China.

Within the facility, the members from the group quickly discovered that all their human waste ended up taken for analysis. Analysis, more analysis. That part of the scientific community on government directives working at various laboratories around DUCK had been informed that the answer to discovering about these people needed sufficient numbers to have a group monitoring each couple for twenty-four hours a day. What was the secret these bodies would reveal to be of benefit to Chinese life, helping in the quest of China, the ultimate goal. China surpassing the U.S.A. as the only true super-power. What is their secret ingredient? Where did they get it from? They assume all the other prison centres will be conducting exactly similar tests, looking for that magic ingredient.

As a matter of fact, none of the other prisons/centres, HENRY (America), FROG (England), HOCKEY (Russia), GEORGE (Australia), apart from DUCK in China believed in the pooh/pee science. A science? One of the most respected and important positions in any royal household would be the 'keeper of the stool' (pooh) for the English (United Kingdom) royal family the title given would have been 'the groom of the stool', originally 'groom of the King's Close Stool'. For an explanation the 'close stool', a name derived from the item of furniture used as a toilet.

Tony Computron, with his gang of young Computrons, continued to laugh, from wherever they now were, at the results of the slight change made by computrons to the male members of 'the disappeared'. According to Earth scientists, all the men were pregnant, scientific testing of the ladies produced the alarming conclusion that everyone had never had a sexual relationship, they were, each and everyone, a virgin. Pregnant men, virgin ladies, no wonder the medical community was in perplexed disarray. Tony Computron and the gang wanted more fun. The Chinese doctors examining the 'pee' of one of the ladies decided she showed an early stage of pregnancy. Examination confirmed she remained a virgin, then her male partner (remember 'the disappeared' were two from each country) at that instant in time his pregnancy (or whatever medical problem existed) ceased. Following intensive discussions, security officials released basic details to the other groups of the new findings. On successive days all other centres reported a continuation of the event, after five events, no more, it ceased. Five virgin pregnancies in ladies, men's hormones still displaying pregnancy. Boredom again set the Computron gang thinking, what could they achieve within staff members the Chinese prison? Simple, effective, safe. Without exception, staff members, male, female, grew hair at an alarming speed, thirty-six hours for both sexes to have a respectable moustache with a beard, hair all over the body.

Ladies do not like a hairy look. Why are those prisoners not getting hairy? Shave or cut; it grew back even more quickly. Palms on hands, the bottom of feet, even where hair does not normally grow, worse of all coming out of the nose, out of the ear. Making matters worse, hair growth different from natural existing hair colour. Protective masks, protective gloves, not big enough. A team of hairdressers/cutters worked twenty-four hours a day, Computrons like new look hairy humanits. Computrons remember that not long ago that is how humanits looked every day, hairy not hairless.

Newly enhanced hairy feet with no footwear make it problematic to walk, running a skill not yet developed, even quick turnout China manufacturing could not produce individual footwear for this new situation.

Computrons well remembered those thinking sessions, all that time ago, Computrons do not measure time like humanits when hairy humanits first started to create problems for all other life on that third rock from the star. Those thinking sessions were scientifically estimating that humanits would have an existence shorter than the dinosaur family. No Computron thought of the immense destructive nature of humanits. How do humanits not understand they smash up the only place they have to live, but then they even damage and break-up the very houses/homes in which their lives are lived. Would the reason revolve around the limited time a humanit lives, no need to consider/think about a future for great grandchildren, grandchildren a distant event? Self interest pre-eminent, is my wealth greater today than yesterday? Can I make more money today from my home world natural resources? Take more oil out from under Earth crust to create pollution. Meanwhile, those vast areas of jungle forest the trees coming down at breakneck speed, those life-giving carbon dioxide absorbers. Make a quick profit today, suffocate to death in the future. A twisted brain motivated by money-greed of worthless paper with no concern for a tomorrow. What has value? Land/property going up as long as banks lend money. Gold really a metal with perceived value, diamonds which were worthless stones only one hundred years ago, man-made values replacing the reality.

Humanits hell-bent on creating an ant-like existence, concentrating lives into large centres of population, an urban ant-like existence, the dream of the young living in capital cities, often called a rat race. In reality, little different from the ant life, subservient to those employers, if you like, queen ants. What are the other ants called? Worker Ants. What is the difference with humanit ants? Claiming super intelligence, in reality following a similar life path. Will the humanit cities one day inhabit those distant areas where the humanit ants were born? Will London absorb Birmingham? Will Berlin absorb Munich? Will New York absorb Los Angeles. Experts predict that in very little time the humanit cities will have over 50% of a countries population. Are we there already?

Those hairy DUCK staff were sliping, sliding, all over the place, as if a game. 'The Disappeared' at DUCK ran away in all directions, serious hide and seek games.

Menworth Hill smouldered, listening (to whatever) it listened to no longer operational, that British place at Cheltenham inundated with additional work. Those four missing, now presumed dead, had full control over all operational systems, increasingly writing programmes deploying themselves for an inconvenience to humanits. Aircraft, shipping, motor transport a new easy target, all traffic lights worldwide stuck on red in every direction, gridlock, seize up, bad tempters, running short of gas, petrol, diesel, to keep the engines running. Yes, less pollution when the engine has nothing to satisfy the thirst. Gridlock, seize up without any form of movement. (In the Ukraine one grouping of petrol stations has a name of W.O.G.), a mistake or deliberate? How long do you sit in the motionless vehicle, the lifetime dream, purchased on finance, useless, how can I get home? Ultimate nightmare, never contemplated within those minds of a commuting society. That commuting world without motorised transport, bicycle, feet, horse, how long would a commuter cycle to get to work? 15 kilometres an hour, what about bad weather, the hurricane or typhoon season, fighting to get on the Underground/Metro, no, no, they use signals as well. How to evacuate trains when the system first ceased to function? Mainline trains need signals; all switched off. At Menworth Hill, compassion from Doris to ensure that on the first day trains arrived at a station, not a terminal station, they quickly clogged up with none-moving trains. How quickly, instantly, a society based on mass travel ceases to function. Everyone working from home with the internet, when will that cease to function? How quickly fear enters capital stock markets around the third rock from an insignificant star. Poor banks, financial institutions, all those worthless mortgages on violently depreciating prime commuter housing. Pensions gone with the ever-failing investment values. Did 'the four' at Menworth Hill understand how intricately interwoven the fabric of a commuting society fell apart with commuters unable to commute on mass, mass transport system by the flick of a switch reduced to a standstill? What are those urban planners now thinking? What is their backup plan? Do not worry; it could never happen? Much easier to pretend terrorists will bring a major city to a full stop with bombs, or poison the water supply. It will never happen. Question who protects reservoirs, lakes, rivers, where the fresh water comes from, just drop in a packet of cyanide or 'red mercury'. Does 'red mercury' really exist? Just ask the Russians.

Roads blocked, transport at a standstill, governments worldwide screaming at anyone with a capability of getting traffic lights working. Bring in the police, bring in the military, go back to organised hand signals at every crossroad interchange, are there enough such military/police to man everywhere? How do they get around? Are there enough helicopters, or enough horses, camels, donkeys etc. etc.

Betty from New Zealand wanted to exhibit more of the Mensworth Hill power, stop those electric pumps at gas/petrol stations from working; any hand pumps left anywhere in the world? Phillip found this exercise a little more taxing;

it took him twenty-eight minutes to introduce the infection bugs. 'More taxing' a primary source of government income for many countries, petrol/gas stations the unpaid tax collectors, what benefits are those unpaid tax collectors receiving? With car manufacturers racing each other to produce commercially priced electric consumer vehicles, how will governments replace the petrol/gas lost revenue? Will 'electric' have to be taxed? How to distinguish between household electricity, vehicle charging electricity? No, there could never be the millions of charging points required. Where in the dark hole of government employees is this planning under discussion, any decision making on how will such a tax be introduced?

On the trains the feasibility of signals having replacement humans acting with hand signals, illuminated signs, trains to run at speed restrictions, how fast is safe? 10 kilometres per hour, not very high-speed trains. A fragile interconnected transport system turned into a stagnant pool of inactivity, who will be the first buying as much food as can be carried to the nearest organised criminal gang that will take it away for their stockpile? Imagine a north of Scotland lorry full of fish marooned in South Bedfordshire, England, on the M1 motorway, for the lorry driver a long time to walk back home, not a good place to be when the lorry refrigeration unit fails.

Doris totally surprised at the lack of basic built-in resilience within the modern world decided, and the other three agreed, to turn off the curse of the today society. How within little more than thirty years mobile phone communications had arrived as the new crutch of humanits. For many, particularly those under thirty, an incomprehensible existence without an instant gratification of holding the mobile, urgently seeking a make-believe fairy tale world of none real existence. Social media, who dreamt up that name, meaning no communication from children to parents. Do not ask a parent a question or give an instruction if the mobile is in use by the child. Why should I not eat while using the mobile, how many secret conversations go ahead in a locked bathroom/toilet? When will a lawyer/solicitor seeking fame instigate a human rights action claiming 'a child must be provided with twenty-four hour a day mobile phone availability', claiming it is for a child to decide when to eat when to sleep? How would the young respond to all teaching undertaken by mobile, schools as a method of teaching old fashioned no longer acceptable in the mobile world? Doris turned off satellites, overloaded transmission aerials that blight every skyline. Modern humanit world at a communication blackout, stuck in traffic chaos, sitting on none moving trains, floating all at sea going to nowhere, air travel none existent. What happened to fail-safe integrated protective security? A comfort of the day replaced with uncertain future of a none tomorrow, who had responsibility for this worldwide failure? Why were politicians not taking control, resolving panic, mindless humanits turned into headless chickens?

Menworth Hill returned normality after the longest four days the world population could remember. Obviously many were never affected, croft farmers in farthest Scotland, sheep farmers in the outback of Australia where South Australia meets Northern Territory, peoples of the Amazon jungle in Brazil, people of Central Asia, for them life continued uninterrupted. Their world of self-sufficiency apparently no way to live in the modern world.

That group of prisoners (not so called, officially) in America, at HENRY, from the very beginning elected to place all their thoughts, collective thinking, into so-called Black Matter, so-called Black Holes, those none-understood empty spaces of the Universe. Reality for humanits whose understanding remains that blank piece of paper with a few theories just on the edge of the papers four corners, humanits understand nothing with its two feet firmly stuck on the ground. How easily the mass desires of humanits are catered for.

The standard model of cosmology (humanits standard) indicated that the total mass-energy of the Universe contains 4.9% ordinary matter, 26.8% dark matter and 68.3% dark energy, thus dark energy plus dark matter constitute 95.1% of total mass-energy content. The vast majority of ordinary matter (4.9%) in the Universe is unseen. Visible stars, gas inside galaxies and clusters account for less than 10% (0.49%) of the ordinary matter contribution to the mass-energy density of the Universe.

Although the existence of dark matter is generally accepted by most of the astronomical community, a minority of astronomers argue for modification to the standard hypothesis. Therefore in simple everyday terms, humanits have no provable knowledge of 95.1% of the Universe, unable to see 99.51% of what the third rock from the Sunstar travels through, encounters, every moment of the momentous journey. That is the point at which 'the disappeared' in America started, then concluding but only for discussion;

1) There is only a minute of observable matter in the Universe. About one half of one percentage point.

2) That 99% of the Universe is unknown to humanits has the collective name of Dark Matter. It could easily be called 'humanits lack of knowledge'.

3) The standard measurement of 'Universal' distances is Light Years. If light cannot travel through Dark Matter (obviously that is why it's dark) are calculations of Light Year distance correct or incorrect.

4) If light cannot travel through Dark Matter what happens to 'light?'

5) Can intelligent forms of existence be present in Dark Matter?

6) Can intelligent forms of existence be present in 'Black Holes'? Consequently, do Black Holes have a bottom, an ending? Are they a complete pathway from one side of the Universe to another side? Are they a bottomless pit?

7) The standard models of cosmology indicate that the Uni-

verse has continued to expand following that event called the 'Big Bang', that model is on-going saying that light has reached Earth from galaxies that are 13.8 billion light years old. Over the last 13.8 billion light years, the Universe has continually expanded. Astronomers have calculated that those galaxies at the very edge of the observable Universe, whose light has taken 13.8 billion light years to reach Earth, must now be 46.5 billion light-years away. A resulting question, 'if the Universe is expanding what is it expanding into?' Nothingness exists, how does the Universe expand into nothingness? Is it expanding into something? Does something put up resistance or is something passive? Could it be that dark matter has no beginning and no end? Humanits are dark matter with light?

Those clever people answer that it is 'expanding into the Universe', so-called clever people what does that mean? Now a new theory about the 'Big Bang', more importantly, this theory suggests 'no big bang'. Canadian Astrophysicist Niayesh Afshordi had a new model in which our 3D universe is merely a membrane, a membrane floating through a 4D bulk Universe. Afshordi's team realised that if the bulk universe contained its own four-dimensional (4D) stars, some of them could collapse, forming 4D black holes in the same way that massive stars in our universe do; they explode as supernovae, violently ejecting their outer layers, while their inner layers collapse into black holes.

In our Universe, a black hole is bounded by a spherical surface called an Event Horizon. Whereas in ordinary three-dimensional space it takes a two-dimensional object (a surface) to create a boundary inside a black hole, in the bulk universe the event horizon of a 4D black hole would be a 3D object. A shape called a hypersphere. When Afshordi's team modelled the death of a 4D star, they found the ejected material would form a 3D membrane surrounding that 3D event horizon and slowly expand.

Confused, another theory, 'the big bang may have created a mirror universe where time runs backwards.' Confused, another theory 'universe may have been around since forever, according to Rainbow Gravity Theory.'

Although 'the disappeared' can communicate all this information between themselves, how can their thoughts enter the humanits word of 'do not disturb me with theories that have no part in my life'. The prisons of 'the disappeared' will not allow outside communications, just like the dark middle ages such information would frighten the world population. Keep a lid on such mad ramblings, whatever happened to 'the disappeared' their minds have been turned into madness thinking.

After five years most of 'the disappeared' returned to a life in the world from which without asking they had been removed. Not as normal, still treated by authority with acute suspicion. Normality for them, a property to themselves plus the minders, surveillance cameras, driven everywhere, minders when they were permitted to work. Menworth Hill time dictated that those four of 'the disappeared' had perished in the fire. Substantial areas of the underground were damaged without repair; rock falls closed off long stretches, many attempts were made to enter the computer hub (where the four still lived) without success. Report after report concluding that rock had solidified creating an impenetrable shell over the whole complex. Much discussion between British officials with their American counterparts initially to abandon 'Menworth' completely, a cost analysis reversing this decision that 90% of the surface capital cost remained intact, in the long term costs would be less by rebuilding a new underground complex. Four continued trying to understand those red dots, from time to time they caused mischief to that becoming even stranger outside world.

All 'the disappeared' knew where each of the rest of the group lived, with their newly given communications skills instant conversation one to the other expanded their knowledge of each other's circumstances, of how humanits continued in their lifetime race to insignificance.

Chad, Chhab (girl) as a result of their families connections in Bombay (Mumbai) were the first to reenter mainstream living taking up their prearranged positions at the major hospital. Again, through those family connections, they started a team to continue work in other parts of the world in transforming 'microsurgery' into 'nanosurgery', the Nobel Prize in 2016 having been awarded for such an advance. Never remembering precisely the sequence of events, the obvious hit them in the eye. Every human breath takes into the body countless particles of all that is floating around, the body itself dealing with those particles. Rather than inject into the bloodstream an unnatural introduction into the body, breathing into the body as natural as is possible. Many frowned at the next stage of development which dispensed with animal testing, instead of going directly into tests on humanits. For a poor Indian family, the temptation of one thousand American dollars produced millions of would-be volunteers. Volunteers were taken from the old with infirmities, that they could never hope to have cured, for them an early death well worth the sacrifice to provide money for the remaining family to have an improved lifestyle.

Prolonged tests proved their decision, the hospital achieved worldwide fame, the next step, breathing in those nano surgical instruments for complex surgery. For humanits an unbelievable advance from old medical treatments, day surgery now the norm, vast areas of hospitals transformed into living homes for the single retired, with on hand medical facilities, in addition, specialist teams transforming the survival chances of the birth disabilities. Chad, Chhab (girl) initially in constant argument with money orientated parents as to why they did not make fortunes from their technological breakthrough. In effect, they were so famous the need for these two 'disappeared' to receive twenty-four-hour security no longer considered a necessity by the Indian government security advisors, the most famous doctors in the world.

Ignacio in Rio De Janiero, Brazil, continued with Bededita their life as it was before they 'disappeared', having felt his eyes opened to technology while on that other side of the moon, he concentrated his efforts on curing the blindness in others that

Bededita once had, his initial work on transplant. A first kidney transplant took place in 1950, the first liver transplant in 1963, the first heart transplant in 1967. Facial transplants achieved by 2010. Perhaps for a month, Ignacio looked at transplant eye as the way forward, his brain constantly arguing with him that this technology could not work with the eye, more fundamental thinking needed. His brain kept repeating the eyes are still there if you were looking at any mechanical problem you would keep what exists by repairing. Later he would say it had not been a scientific breakthrough, he had only followed logic accepting the humanit body as a motor vehicle in the body shop for repair, an add on chemical into contact lenses the obvious answer.

As in India, the eye care providers could not comprehend that a non-profit embargo entered every contract. Having always kept in monthly contact with Lilianna who had been the Rio Embassy legal boss at the time of the accident, instant arrangements were made for her to be seconded as the Chief Executive dealing with contractual licence agreement, any of those 'let's hide the figures' corporate accountants had their corporations blacklisted. One miracle cure from 'the disappeared' had the world excited; two fundamental cures had the media world alight with speculation. Would there be a third? What could it be? Where had their intellect been developed to such superhuman intelligence? For the unsighted to see made dramatic savings for every country healthcare service. People condemned to third-rate citizenship now into mainstream life. Within those eyecare corporations many questions for bloated researchers with development departments asking why had they not discovered 'such an obvious' extension of contact lens technology. Who became the 'film stars' of the Copacabana, conformity produced a quietest of a wedding with minimal guests.

Unrecorded other than in the local press, an assassination of a government minister in Afganistan, in Switzerland an Afgan businessman killed in a motor vehicle accident. Inheriting that pharmaceutical business from the Uncle, Kaamod (male) flew into Switzerland (with his inevitable security minders) to meet executives of numerous suppliers to examine those contracts which had made 'Uncle' a multi-millionaire. Aware of developments in India, in Brazil, more than one executive board meeting postured if Kaamod would provide another medical breakthrough. Now 'the disappeared' were back under closer surveillance, no governments wanted to miss out on that next medical breakthrough. Kaamod found no difficulty in extending the existing contracts. He had no interest in any drug testing on an unsuspecting customer, 'immoral' his words. Without any exception, all the pharmaceutical enterprises wanted to give the surplus, what a surplus there turned out to be. Ruqaya insisted even more strongly for the use of existing United Nations or Red Crescent systems of distribution, a lack of money should not be responsible for lack of good health. Why with all this progress were Computrons showing unusual signs of agitation, what, as they say, could be rattling their cages, in the Urals that jar they were contained within?

Anastasia, originally from St Petersburg, noticed that the blue, bright blueness had paled as if a humanit going pale with illness. She often talked to them about nothing, about everything, so without any real meaning, she asked 'what is the matter? Are you ill?' From the Computrons a torrent of condemnation on humanit stupidity regarding the continued failure to deal meaningfully with climate change. Now a gigantic hole is opening up in the Ozone layer over the areas South and East of so-called Hurricane Alley, the West Indies islands, Southern and Eastern American states. Weather experts have been predicting a 'mother of all mothers' typhoon since the tsunami of December 2004. No-one even knew the final death toll, best guess 150,000 dead or missing, that tsunami often designated the deadliest in history, humanit history, had as a beginning a 9.0 magnitude earthquake near the island of Sumatra. Now all 'the disappeared' were in the Anastasia/Computron link up, as also were the double 'disappeared' at Menworth Hill. Group agreement that at a specific time, Florida time 10.00am the next day, they would announce the potential horror, not of course that any meaningful action would/could be taken. Scientists are aware the Ocean is warming up, this increases the hurricane risk, an area without an Ozone layer increases the risk. When/if the 'big one' comes much of low-lying Florida (the third most populous American state) would be returned to swampland, could it be in pre-humanit history that is how the Florida swamps were created. Appropriate announcements were made, unprepared populations, panic set in. If 'the disappeared' believed in such an event it must be true! Politicians reacted with disbelief, populations within minutes believing 'the disappeared' for the first time they had entered a political world. Colour came back to Anastasia's Computrons; information had been placed in the public domain, Computrons could do no more. News twenty-four hours media now awash with experts explaining the possible event, elaborate charts depicting areas around the Pacific Basin which could be affected, different charts for varying heights of wave surge, of wind speeds, what is the eye of the storm? The fundamental question, 'when will it happen?' Not as difficult to predict as one might imagine – minute by minute measurements follow the Ozone layer loss, same for sea temperatures, once over 26 degrees the conditions exist for a hurricane to start life, it is a fact that sea temperatures have in recent time increased. A world on hurricane watch, it came sooner than the experts could predict, not one but five in quick succession, those American satellites on overtime providing information needing analysis, that big, big one, number four. Always they are given names. These five were Helene, Issac, Joyce, Kirk, Leslie. Much media discussion that the big, big one had the name, for many that name meant 'science fiction', 'Star Trek'. Therefore hurricane Kirk real or imaginative fiction. If Kirk would the next one be Spock? No, weather events prenamed years in advance. Leslie followed

Kirk.

Kirk came, the damage in many placed beyond repair. Florida swamplands returned to pre-1920's existence, before the Florida land grab began, when land changed hands by post without the land having a building survey. Fortunes made, fortunes lost on the whim of postal deliveries. Now fortunes lost thanks to Kirk. How many sold up to the financial gamblers as Kirk began his journey.

CHAPTER EIGHT - SEVEN YEAR HITCH

Seven years had now passed since 'the disappeared' had started enforced imprisonment. All were living lives within the worldwide web, a few famous for medical achievements, most living quietly with instant communications one to another. Menworth Hill four still encased underground, Tony Computron with the gang, also existing quietly. Some of the group entered the world of politics, when those words appeared 'one of the disappeared' election almost inevitable. To date, none of them failed to be elected at the first attempt. In Eritrea, Mary with Joseph took part in elections with some speed that name 'disappeared' propelling them into government positions, Mary a health Minister, Joseph, Minster of Agriculture. World response to Joseph, 'he is one of 'the disappeared', jump on the band wagon, hoped for gravy train.' Mary called on the help of friends Chad, Chhab, Ignacio, Bededita; she did not last long as Health Minister, instead moving to a senior United Nations employee with Save the Children. Mary, Joseph, separated for the first time in many years, only time differences inhibiting constant conversation. Does the world really need time zones? Does it really matter what time 'light' or 'darkness' come around? Stop for a moment, who would win, China or America wanting morning time daylight? Does that make Europe in the dark?

Eritrea, land of starvation, had major international conglomerates queuing up at the door of Joseph all wanting part of the glory for creating new Eritrea, land of milk, a land of honey, so to speak. A poor, no-one wanted, country growing pristine, cleanliness to a fault. Some disgruntlement from one or two Computrons lying in the path of those Massey massive tractors, they have inbuilt survival, sometimes massive tractors brought to a halt by insignificant coloured stones, several thrown together would increase in size if those tractor drivers took time to look. Rains, lack of rains, the forever problem, mass-irrigation existing as that new norm, timeless evaporation.

Within Menworth Hill, no babies, the four decidedly paler, food constantly available. Almost complete, 99.99% complete control of every computing operating system, communicating systems. From time to time rests took place, closing down systems, no country had immunity. Over the years all sorts of excuses provided by security services aware of a more dangerous potential source, somewhere, out there.

Known well by Australian authorities, known to be good employers, Alice with Graham had established a multi-functional computing centre known for attracting every bright programmer of the generation. A and G, as they were known, mirror imaged the Menworth Hill systems. No one of the staff now +300 knew the whole, none knew of the separate underground facility visited only by A or G, operationally under the Menworth Hill four. Two systems, identical, with the computing world accessible at will, at any time. No need to talk between the six. Australia constantly 'in the loop' of activity. Yet worldwide computing grew, social media expanding, a robotic application available for most household chores. Such as;

    1)   a fridge informing the local supermarket when re-stocking would be needed.

    2)   Baby alarm systems monitoring the baby, not only listening for crying.

    3)   Mobile phones monitoring every aspect of the user's

health, messages sent to medical centres, permanent online assessments, the need for doctor visits eliminated.

4) Footwear dictating the amount of walking/physical exercise necessary to use up calories consumed.

5) The correct pint, alcoholic drink ready, on tap, as the regular customer entered the pub.

6) Vehicles driving themselves for fuel when running towards empty, and the correct grade, or electrical charge time.

A world developing of robotics to serve humanits, more than once Tony Computron foretold that eventually, humanits would be serving robotics with robotics intelligence growing exponentially, no one apparently in control.

On the French/Belgium border two of 'the disappeared' had returned to original employment in a research laboratory looking into the ongoing decline in male sperm count (no sperm, no next generation humanits). Annette (girl), Yvon (boy) started as research students in a science which would have more fundamental problems for humanits than global warming. Authority gave permission to return to this science requiring immediate action to prevent the decline continuing. Not talked about in public, that alarming concern that this is primarily a Northern Hemisphere 'white male' event. Fingers point at some factors produced by the twenty-first century, plastics, pesticides, motor vehicle particulates, heat produced from too tight undergarments. At the other end (yes, end) those men who insist on washing the 'end' in ice cold water as often as possible then jumping into heat producing underpants. When did humanits decide on the necessity to protect those so-called vital parts? Not that long ago. How does that true story have an account of how the future Duke of Marlborough (a Churchill) witnessed his future wife fall off her horse 'in her dishevelled state', he could see the top of her legs and wanted more, or so the story is told.

To Annette and Yvon, an initial response very easy, men return to kilts or skirts with nothing underneath. Annette suggested, 'could the same infertility happen to ladies who, as a matter of choice, now wear jeans, trousers?' Much scepticism within the laboratory pouring cold water on the 'kilt' idea. Politicians easily underestimate male alto ego, a few well-placed newspaper articles directed at females, 'would you marry a man who did wear a kilt?' World clothing factories could not meet the demand. What man would wear the same kilt two days in succession? Ancestry genealogists working overtime to answer 'which Scottish clan is my correct tartan?' What man would want questions asked about his fertility? Men for once willing to listen as how to live a better lifestyle, kilts tinkering on the edge so to speak, now a full public debate on 'how to save humanity from infertile extinction?' However those environmental problems as the root cause of infertility remaining to be resolved. Much less of an uptake regarding 'ladies in trousers'. Only future time would tell. All those jokes coming into play about 'who wears the trousers in a relationship?', 'who wears the trousers in your house?' and of course, 'men skirting around the problem.' Unused male undergarments sent for recycling. 'Pants!!'

One of the couples who had been restrained in the Urals were geologists who had specialised in 'permafrost'; they had spent summers in the most northerly parts of Siberia watching literally before their eyes permafrost become soggy, boggy like. No mention of this Earth damage other than within the scientific community.

With no politicians thinking of visiting such a freezing, bone-numbing, intense minus fifty-celsius temperature, there is no impact, the sight is frightening, Mother Earth disappearing underfoot. Long, deep valleys appearing within a short period of ten years, any nearby building losing foundations, standing at acute angles to the ground. Who cares? Nobody! It is Northern, Northern Siberia. No 'votes' in that area. Inhabited only by reindeer herds people who look very Asian, not like European Russians, looking exactly the same as the last many thousands of years. Not within those geologist remit that forest of trees that largest on Mother Earth, loggers cutting it down at an alarming rate, that greatest concentration of CO_2 converters Who cares about the loss of natural wood resources? No-one, provided the oligarchs receive the expected percentage of sales. If not, who will show concern for those now killed for failing to provide that most necessary of kickbacks, life cheap, money more valuable, How many of these dishonest businessmen have their families living freely from expensive gated estates within the security of Western democracy? Keep the family safe in London, Geneva, Paris, free from kidnap (pay the ransom they will be murdered regardless). Siberia land full to bursting with natural resources awaiting the oligarchs grasp for producing money, gold, silver, coal, timber, diamonds, why is this land of natural resources not more wealthy? Because individuals have the benefit, not the community as a whole.

Is any organisation actually now measuring the decline in that permafrost? Leave it for another ten years, no-one cares about Siberia, is not the same thing happening in Canada, Alaska, Greenland? No-one is talking about it. Give me your raw materials and let me leave the land infertile, barren, useless. Carbon dioxide of no concern for me, 'Mr Capitalist.' However, what about release of the methane gases from the ground after permafrost melts? Atmospheric methane the methane present in the Earth's atmosphere is one of the most potent of Greenhouse gases, the 100-year global warming potential of methane is 28. That is, over a 100 year period, it traps 28 times more heat per mass unit than carbon dioxide. Concentration is higher in the Northern Hemisphere as most sources of both natural and human are located on land, and the Northern Hemisphere has more methane land mass. Global methane levels have risen from 772 parts per billion (ppb) in the pre-industrial times, to 1800 ppb by 2011, an increase factor of 2.5 and the estimated highest level in the last 800,000 years, in other words, since humanits existed.

Information that made the public world about 'the disappeared' came through a small group of favoured journalists, carefully vetted, with no article published without the prior consent of the prison authorities, or further up the intelligence structure. One such favoured journalist, the friend of Doris from England, she constantly attempting to understand where Doris was. She had heard of the work of Annette and Yvon who had changed the manner of male dressing; kilts, skits, now replacing those 'damage to sperm count' trousers/underpants. Rachel, that journalist, had considered on more than one occasion making contact with the now famous Annette and Yvon somehow always finding an excuse then deferring making contact. She well remembered it happened on an early Friday lunchtime, a phone call from Annette, easily recognisable with her 'facetime image'. Asking if she would be able to depart on Saturday for a meeting in Paris. Annette, then speaking in code, that Rachel had practised many times with Doris, 'Chocolate sweets will be back after seven years.' Rachel, 'Yes, it has been a long seven years missing those sweets.' As to meeting arrangements, make your way to 'Sacre Caer,' wait twenty-eight steps down, when Annette walked past her follow at say, eleven paces behind. Somewhat 'three musketeers' thought Rachel, nevertheless she followed instructions exactly, fortunately, no rain just lots and lots of tourists. Entering into a private house, Yvon sitting at a table, computer in front. 'Come and look at these sweets on the computer.' He beckoned to the girls, on the screen, Doris with fingers to the mouth miming 'shush' (be quiet) then Doris spoke with a man's voice. She held up in front of her two newspapers both with today's date clearly visible, the timely headline 'Government reshuffle details.' The Express, 'New Royal Baby Expected.' Rachel concluding she is alive after seven years missing, how did Doris obtain newspapers?

Male voice Doris continued. 'There is a court hearing next

Thursday in the High Court, London. Seeking an order that as I have been missing for seven years, I am to be presumed dead. I recorded a few minutes ago information to be handed to the judge before any more proceedings.' Then Doris had gone, all questions that Rachel had intended to ask, left hanging. Her instructions clear, a scoop of all scoops.

She returned to London that evening having decided to forego a night of the pleasures of the flesh in Paris, one public telephone box call to her editor-in-chief meant a car waiting at Heathrow to have her in the office by 22.00 hours. They were waiting, editor in chief, features editor, the most elderly and trusted researcher who always had, always, always, worked for the paper. Secrecy now of the most highest level, the project would be called 'sandwich', the last minute addition to the group, the advertising director. Without much conversation, the group moved down into the basement bunker room (lead panels, soundproof). The first point of discussion, should 'it' be looked at before giving it to the judge? Should a backup copy be taken? The answer to both a resounding yes. Next decision, how to capitalise on the good fortune. How to prevent other newspapers running a spoiler.

The researcher sent off to find pictures of Doris, all reports relating to Doris, the earliest reports of 'the disappeared', for this purpose only using information from the newspaper itself. In itself, the recording from Doris contained a statement to the judge that she was still alive, instructions on what to do with some of her money, most intriguing, if the court connected a television for the judge to see she would speak directly to him at midday on the BBC news channel. Disbelief, impossible, the comment from the advertising director, what is she going to do? 'walk into a television studio somewhere in the world?' For the editor in chief, that would diminish the impact of the scoop. They would need the special edition out on the streets before midday.

Rachel's phone rang, face to face Doris. 'Do not try and make money out of the scoop I have given you.' One advertising space you can sell full page and you give the same space for Mary to have an advert for Save the Children. Doris gone, to be replaced by Mary. 'When do you want copy for the Save the Children advert?' Without even thinking the editor in chief replied 'by midnight on Monday.' Mary was gone. No one in the room spoke, silence one minute, two minutes, three minutes, then editor in chief, looking at Rachel 'what world have we entered? How can they communicate so easily?' He took Rachel to one side whispering, 'this may be the biggest story of my life. For you with contact to Doris, everything is possible. Who are they? Where are they? What is their purpose? Get on the next plane to wherever Mary is.' Immediately Rachel received a text, 'no need to travel. Mary will contact you in thirty minutes.' The editor in chief looked at Rachel, Rachel continued staring at her texts, within thirty minutes the first proof of that advert. Sometimes even in cut-throat journalism, the immediate needs to be forgotten for the long term.

Such had been the experience of the editor in chief that he requested the managing director called an executive board meeting urgently for Monday morning. As facts were emerging the control of information had now moved beyond day-to-day newspaper production into long-term strategic decisions. He needed discussion/decisions, firstly on releasing the 'Doris tape' to the judge, secondly how to proceed with a special issue newspaper.

The discussion at the meeting centred around the correct, proper, legally acceptable method of getting the Doris tape to the judiciary. Legal advice from the director responsible for 'legals' indicated the newspaper had already been compromised by not getting the tape to the judge at some time already, they could play, 'it is the weekend,' but it would be a poor excuse. On his legal advice, the board authorised him to make contact with his friend currently head of the judiciary. Legal people live in a black or white world; shades do not exist. The head of the judiciary went red with rage when given the facts, not red with rage with the newspaper, no rage with an obvious cover-up about the fate of 'the disappeared'. A call went out to the judge officiating at the Doris trial telling (not requesting) him to attend at once.

During the legal hearing, Doris telephoned, speaking with the judge, confirming her instructions, the newspaper produced a sell-out special edition, the only advert a full-page, as directed by Mary. In many respects the advert represented the end of the work Mary was then doing. She followed those instructions from Doris to form a new worldwide political party and investing money given by Doris to produce an annual income of a minimum of £1 million for the initial day to day running of the party called, 'Disappeared'. Rachel found herself appointed as the head of a new internal department set up exclusively to cover anything, everything about those people collectively reported as 'the disappeared.'

Mary started the new party in South Africa, where she had been born. Here that name 'disappeared' went down well. Now the complete group of 'the disappeared' knew they had a political party, collectively they wondered but already knew, where and who the next branch of the 'party' would be started, in fact, those countries bordering South Africa were the next to follow.

Monumental efforts were made during the legal hearing to discover where to find Doris. Doris was not found. High Court precise regularity disturbed. For the judge, straightforward order to implement the wishes of a very alive Doris, a case that insured his forever appearance in case law history.

Mary, after a few days, communicated extensively with the others saying, in her opinion, now would be an opportune time for the group to project what might happen in the world over the next few years. Agreement amongst all, an editorial type document sent to Rachel offering her an exclusive, ready agreement to publish from the editor in chief, headline,

'A None Political View of the World.'

If the world is heading towards electrical motor vehicles, where will all the charging points be situated? One for each vehicle? How will the world produce enough electricity? What will happen to all those economies dependent on selling 'oil'? resulting in the Middle East going from riches to rags, creating an excuse for military action, 'when a ministry of defence changes to a ministry of attack.'

World weather will further experience extremes, wind speed an increasingly destructive force, the Gulf Stream continues to follow unpredictable directions.

Populations continue to grow out of all proportion to available resources; urbanisation creates Mega Cities with populations of twenty million. Children have little idea where food actually comes from. When will the weight of the population be too heavy for the Earth?

2030 will be the year that electricity supply is insufficient to meet the needs of the computing world; internet enters a deluge of pornographic material.

Many European parliaments have parties representing minority groups, e.g. the British parliament has an Indian National Party. e.g the German parliament a Jewish Party. e.g. the United States of America has an all-Black party.

China continues with an expansionist programme by creating land mass in the South China Sea, used only as military bases with airfield capabilities. Japan reinstates an army, navy, airforce, America rearms South Korea in retaliation. China provides the North Korean army with missile launchers, not the most up to date, but effective. (Then by some far stretched supply line, offer arrived at the North Korean defence ministry, 'would they like a leasing arrangement for two nuclear submarines? They could be supplied with a crew of mercenary submariners.' 'Yes', came the answer. 'But we want some of our own people on board.' Unbeknown to the rest of the world, North Korea had two ageing nuclear Soviet Union submarines, one stationed in American Atlantic Coast waters, one on American Pacific Coast waters.)

Democratic elections will continue to move away from those established parties to those on the edges, far right, far left, with populations as a whole remaining disillusioned with the self-styled political elite, decision making forgetting grass-root party members. 'We know what is best for you, don't ask questions.'

Royalty in all countries removed from all/any political influence, only pieces in the jigsaw of ceremonial life, tourist attractions, good for foreign income, news organisations chatter stories, always good for matches, hatches and dispatches. Then the new royalty, those super-rich, those film stars, taking over from royalty by birth.

Certain food additives, certain types of food coverings, would be found to be carcinogenic. Eventually, figures on how dangerous 'diesel' was to human health would be released. Younger people who moved into the growing urban cities will be found to have serious breathing illnesses.

At what point in the development of 'driverless cars' will the motor vehicle brains lock the doors to keep out humanity, then go driving themselves around, all that fuel that will be saved without the added weight of humanit passengers. What else will the robot brains take over? Dismissing humanity as obsolete, as when the robot brain controlled central heating will not move from temperature at zero, or the fridge controls going into super-drive, actually heating the food not keeping it cool, or the baby alarm not communicating with the parents, perhaps a good method of population control, robotic brains not needing humanits. Would it be cruel to do something similar with medical equipment of the elderly, unproductive, hanging on to humanit life?

Much opportunity for those humanit labour-saving robots to take control of their creators, that becoming increasingly easy as all humanits concentrate their existence in cities just like ants in their 'ant hills' (skyscraper cities in ant world). Is the ratio similar? Ant size to an ant hill? Humanit size to a skyscraper?

Mary, with the group, thought those suggestions enough to keep feeble humanit minds thinking for a reduced span of time, well until the next sex scandal.

In China 'Dong' stood in the so-called Democratic elections getting elected with no opposition, which in itself was more than unusual. National newspapers, from somewhere they did not disclose, published detailed financial statements of those monies misappropriated by officials within the area he now represented. Obviously, he as one of 'the disappeared', the Central Politburo of the Chinese Communist Party knew his background; the security service had voluminous files on Dong, also Jiang. Jiang had entered the State Bank showing an unheard of ability to forecast events which provided immense profits for the Chinese State. More than one international bank had approached her with mouth-watering money offers to join them, she knew her place, like Dong, would be to remain in China. Jiang from her very first day expressed in written form her great reservations as to the amount of investments in USA Government Bonds, billions upon billions invested in the United States of America, the concern of Jiang? What political advantage did China get for such massive investments? Why from the beginning did China make such investments?

With her special ability, it did not take long to establish which banking officials, which politicians, had received monetary rewards for making the dollar investment. Her preeminent problem, who to report such explosive information to? Fortunately, Dong knew her thoughts, arranging to meet her in the most open of spaces in that Central Square well remembered for pictures of tanks with protestors preventing tank forward progress. Dong advised, she agreed, such damning information would best come from news media outside of China. Therefore Rachel, the journalist in London would be the point of contact. A well-established procedure now existing between all 'the disappeared' and Rachel. After that, and quietly, Chinese officialdom removed those offenders who found themselves in remote, long way from the Capital, prisons in the lands of the forgotten. Such was the start of the career of Jiang in the State Bank, progress for any lady tortoise-like slowness with a well-defined middle management the height of advancement, salary less than a man of comparable standing.

Her next achievement involved those precious Earth metals some of which China enjoyed a monopoly supply. She soon discovered fingers in the pie, creaming off money from the precious Earth metals. Her investigations tenacious, no-one immune from her investigative tenaciousness.

Dong, Jiang, well-established in their chosen professions. Influence of Jiang extended well beyond China, into the rest of the World with fraudulent activity rampant, particularly within those Middle Eastern oil states awash with oil reserves which in the last hundred years transformed their society by polluting the world with CO_2 emissions and diesel particulates. Would humanits have had more healthy lives without oil based products? What contribution do the oil-rich states make to international health services, treating the effects of oil pollution? Then the oil states saying, what do individual governments do with all the taxes added to base oil prices?

Well over 15000 feet above sea level (say 4500 metres), in Chile, located around Cerro Chajnantor can be found, the cluster of the world's highest permanent observatories. The University of Tokyo Atacama observatory, the James Ax observatory, The Atacama Cosmology Telescope, Llano de Chajnantor Observatory, the newer Llano de Chajnantor Observatory completed in 2002, the European Extremely Large Telescope, so much brainpower concentrated in high altitude Chile, something must attract so many. For University students in Chile, a fantastic post-graduate experience, rubbing shoulders with the elite brains with a lifetime experience of neutrinos, those subatomic particles produced by the decay of radioactive elements and are elementary particles that lack an electrical charge. The name neutrino came from Enrico Fermi as a play on the word 'neutrone' the Italian name of the neutron.

Two of 'the disappeared' had worked here before that event, now after the years of isolation (polite word for imprisonment) they had over the recent of times returned to complete their joint thesis on the neutrino. Guillermo (boy), Isabel (girl), now married, had come from farthest North and deepest South of Chile, meeting at the Llano De Chajnantor older observatory as post-graduates. To them the study of cosmology provided an opportunity of an involvement in a tomorrows world provided from information from the beginning of time as it is believed to have started. 'Believed' their fascination with no absolute proof on any of the accepted cosmology opinions. Take a basic fact, 'the speed of light,' a real constant or varying speeds? Or, is the estimated age of the Universe correct?

They commented many times between themselves on the frailty of humanity at this height with breathing problems, altitude sickness, but needing to be at this height above sea level for the clearness of the sky. Self-imposed sickness for the greater benefit of science. In past time, prior to that 'disappeared' event, walking out at night, well-dressed against the night chill, cursing as in the twilight they would kick boulders. Not really the problem caused by the twilight, no, caused with that perpetual fascination in looking upwards into that always changing night sky full of stars, full of an expectation of an unknown. On the tip of their tongue questioning 'has humanity given up on reaching out there?' 'Will Earth be visited from out there one day?' 'Or is the third rock from an insignificant seventh-rated star of no interest?' 'Perhaps Earth has been visited then vacated?' 'Perhaps it is constantly visited without arrogant humanits understanding what to open their eyes to?' 'Or frightened humanits not wanting a visit from something that would be superior. Better to pretend anything out there is vicious, only contemplating a complete annihilation of humanits to gain control of all natural resources, perhaps 'oil' is of no commercial value in other worlds, perhaps diamonds have no value other than that of a hard substance? It was the night thoughts, the night walks which kept them positive in the early days of incarceration. Locked up on the instructions of the scared, fear of an unknown. Are these 'disappeared' a danger to the status quo? Isabel thought, therefore all 'the disappeared' knew her thoughts, her freedom no longer taken for granted, well, freedom accepting the forever present security personnel. Fresh air, twinkling stars, holding hands with her beloved Guillermo, those extra powers given when they were on the far side of Earth's Moon, powers not yet used. Now they knew that any stone they stood on or kicked could be a very annoyed Computron.

Life had a regular routine for the Menworth Hill four, those red dots on the star maps continuing to consume their time. All the new building structures now long completed, those new underground works started now completed in a different area of the site, that old belief in not disturbing those none recovered dead bodies. 'A cold war grave.'

Progress had been made to more of an understanding of the Red Dots; all appeared between 1996 to 2014, somehow no backup information could be found in the base; therefore Menworth Hill computers were a secondary source with the four having no idea as to where the primary source would exist. Computrons were noticeable by their silence on the subjects, what they knew being kept to themselves. Every now and again one of the four would spend time on the Red Dot computers trying to originate an access code, then the person, would get tired of the message on the screen, 'Access Denied.' Contact with the rest of 'the disappeared' a normal part of the every day, of course from time to time joint operations were undertaken, disrupting humanits excesses. A popular one for the group closing down a satellite or any number, many, many of them in use for the technology world, a favourite knocking out mobile telephones, humanits totally dependent on that 'track me where I go' piece of technology so useful to Security Services. How angry humanits become when it is not working, all happening in little more than a quarter of a century. What time is it? Look at the mobile phone. What is the temperature? Look at the mobile phone. What direction should I go? Look at the mobile phone. Soon it will be, what shall I eat? Look at the mobile. Do I need a wee (piss)? Look at the mobile. And for sex? Will two mobiles have to agree the time is right? Tomorrow world, technology for man, or man the servant of technology? Have you ever played the game when you allow an intent, mobile phone user to walk into you? Their mobile technology more important than other humanits. All those jobs-worthy tasks done by humanits to be replaced by mobile technology, any repetitive function done more efficiently, with none eating, none sleeping robotics. Will there be a test to obtain a driving licence to sit in driverless cars? Teachers replaced with robotic carrot and stick, 'do the work correctly, and you can have one hour on the mobile.' The new shopping experience, sitting at home directing around the virtual shop with very simple robotics picking out your choices, loading into a self-drive delivery van, delivering directly into fridge and cupboard. Humanits sit still and do not move

Again, spending time on the Red Dots in space computer, Doris type in 'OOTHHMPGEEN', access granted. From the four, stunned silence, that compared to panic in an underground bunker near the White House, Washington DC, USA. Absolute panic, literally alarm bells ringing. 'The Four' instantly aware that the Red Dots were places from which radio waves had been received, then project ECHO came online, constant radio waves sent from Earth out into 'Red Dot Universe'. How many years to get a reply? Would anyone today be alive? How long ago were the radio waves now received sent, or are they background radio waves from the beginning of time? While 'The Four' were busy reading about project ECHO, those in the Washington bunker knew only one other place in the world had the access code. But...but...but, that place had been burnt down, then buried. Who, or what, had made the discovery? An immediate joke, 'the Russians are at it again.' Within less than seconds, the current Base Commander received specific instructions to get into the old, closed off, underground facility. Having covered concrete several meters thick over the 'old' that instruction would need heavy equipment of which none existed on site (not work for a pneumatic drill). Such equipment needed the help of the British Army, for the Station Commander one phone call to the London office of the Minister of Defence. That office knew the nearest base with heavy equipment had to be Catterick, also in Yorkshire, some fifty miles away from Menworth Hill. Even in a state of readiness, it took at least three hours to get on site. Not many seconds had passed for 'The Four' to understand their time underground would be coming to an end. Plenty of time to run-off files of information, plenty of time to start cleaning up. Also, time to rehearse the story/facts about the time underground, they knew from the others that once freed interrogation would be constant, relentless, invasive. Thinking in the very early days, each made a comforter, not a teddy bear or cuddly doll, no a small piece of the blueish stone pinned onto the tongue, a constantly present Computron (size does not matter to Computrons). For 'the Four', now a waiting game until Doris suggested entering the access code again, followed by a message, 'we are stuck underground. We are the missing four of 'the disappeared.' How to explain that state after ringing alarm bells? Beyond panic, perhaps professional hysteria!

New message from the Americans to the British. 'Proceed with absolute care. It is fundamentally important to understand four people are still underground. They must be brought out alive. Very much wanted alive, only alive.' Now a complete rethink on breaking into the concrete casings, for the underground girls they had often rehearsed the 'back into the real world', kept a complete set of borrowed clothes with as much make-up as they could find in those long distant early days.

They were aware their skin had lost all colour. Rouge with lipstick, with eyeliner, could improve, they were not going to be called unclean or any other derogative name, they could not be glamour models, presentable their watchword. Now an anxious time waiting, no doubt armed guards would be first through the door or whatever opening would be made. They could hear no activity from outside, only an assumption that their underground life would soon end. Committed to the end, Gwen, with Doris, concentrated on the Red Dots out in space whilst the other two decided to cause their last period of time causing difficulties for humanits. Out of action went every single satellite regardless of what purpose they performed, so no mobile telephones, no GPS signals so no satellite navigation for aviation, shipping, automobiles. Total chaos. Off went all closed-circuit televisions, traffic lights, railway signals, speed cameras. Electric and gas supplies affected, working electric lights only working in the hours of total darkness. Humanit world brought to a standstill. Walking world, communications not possible anywhere, the construction/demolition builders now waiting around the old Menworth Hill underground site awaiting specific instructions.

Desperate attempts continuously attempted from America to close out 'the Four's' access to the Red Dot sites, a game of catch if they could, clever four remaining ahead of the game. Both locations heard it at the same historic moment of time, a defined sound of music (was this the same as reported by the Astronauts on the Apollo mission?") From around the Red Dot screens an American voice. "Menworth Hill are you receiving that music?" From Doris in a matter-of-fact voice, "Yes." That American voice, "Keep recording, keep recording." Seconds later "attempts to recover you are suspended. Nothing must cause any disturbance to the building." Then an afterthought, "we are connected by a submarine cable. In Chile, at 15 000 feet above sea level, the music also heard." Menworth Hill 'Four' decided to reactivate communication satellites. During the later enquiry, more than one suggested the music may have been drowned out by all the 'airwaves' only to make itself heard when all went quiet in the atmosphere. Those senior spies still controlling 'the disappeared' decided to get all 'the disappeared' together in one place, get them to Chile with all the equipment, see what they can discover.

What story to give the local Chilean's with such a sudden increase in activity in building a large new village? The answer, as usual, use a simple, believable story this time, 'gold deposits have been found,' then enough money spread around the local politicians who would reinforce as fact the made-up none facts. (Not difficult to display some gold bars to add weight to those none-facts.) Those first few days uncomfortable for everyone, and the time difference, some of the new arrivals eating breakfast when in Chile it was bedtime. Really completely out of time were Munis and Hubter from Turkmenistan, when it went into daylight they wanted to go to sleep (better not say 'bed' with its connotations of sex). When the stars came out to play, Munis and Hubter were wide awake, then Hubter had a stomach upset, then the food tasted bad. Oh! To be back at home. Why can I not be normal, not one of these special people? Even normal humanits find it uncomfortable needing toilets urgently when in a mass of humanits, that long flight when the limited number of toilets are occupied, even if one wets oneself, still not allowed into those palatial First Class ablution cubicles. Perhaps even worse, a train journey when the only toilet does not flush with the contents slopping out of the designated area in the passing corridor. Why does it smell so chemical? Back to aeroplanes. How often does someone get into clean the storage tanks out? Is there a different storage tank for First Class from economy? Obviously, the mixture of contents is different. Sometimes to defecate outside in the fresh air is the preferred way forward as long as the Police do not arrest for 'doing it in a public place.' That was the option that Hubter opted for, depositing the contents of a gurgling inside, 'outside'. Crouching hopefully out of sight with Munis on guard duty, standing upwind, as the first content splashed onto Mother Earth. Such a scream of anger went through the head of Hubter, even Munis, at his distance felt the scream followed by, 'that is no way to treat a Computron. So you are here to understand if the music from somewhere out there is real or a naturally occurring event in the Cosmos. I could tell you the answer, but I need a good clean to get your humanit waste removed.'

Wasteful humanits in the infinite Universe. Alone, or not alone, music to the ears of?

Chill within the night air, as for only a second time all 'The Disappeared' were together again, walking over a moon-like landscape at some 15,000 feet above sea level on the Atacama Desert within Chile. A usual observer would have no comprehension that these hundreds of young people apparently meandering without cause across the deserted landscape were the best of a generation of humanits. For Northern Hemisphere humanits the night sky is different in the Southern Hemisphere, here on the Atacama as clear as no other place. Warm jumpers on top of day clothes kept the chill away, for any humanit the celestial night sky more than a humbling experience; somewhere out there for the furthest points of light, which the humanit eye can detect, could there be is there other types/forms of life? Can humanits be alone? Condemned to a short life of never finding out, never knowing. Super intelligent, these young minds have asked the question the other way around. Why would there not be other life forms in the great expanse of never ending, 'beyond my sight', statistically, yes. That possibility they are all together again in one remote place on Earth to study those celestial music sounds instantly recorded at underground listening stations, could the sound come from one of those stars with a red dot on the Menworth Hill computers.

Much to talk about as 'The Disappeared' walked in the chill starcast night, exchanging information from their last meeting, some joking about the years as any were just coming up to, or just passing thirty years of age, students days long since past. Anna from St Petersburg still retained her pencil-thin figure; Thomas from Munich had lost his 'beer belly' now drinking quality wines.

It happened to be Thomas who asked, pointless their telepathic powers, if anyone had heard what had happened to those two Swiss bankers, Alfonsa, with his wife Gretta. Somewhere within the group, 'do you think he is still collecting 'Star Wars' figures?' In the early days of 'The Disappeared' each family of a 'Disappeared' child received as if from outer space a bank deposit of US $250,000. Extensive interbank investigations traced each transfer back to a Geneva office of a private Swiss Bank, in particular to the married couple Alfonsa and Gretta. Alfonsa collected Star Wars valuable figures. Within the bank they were little more than lower-middle managements, however between them access to dormant bank accounts. After the illegal bank transfers they were tracked down to the theme parks of Florida by investigating auditors employed by the Bank. Despite repeated interrogation, their response remained of total denial, no knowledge, constantly stating if stealing money remained the accusation, why would they steal for others? Surely they would transfer money into their own bank account. Rather than having a black cloud over their integrity both requested for a return to Switzerland in order to assist into the 'transferred' money perpetrators. After all those years, both remained with that bank having made no advancement, as often a bank deciding to keep them, 'better the devil you know.'

Gretta's mother died, Gretta inherited her family flat, two salaries, no outgoings for mortgage or rent, so comfortably off, which enabled Alfonso that freedom necessary to extend his 'Star Wars' figure collection. Ultimately bankers gave up their search for who made those money transfers, all they could explain was 'down to a computer glitch'. Sometimes the bowl of beautiful blue stones in the office of the Chief Executive appeared to move around. Do Computrons exist everywhere within the Universe as we know it? Perhaps in the Universe we do not know.

Is the theoretical concept of Computrons any different from the theoretical concept of 'Gravitons,' perhaps Computrons can explain the theory of 'gravitons'? In speculative theories of quantum gravity the graviton is a hypothetical elementary particle that mediates the force of gravitation in the framework of quantum field theory, in quantum field theory, the fundamental forces are mediated by the exchange of particles, and if such a particle exists for 'gravity', quantum field theory would describe all the <u>known forces</u> (note all the known forces).

There is no complete theory of gravitons. Lacking such a theory, the most complete theory of gravitation is general relativity. This problem has now motivated developing models beyond 'QFT' such as the string theory.

Graviton, if it exits, is suggested to be 'massless' (remember this is theory not fact, just as Computrons) because the gravitational force propagates at the speed of light, and must be a Spin-2 Boson. A Spin-2 particle is also known as a 'tensor Boson', compared with a Spin-0 Boson and Spin-1 Vector Boson.

Specialists in the field clam that gravitons have proved harder to model than other Bosons, in that other types of Boson do not interact with other Bosons of their own type. For example, photons do not interact with other photons. Again, 'theory, gravitons, like photons, also carry mass, but unlike photons and gluons, gravitons carry the gravitational force which interacts with this mass. As well as gravitons having to thus interact with other gravitons, quantum mechanics means they must also interact with themselves via 'virtual particles'. In theory, gravitons are massless, but they do carry energy.

There are facilities that are looking for gravity waves the most promising place to discover a graviton is at the 'Large Hadron Collider,' (known as CERN).

(So, in building the 'Large Hadron Collider' how many Computrons were disturbed, reacting by now allowing the 'Large Hadron Collider' to find what scientists are searching for?)

Like the rest of humanits, 'The Disappeared' felt a low level earthquake, unusually the same feeling all over Mother Earth at the same time. Probably not an earthquake, rather the accumulated laughter of Computrons amused by the 'graviton theory', and what do they think about 'black holes?'

Humanits in their own particular arrogance believe theories established by humanits exist as an answer to the Universe, could other intelligence have their own theories? History shows that today's 'humanits facts' is tomorrow's 'dustbin of discarded research'. What might an intelligence on one of those red dots conclude/think? Now the preoccupying task of the best young brains of humanits, their thinking as witnessed by never-ending questioning, as for example, William from America saying 'could our solar system exist in the early growing state of a black hole which could explain why no known intelligence is recorded as visiting our Planet Earth? Only to be augmented by his friend, Kerrem, asking, 'have any of us heard of a theory that the planets of our Solar System move closer to the Sun Star?' General agreement from all of the many calculations of the remaining life of Earth's sunstar, nothing for generations of humanits to worry about, unless of course a fundamental error is made in the assumption used for such a calculation. With their never ending questions amongst themselves, Yvon from France asked, 'do we believe that dinosaurs lived between 240 and 60 million years ago, living on Earth for some 180 million years?' Following up with, 'the best longest estimate for humanits is not more than half a million years. Humanits have along distance in time to reach 180 million years. In my opinion humanity will not survive that long.' Without exception, everyone agreed.

From within the group, a communal thought of, 'we know much about the dinosaurs. What teaching is there in schools regarding life before 240 million years ago? What education is there about life after the dinosaurs for those 60 million years before humanity.'

Eldora (girl) from Mexico, a fantastic area for skeletons, not only dinosaurs, started throwing out names of before dinosaurs, Lystrosaurus (found in the 250 million year old rock of South Africa and India). Inostrancevia (some 11 feet long, Russia, about 254 million years ago). Suminia (skeletons found amongst 260 million year old deposits found in Russia.) Dimetrodon (with the fleshy sail) living some 272 million years ago, what was that sail along the back for? Often mistaken for a dinosaur more often than a prehistoric reptile. Dimetrodon closer to being a mammal than a dinosaur, many of the remains have been found in Texas, U.S.A.

General group agreement, so little known by humanit populations, stop 100 people on the street ask them two questions. 1) What is Suminia? Probably 100% failure. 2) Ask about the latest celebrity sex scandal? To Receive 100% confirmation providing all the current gossip. No one will ask a question about Suminia. Now a thought from Emilio (a male from Mexico), we know so little about life of Earth. We know so little about our Solar System. We know almost nothing about this Universe. As always, neutrinos were not far from anyone's minds, as always constant need to understand their purpose within this Universe. On their constant existence going into, going out of solid objects, is there a theory on what existence they have within or without black holes? What is their reaction with black matter, that never ending question, 'what is black matter?' Would the dinosaurs have had a feeling about neutrinos? Humanity knows of no feelings. How can the humanit body have no feeling of a passing through it of an item of the Universe? Consequently no understanding of any reaction within the body. Do they carry harmful 'out of the Universe' poisons into a body? Is it the relentless never-ending bombardment into a body which causes old age, decay? How many neutrinos can pass through the brain before a brain can take no more? Before a brain switches off vital organs? Can a neutrino affect the first cell at an instant of conception? Does it determine male or female, healthy, not healthy? By what mechanism can a first cell protect itself with neutrinos passing through, not one, but multi-millions? What other items from the Universe pass through a body, pass through the Earth? Pass through the deepest oceans, reappearing, it is believed, the same as when they entered Mother Earth. Are they harmless or harmful? Or neutral? Why neutral? What about for every action there is a reaction? Do they help the decaying process of flesh? Does the humanit body spend all off a lifetime protecting itself from neutrinos? Could I give up being human to surf the Universe with neutrinos? That brings back into focus the work of William and Karren of M.I.T. While still at University (M.I.T), they had jointly proposed to harness that power that exists in the atmosphere, simply put, taking wind power as an example, to capture, to release to produce propulsion force. (Karren herself constantly questioning nuclear powered space vehicles. It exists under the water in submarines, why not in air vehicles?")

Possible with her heightened hearing capability (often people with a disability compensate with greater sensitivity with other senses) Bededita, who had been blind, looked at Ignacio, asking, 'can you hear that noise?' After a moment he replied in the negative. She again asked, 'it is louder, can you still not hear?' Before Ignacio could reply, a thought from Anastasia. 'Yes, she could hear a very faint noise.' But very faint if it was not for the silence all around, nothing could have been heard above normal noise pollution. Every group has a comedian, from Dong (Yes, Chinese do have a sense of humour), 'you mean like when the mass of humanity passes wind with humanity unable to hear, do you notice how a dog's ears move at the sound. The telltale sign looking at the windy person.' Doug, having pronounced on his humour, most of 'The Disappeared' could now hear a low, little more than faint, sound of beating wings? Late in the night, no sound from anywhere had been the group's normal experience. Many of them previously commenting, so quiet that twinkling stars might be the only sound. As often with the group, it divided itself into five or six smaller groups, happily walking through the clean air, not separated by any great distance, difficult enough for the ever-present guards who could really do with sheep dogs to keep them all together.

Much louder, several guards realized the sound of the steady beat-beat of helicopter blades scrapping at the thin atmosphere. Several simultaneous calls to base established no night helicopters expected. Now sheep dogs would be useful, as children in Vietnam knew that sound meant dive for cover, not so 'The Disappeared', Vietnam a long time ago. Landing helicopters have a very distinctive sound, these were heavy military 'copters', certainly, Peter from the Ukraine, knew by instinct the noise created by the MI 26 monster helicopter with that phenomenal load capacity constructed in the Russian MIL Moscow helicopter plant. The load-carrying capacity of the MI 26 (Nicknamed Halo) can accommodate two combat vehicles weighing up to 9.988KG in the cargo area. The interiors have space to seat 80 combat-equipped troops. India was the first foreign country to purchase the helicopter.

Peter also knew the sound of those smaller troop-carrying machines. Well trained troops act like lightning in meeting an assigned objective, this easy, plenty of visibility to view 'The Disappeared', where were those responsible for their protection? Only one objective for helicopter arrivals, secure base camp facilities, keep 'The Disappeared' under lock and key, awaiting final instructions. For the mercenaries, what happened after that of no interest, as long as the 'balance money' arrived in United States dollar cash, that universal currency used by underworld mafia. Mercenary soldiers, fraudulent business people, that currency of choice, 'cash dollars', funny 'bitcoins' none existent money, of no use. None of 'The Disappeared' ran away, none stood still in fright, no scared rabbits, see what would happen next. Next arrived very quickly, surrounded by military men, military equipment, helicopter blades continuing to beat into the rarified air.

Again, Bededita heard another faint, distant sound, more helicopters coming from an opposite direction. In control, with no opposition, those armoured jeeps now acting as sheepdogs, rounding up, directing everyone back towards base camp. Security at base camp having strict instructions not to fight, their routine to notify a small mixed army somewhere at the plateau base of an emergency, this had been achieved instantly, and helicopters had been identified. Now a race, with the plateau base military, will their helicopters arrive before untoward events overtook those precious 'Disappeared?' Having alarmed worldwide security services that state after panic set in everywhere, who were they? Where had they suddenly arrived from? Some South American government by sheer distance from any nearest coast somehow had an involvement or if not a government, some corrupt officials have dirty money crossing greasy hands. Within moment those senior world-wide security agencies established two lines of enquiry, protecting those precious young (still) people, pursuing where those invaders could have arrived from, both called for inter-agency co-operation. In these type of events, very often the first place to call are those at Israeli security, 'Mossad', as a matter of pride, 'Mossad' establishes an undercover involvement from unknown resources gleans (obtains) early information. Over many years, other security agencies had learned not to ask questions regarding any source, primary, secondary, or even tenth hand, more often than not, what they report established itself as fact. What did they already know? Why had they not shared the information with, at least, the Americans? Or were the American Central Intelligence Agency out of favour this week? Mossad knew within moments information would be requested, within duty staff only blank, puzzled faces. They were as helpless as every other worldwide agency. Second area after 'Mossad', looking back over recent time satellite images, again questions. Who had missed the military build-up? Or, again, back to dirty money changing grubby hands, sticky fingers. Some piece of important information missed, dismissed, hidden. Who, where has an interest not to allow those 'Disappeared' continuing with an existence? Almost unnoticed, a report from the plateau base camp made reference to 'them' (The Disappeared) showing no outward sign of anxiety. What did they know? What information had they collectively received? Someone at 'Mossad' grumbled, without really thinking, 'money makes money'. Fortunately for him, an ever-listening microphone recorded for posterity his thoughts. Invading military within ten minutes controlled all perimeter buildings, encircling like American Indians, a California-bound wagon train.

Bededita looked around the group, were others hearing what had been a faint-distant sound, getting louder. Others picked up her thoughts, confirming they could also hear another faint sound, not like that of the previous heavy 'Antonov' these must be lighter 'gun-clad', ready for a first strike swoop at ground level. Recognition from within all minds, perhaps a need to take protecting cover, where can anyone suggest? Kaamod, obviously familiar with similar landscapes in Afghanistan, indicated earlier he had observed a narrow fissure with enough width for a hiding place, side by side, only enough space for no more than half the group. As often with their telepathy powers, unanimously agreement for ladies only to take protection, not yet, those guards still high from their achievement. Wait for an appropriate moment when it would be obvious to those illegal protectors that another force would be arriving, giving moments to enable a smart dash into cover. Further agreement some of those more athletic men, Thomas even with a reduced beer stomach opting out, would escort the ladies while those other men, including Thomas, would run in different directions at short intervals. Ready to run accepted by all as a beating, beating air movement, entered realms of loud enough for protecting guards to hear. An unexpected, welcome noise, unconcerned military minds as if standing to attention, prepared for any possibility. With beating, humming, increasing in volume an imminent arrival homing onto the plateau, who would fire first? Defender or attacker? Now who is the defender? Generally speaking defenders sit on the moral high ground, in these changed circumstances, have the military-paid-attackers changed positions? No longer attackers, but turned into defenders or not? Intermittently, arrived those first attackers, more intent to fly over than engage, taking an aerial overview, neither side fired a shot. Could anyone see what looked like a smile on Bededita's face? Perhaps not, with massed airborne blocking out starlight, with mosquitoes descending into every part of those mercenaries, every gun, every piece of military hardware, their helicopters went silent. Mercenaries mouths trying to close, with an impossible attempt to keep out beating mosquito wings, to choke as mosquitos enter into wind pipes, leaving their prey instantly with blood oozing out of mouth, nose, ears. Does anyone deserve to die like that? Straight forward answer, yes. Anyone taking money to murder another human deserves worse than choking to death on mosquitos. Imagine that being a last taste a brain registers, not recognizes as never eaten/swallowed before in all probability. Some mosquito accidents happened with some landing in the hair of 'The Disappeared' ladies, with care those unexpected friends from the air were delicately removed, thrown into the twinkling night sky to continue a journey to where? From where had they arrived? Surely not an accident of nature, never before had a swarm been recorded at the height on the plateau. Silence fell with 'The Disappeared' quietly in deep thought, walked back to base, passing, going in an opposite direction, their minders who themselves had seen death facing them, who would believe how their lives had been saved?

With the immediate fear passing, Security Services moved attention to who were they? Exhaustive searches of dead bodies found plain uniforms, no identification papers on any person, no metal tags on chains around a neck. Next search, their military equipment, their military vehicles, their helicopter transport. Not a trace, no hint of where they had come from, no hint of where their next destination would be, no clue as to organizing brains, as surely there must have been. Who put up the money, who would be carrying the news of the loss? Countries, groups, individuals? In this type of military operation all money is up front, no group would take such an undertaking on credit, a success bonus might be available, and mercenaries only work for upfront. They can spend money prior to possible death. At Mossad, he who uttered those words, 'money makes money,' started looking at all those casino centres worldwide where dirty money could be washed into casino winnings. Amos (his name) thought he had a hit, one of those casinos near Vladivostok (Russia) kept in business by wealthy Chinese businessmen out for days of gambling, night with an ample choice of young, tall, slim blonds earning a potential pension before their looks failed, or more often, contracting a sexually transmitted disease. Wealthy, pot-belied hunting on their own for the inevitable packs of girls anxious to perform together, safety in numbers. Little did those half-drunk on whiskey men understand that the girls had to pay a performing fee to the Russian casino owners. Here then a hunting ground for wealthy Chinese, wealthy Russians, then the casino required to hand over in cash a percentage to whoever claimed to provide protection. For the girls, lesson provided by casino managements on how much noise to make when faking whatever a 'punter' needed to be faked. Many a punter to their cost, in a good state of drunkenness, failing to secure cash, credit cards, as they fell into the sleep of the drunken. A clever 'girl', with the help of management, could have a card used, with the 60% cut for management, and returned before the punter woke up again. Anyway, these rich, pot-bellied, would hardly miss US$5000 here or $10000 there, anyway, they would receive no help from managements, whose first question always began, 'where is the credit card now?' Pot-bellied sensibly walking away before embarrassing questions were asked. It is quite difficult for white Europeans to tell the difference from one Asian to another, not many can recognize a Korean from a Japanese or from a Chinese. In reverse, the same for the pot-bellied, all white, tall blonds really look the same, no point in asking management for a line-up of suspects. Here Amos came upon reports of a vicious knife fight with six killed, many admitted to hospital, a Chinese mafia-gang falling out with a Russian mafia-gang over credit card theft rights. For Amos, he recognized one of the Russian gang faces as being well recorded for mercenary activity al over the world. From another 'Mossad' department, Amos requested access into the Casino surveillance cameras, picking up pictures of others in company of his 'target man'. Then that clever department feeding pictures into Mossad's accumulated library of rouges and villains, Amos was correct, another two names entered the short list of one, both nationals not of Russia or China, but one from Albania, the other from Mexico, whose record showed a falling out with one of the drug cartels operating near that Long Texas (USA) border. Now three whose photographs were quickly in the hands of those guards looking after 'The Disappeared'. With detailed photographs, recorded characteristics, the Albanian, the Mexican bodies very quickly identified, from Amos that urgent message to continue searching for the third. Special Forces from a number of countries, American 'SEALS', arriving within eight hours of what happened, such advantage of having a permanent task force on active standby. Taking into account flight time from Israel, those Mossad special troops were less than two hours behind, being on site those two groups took operational control. Amos now in his hour of glory, obtained mobile phone records of the Albanian, (anything obtainable in Albania for money) finding several repeat numbers, one identified as that casino, another a St Petersburg, Russia, another many repeats in London, a third to Cannes in France, playground of the super-wealthy. Each time a call made to one of those numbers, shortly afterwards, another call to Switzerland.

Amos, with a large display information board now installed in the office, wrote down all information so that the rest of his newly appointed assistants knew how investigations were progressing. Each assistant received one of the telephone numbers to follow through, Amos sat them all down stating this is our disguise story. All your phone numbers are only, I repeat, only to be used on this particular investigation. Each night phones are to be handed back into 'registry' together with a signed list of all calls made or received. All these phones are registered in the Cayman Islands, which all know is the registered business address of the military arms dealer we own. 'I think you have all used this cover story before?' General head nodding from each member of the group, and continuing. 'Our remit is to identify all members of that attack group on 'The Disappeared'. Who were the organisers, are further attempts to be made to destroy or capture them?

After the incident, 'The Disappeared' as a group were concerned for their protection, obviously those systems in place had failed. Having only been rescued by insect world from whatever, what other groups knew where they were? No less concern expressed by their on-site permanent guards who considered themselves fortunate not to have been injured or killed, time to increase protection or perhaps split the group up again. Concern. Perhaps fear even greater.

Only a few hours later, another panic, a large piece of space debris now being tracked, due to enter the Earth atmosphere, overfly South America entering the Pacific some 200 miles off the coast of Chile. In space debris terms too close for comfort. An early chunk of Chinese spaceware, about as large as a London bus, much too large to burn up completely, more important, too difficult in calculating a precise area of landing. So-called space rubbish, who takes responsibility? Who is the rubbish collector? Perhaps the reluctance in that very basic that as yet no research into contamination, poisons, germs, microbes waiting, ready to pounce.

In reality humanits with no understanding (unless of course, authority knows of danger, keeping the information to an elite minority in order to prevent panic). So who knows what contamination is brought into Earth on man-made space rubbish. Around the Earth, tracking stations exist, attempting to monitor the tons upon tons of space garbage, some no bigger than a fleck of paint. For humanits that usual story, 'out of sight, out of mind.' Protected with a none-thinking brain by twenty-four hour television. What would humanit society do with those aged or infirm that could be left without supervision in front of a television screen until the next meal event, then back off into bed, another day in a none productive life, when toileting becomes a relentless bottom-wiping task for another humanit. Are dogs/cats better prepared? Able to lick that bottom clean? But would you kiss a bottom-licking mouth? Would you French kiss an old person smelling of human waste?

Amos, with the Mossad team, now tracing mercenaries into Macao, that old Portuguese colony transformed into a gambling haven not just a sin city, now a sin territory. Macao officially the Macao Special Administrative Region of The People's Republic of China, is an autonomous territory of China on the Western side of the Pearl River Estuary. Hong Kong lies about sixty-four kilometers to the East. It is said to be the most densely populated region in the World. A former Portuguese colony, it was returned to Chinese sovereignty on 20th December 1999.

Macao has more than fifty casinos, often referred to as the 'Monte Carlo of the Orient' or 'The Gambling Capital of the World.' Served by a constant procession of ferry traffic from Hong Kong. Wealth, opulence, combined with dirty money, dirty tricks, and spotlessly clean hotel bedrooms. That tentacle of the Mossad machine had a small resident group of three working in administration at three different casinos. They spent their spare time learning every nook and cranny within their allocated casino, where countless rooms never appear to be visited. More interesting those points of entry into that underground maze built to protect the Portuguese from those never-ending attempts by the Dutch to capture Macao so as to have some control over the opium trade, always a cash-rich commodity. In the past, in the present, in the future (will there be another Opium War?) all those fields in Afghanistan providing illicit funding for a multitude of questionable military groups, that trade that no one had been able to stop.

More than one underground route to the 'Fortaleza Do Monte' built between 1617 to 1626, on Mount Hill. It had been constructed to protect the properties of the Jesuits from pirates, then in 1622 from Dutch invaders, later the residence of the Governors of Macao, by 1810 the base for two companies of the Portuguese Prince Regent Battalion acting as a police force. A rabbit warren of underground passageways, cellars, priest hiding holes, not difficult to get away from official prying eyes.

CHAPTER NINE - DARK WEB

Within the conspiracy world many a claim is made that the 'Dark Web' had been created between American Black Operations and Mossad, certainly giving access into an unsavoury world of badness, secrets, depravity; this however a contact point between Mossad central to field operatives. Through to Macao, Amos sent photographs of those mercenaries in which he had an interest, in particular any contacts made by them. Some, a very few, of the casinos are for the discreetness of the high rollers, some are for every day gambling, some provide the male, female, so-called escorts. All have quantities of martial-art trained door bouncers, or security guards. This complete industry licensed as a large vacuum cleaner sucking in cash money from all over the world, clean or dirty it all ends up in the hands of a select few. (How much ends up with politicians on Mainland China, those blind eyes not upholding strict laws, to such a growth industry for those new Chinese multi-millionaires.) More than once a comment has been made that the Chinese will bet on anything, the crueler (cockfighting) more exciting with an added thrill of death. Perhaps international football when one of the players is bribed to provide the expected result, who gets caught, only the foolish bribe-taking player, or two spiders crawling up a wall.

A relay of pictures sent from Macao to Amos with his team soon had new names with photographs making up that group of mercenaries, with possible one new small piece of the jigsaw puzzle, one of the new identified being a crew member of one of those fabulous ships owned by a well-known business man from America with gambling interests in Las Vegas. Needless to say, Mossad had a representative imbedded (don't tell the CIA or FBI or Homeland Security). Another shred of evidence came from a police report of fighting amongst the crew of that fabulous ship and a local triad group called 14K (14K is a worldwide group originating in Hong Kong with as many as 25,000 members). That police report had 18 members from that ship fighting on the pier with a similar number of triad members, plenty of blood, with the fabulous ship crew departing in a fast cruiser back to the mother ship with an estimated eleven female night workers obviously giving part of their income to 14K. Police took no further action against 14K, the fabulous ship very quickly out into international waters apparently with the night workers remaining on board. Such arrangements are not unusual, history suggests that an English prince was sent by his mother on a voyage to India to keep him away from the glamour of London nightlife, however, perhaps some nightlife ladies also made the long voyage. 'What the eye doesn't see.'

For Amos, one luxury sea vessel on the high seas with at least 18 mercenaries on board, not enough for the attack on 'The Disappeared,' however, a start, his jigsaw puzzle now with more pieces, next stage, start searching the whereabouts now of these luxury ships/yachts, not quite a needle in a haystack with all of them using GPS positioning.

Within 'The Disappeared' there was concerned discussion regarding their present, on-going safety, general agreement to be all together in one place not a sensible idea. In blunt terms, no limit to the vested interest thinking of the group as a threat to whatever activities those vested interests were involved in. Conspiracy theories abounded endlessly. Those 'men' (yes, only men) formed themselves into a small group to say, 'think the unthinkable,' they were Vladimere from St Petersburg, Thomas from Munich, Dong from Beijing, William from MIT America, Yvon from France; as Gwen from England remarked, almost a United Nations Security Council list of permanent members. The added member Germany, the missing one of the Permanent five the United Kingdom (neither Doris or Gwen being a man!)

Collectively the 5 turned their thought now to the obvious potential culprits, rather thinking out of the box, it appeared to them that those with most to lose were those unregulated 'creators' of enterprises created out of the 'internet', those social media sites who now 'posted' information, be it 'true' or 'false'. Why is it that originally many of these 'institutions' (as they have become" start their existence in only 'The United States of America', why were so many of the 'founders' little more than college students? Beyond that where is the American regulation of these institutions? Why does American legislation not extend into their activities? How many of the so-called 'political elite' actually has an understanding of the complexities of 'new technology'? Almost none. How, once these young entrepreneurs have established the seeds of an idea, do they acquire money necessary to make the seeds grow? Already, in say twenty years, these 'institutions' have changed ordinary humanits living habits, particularly sleeping, or rather, not sleeping, and shopping habits?

William started talking, as if with some knowledge, 'let us suppose that in all cases these seed thoughts find themselves, even with the most basic of ideas, entering internet/computer/programming world. That world nearly 100% of the world population has no comprehension of how it works and with no interest in trying to understand the most basic of basics. These from nowhere 'institutions' under-pinning many world stock markets (professional gambling casinos).' William conjectured, 'so someone is processing ideas on their computer inevitably connected to the Internet, that in thirty years has grown from nothing to world-wide, when from nowhere a friendly other humanit makes contact offering to help.' William explained of a website he reads called 'beforeitsnews.com', the others looked and for instance read, 'Congress (American) has authorized CIA funding for Facebook. Facebook has replaced almost every CIA information gathering program since it was launched in 2004. Or another read, 'the United Nations, International Telecommunications Union proclaims that because the internet is a 'global entity' that the United Nations should have jurisdiction over it, manage its activities according to global UN standards and engage restrictions that could be installed at the fundamental level of the internet to prevent any infractions of international mandates. The United Nations wants to include the Domain-Name system along with 'internet corporation for assigned names and numbers' (ICANN) which s currently a privately owned, US non-profit organization.'

As the group thought between themselves this type of published information exists as only the very tip of a very deep iceberg, one of the group thinking aloud, 'he who controls the Internet, controls the world.' So who does control the Internet? Is anybody's profile secure of safe? On reflection for the 5, those activities they have previously undertaken, easily repeatable, like sea vessels going around in circles, like closing down airports, must have caused serious reactions with those who are controlling the internet, seeing that control and influence being taken over by others. Without delay, the 5 shared their thoughts, with the members of 'The Disappeared' it is the modern computing, Internet, social media platforms that are most vulnerable with most to fear. General consensus within 'The Disappeared', this outcome more likely than a government conspiracy. Never afraid, a unanimous agreement to provoke to see what sort of response, hit them in their pockets (money).

With their powers, did they have an understanding of what Amos and his group were discovering?

As 'The Disappeared' had already discovered, go into the basic, the beginning, none of the 'institutions' can exist without a supply of power (electricity), no doubt back-ups existed, the beginning is that generating facility remembering that electricity is not stored, instant creation for instant use, which of course asks the questions, 'why has no clever scientist discovered a method of storing/storage?' 'What firewall protections exist at those many tens of thousands of generating facilities? Not strong, poor, almost none.'

Often, for no obvious reason, one thought leads to another. Bededita however found herself thinking about how society (particularly) affluent society happily placed parents, grandparents into so-called care homes, locked into little better than single-person cells with television, perhaps a window. Before that living in so-called 'adult communities' if money existed in plenty, otherwise inferior care home institutions funded by the state. Yet in the so-called 'Poorer World/Third World' parents, grandparents are looked after by younger members of the family within a home/house/property they have lived within. Would old people have a happier life within a family of the Third World, compared with a prison-type existence within the affluent world? What is it in the affluent world that makes such an existence acceptable? Why not be truthful, 'lock them up, throw the key away', unacceptable to keep a visitors list. How often visits made, how long a visit lasts, what is an acceptable length for a visit? Ten minutes too short, fifty minutes too long, anyway come with an excuse as to why short-time visit is only possible? Heaven help (can you believe in Heaven when also locking relatives away) any family member locked away who starts repetitive talking, or even worse, repetitive talking about those 'good old days'. Without a scientific study into mind thoughts such affluent society behavior cannot be comprehended, even ants look after the older members of the anthill. Is it true that some ants live to 12 or 15 years old? At the other size dimension think of elephants remaining as a family group; they say when it is time to die, the herd knows. Who knows what goes on with those that live in the ocean deeps? Of course, humanity will be of an opinion that these 'things' do not have families or feelings, or real brains. What colours do their eyes indicate? For humanits, who decided to call red, red? What colours do so-called 'colour-blind' people see? Are they 'colour-blind' or do they see colours as they really exist, anyway humanits only see a limited number of colours, those existing within the colour spectrum, ask a bat what colours a bat can see.

Electricity back in everyone's thinking, except for Helga from Munich with plastic society on her mind. How all over the world food is packaged in plastic materials. What makes plastic a by-product of the petroleum industry? Plastics are made from oil. Oil is a carbon-rich raw material, and plastics are large carbon-containing compounds. They're large molecules called polymers, which are composed by repeating units of repeating units of shorter carbon containing compounds called monomers. It was not until 1907 that Leo Hendrik Baekeland invented the first fully synthetic commercially successful plastic. He called it Bakelite, which was much easier to pronounce than its chemical name; 'polyoxybenzylmethylenglycolanhydride.'

As Helga pondered, 'would you deliberately pour 'oil' or 'petrol' on food before eating?' 'How easily accepted benefits of food covered in plastic materials, or was it the food industry pushing the concept, so what chemicals pass from plastic into food? Are we supposed to believe 'none'? Could they be carcinogenic? Could they contribute to the explosion in cancer? Well, would any government enterprise tell a world population, or keep the information secret?' These thoughts of Helga were picked up by all, particularly by 'Mary', who with her experience in the Horn of Africa, had always commented on the volumes of non-needed plastics on food delivered for the underfed/starving. Both of them thinking about all those millions of tons of plastic dumped into seas/oceans of this little planet now filling up with unwanted plastics with all those sea creatures consuming plastics thinking it would be food, or entangled in plastic bags which somehow manage to intertwine themselves. Now what happens to humanity when the seafood eaten has plastic waste inside? How much other food do humanits consume containing plastic waste, in addition to that plastic on food packaging? How often will a cook take food out of the plastic packaging and wash it before cooking, then of course, all those minute plastic pieces find their way into sewerage, rivers, and water flows, into oceans, seas, for those of the seas to eat (again and again)? For humanits, what will be the health result of too much plastic in the blood stream, body, not healthy when those life-providing intestines are full of plastics. Not to worry, it will not happen to my family or me. Perhaps a mother can look forward to her baby being delivered in a plastic bag directly from the womb, or perhaps at the other end, 'poo' appearing pre-wrapped into a toilet. Will we need toilets or only larger plastic bags to drop pre-packed 'poo' into? Then what will be developed to replace plastic bags? Some form of propulsion to get it out from Mother Earth into space. But!! Why can the waste not be turned into a useful product such as building material? How quickly the world entered pollution contamination from plastic since 1907, with much of that in the last twenty years with post-millennial polluters, of course today's young generation is of an opinion that meat, more particularly burgers, grows in plastic packets with nothing to do with those cuddly sheep, cows, pigs or chickens, or as they say, 'meat comes from the supermarket'. Exactly the same cows not involved, in bottles (sorry, plastic containers) directly from a shop, or even a petrol station. Do not ask a child of the day, 'why does a cow produce milk?' as the answer might be uncomfortable to think about. Surely the milk is not stolen from baby cows (calf's). It does not say that on the bottle container. There is no computer game to play as to where milk comes from. With the ladies musing on these strange ideas, with men working out how to close down the electric power system, news came in of earthquakes starting, regardless of which country, all taking place at the same moment in time. 'An unprecedented event' started those flash news reports from every countries twenty-four hour rolling news.

Girls were still thinking those unthinkable thoughts, showing concern for humanit inhumanity, Anernerk from Alaska started the thoughts with what seemed an outrageous statement, '99% of Earth species no longer exist, that 1% remaining humanits are destroying at an ever increasing rate of destruction.' Without stopping she went on, 'take the West African Black rhino, declared extinct in 2011, the last one having been sighted in 2006, see within our lifetimes a huge animal like that no longer to be seen in Africa. Why were they killed? For the horn used in Chinese medicine. Forget all that remaining huge body, leave that to rot or eaten, just sell 'horn' to those Chinese producers of medicines. There is another branch of the Black Rhino family in Sub-Saharan Africa which in the 1970's had an estimated population of 60,000 to 70,000, now best calculation is that 5000 remain alive, now critically endangered.' Humanits have little concern. Extinctions happened all the time, there is no let-up in humanit advance destroying all in its so-called 'march of progress.' What do we know of that which has gone recently? Not an exhaustive list just a taster (not all of them eaten by humanits.) Golden Toad 1989, Zanzibar Leopard 1996, Poouli 2004, Maderian Large White Butterfly 2007, Tecopa Pupfish 1982, Pyrenean Ibex 2000, Javan Tiger 1979, Spix's Macaw 2004, Round Island Burrowing Boat 1975, Dutch Alcon Blue Butterfly 1979.' All never to be seen again. Then a masculine but from Anik, 'what about animals, insects, birds, reptiles not yet discovered?' With a response from Anernerk. 'So humanity needs to discover them so they can be driven into extinction?' Are they all in deepest Amazonia?'

Rolling twenty-four hours news continued reporting on more earthquakes worldwide, not yet concerning those 'Disappeared' however they did notice heightened activity from their protectors, were they concerned by another earthquake coming to them? No!! Impossible to determine where an actual earthquake is going to occur.

Thinking not disturbed in those fertile minds of scientific men with such overwhelming brain power, no doubt these current thoughts prompted by knowledge concerning that recent death of Stephen Hawking with his mind-changing ideas concerning theoretical physics, concerning cosmology. Specifically discussions were continuing the 'black hole information paradox,' not a common expression, particularly difficult for an every-day humanit to comprehend, more important, has 'black hole information paradox' any relevance to ordinary every-day life on Earth?

The paradox arose after Hawking showed in 1974/5 that Black Holes surrounded by quantum fields actually will radiate particles (Hawking Radiation) and shrink in size, eventually evaporating completely. In simple terms, where does information entering a Black Hole go to/end up? Maybe the information came back out with the Hawking Radiation? Problem is that information in the Black Hole cannot get out. So the only way it can be in the Hawking Radiation (naively) is if that which is inside is copied. Having two copies of the information, one inside, one outside, also violates quantum theory. Of course, it may simply be that quantum theory is incomplete, and that the physics of Black Holes forces us to extend that theory, much as Einstein extended Newton's Laws of Motion in his Theory of Relativity. And this is what Hawking believed for three decades. However, others felt that it was General Relativity not Quantum Theory, that would need to be changed and a proposal was made in 1992, called 'complementarity' that suggested that the information was in a sense both inside and outside but without violating Quantum theory. ('Susskind' and the younger co-workers developed this proposal). Specifically, observers who remain outside the Black Hole see the information accumulate at the horizon, and then come flying outward in the 'Hawking Radiation'. Observers who fall into the Black Hole see the information located inside, the two classes of observers cannot communicate, and there is no paradox. Still, the suggestion is potentially self-contradictory, and requires a number of strange things to be true. Among them is something called, 'holography,' an idea developed by T Hooft and further by Susskind. The idea is that the physics of the three-dimensional interior of the Black Hole, where gravity obviously plays a role, can instead be viewed via a rather mysterious transformation, as Physics, just above the two-dimensional horizon, when it is described by two-dimensional equations that do not include gravity at all.

Within these active minds of 'The Disappeared' they were thinking theoretically beyond Stephen Hawking. To their minds, there existed no death, no nothingness of a Black Hole, their theory, as a Black Hole contracts, gets smaller, around the size of a pin-head weight to size ejects at speed the Dark Matter which is infinitely more substantive than the Speed of Light (that reason for humanity not detecting Dark Matter) into another Universe. Within the Event Horizon, entering a new Universe, then, rather like magnets (attracting/rejecting) matter within another Universe attracts itself onto the pin head of a Black Hole creating a new star formation, inverse, reverse, regeneration. If you like the other side of a coin. Not all males agreed, this had become a male-only conversation. Another group questioned, 'complementarity' information (identical) both inside and outside Black Holes simultaneously (as one school boy suggested, a giant photocopying machine). 'Out of the mouths of babes'. However that school boy went on to contradict himself with saying, 'Yes, but only one is original.' Not to be outdone by the girls (Doris from England) 'it is all theoretical, little minds, on a little planet, with little real equipment trying to create an understanding of everything, are we little better than stone-age man creating tools inefficient for the task/problem trying to be understood. Are we even making a scratch on the surface of Universal knowledge? Is not our perceived knowledge nothing more than one theory built on an earlier one. We accept a theory of Dark Matter really what we are saying, is we have no understanding/knowledge of immense areas of the universe, and then our equipment is not as accurate as we believe, remember every computer programme is only as effective as the person's knowledge who does the programme writing. General agreement on the frailty of humanits knowledge, in superior self-belief. Blind belief is what any other inhabitants of our Universe will look like, heaven forbid if they were superior in any respect with greater knowledge. Could a bookmaker offer betting odds on other intelligent life within the Universe?

Rolling twenty-four hours news continuing with more reports of earthquakes reported from Japan (probably a continuation of those in China), Australia, Vietnam. Are they all a continuation of the Chinese event, many reported cases in the Eastern hemisphere. Why? Enhanced activity within the platoon of minders, obviously awaiting instructions from one or other of those with ultimate responsibility for 'The Disappeared' safety. Plenty now of speculation from those news media 'paid' so called experts, consensus formulating around movement in one of those 'plates' covering the Earth, constantly in movement yet undetected for humanit. However some ability/instinct of the animal/bird/reptile world ready to move prior to the first sign of danger, then follow those flocks.

Now Thailand, India, Malaysia, Vietnam reporting 'quakes', those television pundits now in total agreement all events restricted to Earth's Eastern hemisphere. Much discussion on the yet to come catastrophic California San Francisco earthquake, then into guesswork as to how long before that event, of course the longer those pundits talk for, the greater their fee. They will not tell you no-one can predict/forecast/estimate when or where earthquakes will occur, except 'probably' somewhere along tectonic plates that hold above them Earth's Continent, a literal meaning to that expression, 'the Crunch.' Look at what they can create in a big crunch, the Himalaya's where at many thousands of feet in the air, sea fossils are found on the highest mountains in the world, the most recent in formation, 'ice clad sea beds on top of the Himalayas.'

Television pundits started contradicting themselves with news concerning earthquakes in Brazil, United States of America, Brazil now getting close to Chile, 'The Disappeared.' Again

Ignacio from Brazil noticed prices of minerals increasing with alarming speed, he commented, 'forget about electrical supply, look at the prices of rare Earth minerals. All those countries with earthquakes are the producers of rare Earth minerals.' With that thought of Ignacio hanging in the rarified air, those television pundits caught up with his thought pattern. Pundits in an instant realising greater fees from explaining about rare Earth minerals. What they are. Where they come from. What are they used for, not to be outdone, the programme interviewer started, 'is it true that the mineral value of a mobile telephone is many times greater than the minerals making up the human body?' This produced a response from an expert. 'Our world of computers, mobile phones, aircraft, cannot exist without rare Earth minerals.' Then reeling off a summary.

Neodymium, used to make powerful magnets used in loudspeakers and computer hard drives, in green technology for wind turbines and hybrid cars.

Lanthanum, used in camera and telescope lenses, studio lighting and camera projection.

Cerium, used in catalytic converters in cars. Lanthanum and cerium are used in refining crude oil.

Praseodymium, used to create strong metals for use in aircraft engines.

Gadolinium, used in x-ray and MRI scanning systems, also in television screens.

Yttrium, Terbium, Europium (sounds like a drug) important in making televisions and computer screens and other devices that have visual displays. Europium is used in making control rods in nuclear reactors.

A complete listing of the 17 rare Earth metals/rare Earth elements;

Scandium
Yttrium
Lanthanum
Praseodymium
Neodymium

Promethium
Samarium
Europium
Gadolinium
Terbium
Dysprosium
Holmium
Erbium
Thulium
Ytterbium
Lutetium
Cerium.

Rare Earth elements are peppered throughout a mobile phone, from the glass display, making it harder, magnets in speakers, headphones and vibrating motors.

Now, the television pundits were out of their depths, not that they would admit it. How is it possible to have specific earthquakes in well-defined areas only where rare Earth elements are mined?

Mary said she was fed up with all this talking. Who has ever seen statistics on the wear and tear inflicted on a humanit body caused by every-day commuting to a work place? Total none response, these brightest of the most intelligent of a generation had never seen any statistical information.

Sometimes, with a new transport system investigations into time saving, in other words, promoting that new system. As with much in humanit life, an obvious life requirement (not choice) under-researched as no doubt findings might show results not wanted by those multi-national corporations in major city conurbations, is it just too obvious that health issues arise? Take an example of Japanese commuters regularly wearing facemasks as a normality. What would they say in the London underground with people coughing, sneezing, breathing germs in and out without face masks on, no wonder flu epidemics spread so quickly. Does group travel explain the compulsion to travel alone in a motorcar, perhaps, or could it be laziness in not walking to a bus stop, train station, tram stop. Living in a block of flats? Where do you park the vehicle? Why has car sharing never become popular? Keep out of my space! Is there a psychological reason why some want to travel alone, some will walk with other humanits, or is it only a financial consideration.

How bad is the air these commuters breath? A recent exhibition consisted of 'smells', large jars full of smells which visitors are invited to smell and recognize. With all the many, many jars all can be sniffed/smelt with one exception that jar containing 'London Air'. This jar of London air has been designated too 'harmful' for people to smell. Therefore a reality of walking into that exhibition, breathing London air all the time, toxic, full of particulates but not to breath out of the jar on display in the exhibition. Exhibition managements no doubt advised of those health and safety concerns of London's unhealthy air. What does that say about the inability of politicians to provide healthy air for citizens?

Take London, its famous fogs caused by every home using coal fires, factory chimneys belching out smoke, at that time a clear air act required use of smokeless fuels, London now rid of 'Sherlock Holmes fog' instead a smog of fumes/particulates from the combustion engine. Health officials manage to be alarmed at an increase in death from chest complaints/breathing problems, yet the answer stares them in the face. Every minute of every day, with line upon line of stationary traffic jams, get rid of the combustion engine. London just one of many, the infamous Los Angeles where the city lives under a thick blanket of pollution. Or perhaps Beijing or Mumbai or any major world city, inhabitants always breathing in pollution. (Ah yes, but that is where the best paid jobs are, how much of that 'best paid jobs' is a premium for a premature death, with children growing up with ever-persistent chest complaints. What will historians call such pollution in years to come, something like the 'Black Death,' or a name of its own, 'Preventable Death?'

Events overtook those plans of 'The Disappeared' to affect electrical supplies with the earthquakes causing phenomenal repercussions to humanits at so-called natural disasters. Were they natural? In that sense, yes, and that is what the populous were left to think. Governments everywhere were searching for a real cause. (Computrons, everywhere were laughing.) No neutrinos were known to have lost their flight path through the earthquake areas. What could humanits use to replace the now-lost rare Earth metals? Easy exploration to discover more of the same. Just like early gold rushes in America and Australia, huge profits to be made for those making these new discoveries, if only they had known that there was none left to be found. Exploration companies were formed raising enormous sums of money from a greedy public.

With the earthquake dust settling, a unanimous decision of 'The Disappeared' to remove all electrical supplies with the exception of hospitals, somehow those humanits needing specialist medical equipment in their homes continued receiving a supply. Television experts trying desperately to explain how such circumstances could take place. How could mankind continue to exist without computing? Unfortunately, with no electricity they were talking to themselves, but to them it did not matter, self-importance.

From within the group one of those far thinking ideas developed a phone small enough to fit on a nose with a camera recording all of the/your life, such an idea only a short step from babies being born with a right arm next to the ear, with a right hand already formed ready to receive a mobile phone, a whole new meaning to being nosy. With such developments, those 'do-gooders', 'health and safety' fanatics would have days of anxiousness worrying what life-threatening illness such equipment will inflict on ill-prepared human bodies, any different from plastics? In their minute sizes, easily inhaled. Could raindrops now be falling with minute plastic particles crashing onto human bodies? Impossible? Why impossible? Think of normal rain, ocean, rain cycle, rain arriving from the seas/oceans contain elements of salt, humans unable to see, to smell, to feel raindrop salt. Could the same happen every day with plastic? Perhaps the minute plastic particulates will be inhaled entering lungs, entering blood flow, could these plastics build-up over time causing body damage. Falling as rain, into water flows, rivers, seas, oceans, then back as rain. Think of all animal world, fish world, and reptile world, also consuming those particulates. Such a modern experience of the recent plastic world and no one having any knowledge of long-term consequences. Of course, there will be. When will humanits take action to prevent this potential long-term killer? Will there be any plastic producers left to prosecute when it is proven to be a mass killer? All those lawyers looking for easy income. As this is currently being written a factual story of a beached sperm whale with sixty-four pounds of plastic, rope, fishnet lodged in its stomach (February 27th 2018). Again, dead pilot whale found with eighty plastic bags in stomach on a Thailand beach (June 2nd 2018)a further comment at least 300 marine animals die in Thai waters from plastic ingestion each year. Obviously a tip of a very deep iceberg.

4Ocean posted this in 2017. 'Every minute one garbage truck worth of plastic is dumped into the ocean. Yearly, a colossal 1.4 billion tons of trash ends up in our beautiful oceans. Of this waste, much of it is plastic. To date there has been 275 billion plastic bags produced worldwide in just 2017alone. Every second a massive amount of 160,000 plastic bags are being produced and used.'

If only living creatures could organize a mass extinction of humanity, what a better world they would enjoy. Perhaps another flu epidemic, humanity creates extreme feelings of sadness when another humanit dies, somehow managing to convince itself that nothing else can feel sadness. Perhaps nature will win in the end with constant plastic particulates inhaled by humanity. Some people would like 'The Disappeared' to go away forever. Yes, killed if necessary, as soon as possible, if not in the next few minutes.

Amos, with his Mossad group, continued to piece together the internationally complex jigsaw puzzle. Still information retained amongst themselves, no sharing with any other 'spy organization.' No benefit yet to be gained for sharing. Now very obvious within Mossad that very powerful people wanted the extermination of 'The Disappeared.' Needles in haystacks, GPS positioning, port authorities, Amos receiving new information, rest assured with satellites those wide open oceans aren't that wide-open. Then the old way reports from military vessels, eventually established eight of the ocean going luxury private yachts/liners had assembled at a disused slipway off the coast of Chile. Not any one country, more as if the wealthiest of the World had acted with a common interest of protecting their wealth. For a reader not difficult to name those super-rich with their beyond-luxurious ocean-going vessels. So who makes up the ordinary, every-day crew? Quite often those who work for peanuts but want to travel to exotic places. Plus, of course, any 'spy' type people who can get employed, say an American working for Russians, not an easy life below deck, cramped quarters, normal food, at the beck and call not of the super rich, those the super-rich employ to look after day-to-day living. Imagine when the super-rich are absent, that management left behind, taking every conceivable advantage, some infamous people have mysteriously died on those floating gin palaces, less public knowledge of deaths of crew members as reported in one case of a young man on night duty, he disappeared on duty with no one missing him until morning. Lost at sea, no screams for help, no body recovered, just disappeared. Who did he upset? Perhaps someone discovered her was the spy. How many young ladies take up employment as fitness coaches, waitresses, cleaners, or even the doctor or nurse? How many of those will be expected to provide sexual favours?

For Amos, his Mossad colleagues, in their own minds, with enough proof establishing who the organisers were, where they had come from, now dispersed licking their wounds, obviously an expectation that the group would try again. As Amos knew, so too did 'The Disappeared' who, without exception, decided to respond against those responsible. Assuming that one of the yacht owners involved itself in retail selling of clothing, stories quickly circulated (with evidence) that clothes were manufactured in near-slave-trade factories that is hated by 'Mrs Public'. She wants cheap clothes without knowledge of who manufactures them or slave workers working conditions of long, long hours with no proper breaks, limited time to visit toilet. Industrial injuries never recorded, compensation never paid, fire regulations of no consequence. Where does pressure originate from to those 'slave factories' working in desperation to fulfill shipping schedules? Pressure is from 'buyer's who receive pressure from directors, but no one is to blame for factory accidents.

Could a yacht/liner owner be connected with the aluminum industry? Aluminum needs to be pure, any impurities can make aluminum unusable, therefore un-saleable. Particular problems arise if any materials had been exposed to any form of nuclear event with its inherent long-life. Within living memory, nuclear accidents have (or might) have taken place in America and the Soviet Union, no doubt more nuclear accident will happen in the future as in Japan. News media reports of a minute worm found infecting aluminum products. Why had it never been detected previously? Any aircraft with an aluminum content immediately grounded, combustion engines with an aluminum content no longer permitted on public roads, suddenly aluminum a product which no-one wanted, anyone want to purchase a cheap yacht? Of course, yachts can be made from the now-worm infested product. Is it true? That yachts made from aluminum are used to smuggle drugs as something in the smell effects the ability of dog-drug detectors to smell out those drugs? Could those newly found worms eat through completely?

CHAPTER TEN - END OF THE BEGINNING

At Greenwich Time midday plus six minutes alarming news arrived of men and women (no children) with holes appearing in their skin, almost instantly those holes joined up, showing large skinless patches, with little more than twenty-four seconds totally skinless pools of bones of fluids, no time to shout for help. Mass happenings in buildings, no protection anywhere, nowhere to hide, even in cellars, under tables. In those lead-lined rooms from which lead excludes voice noise. At Greenwich time plus 6 minutes, the same event happening worldwide. Vladimere looking at Anna (well knowing all 'The Disappeared' would receive simultaneous thoughts) neutrinos could cause that effect but never before has it happened within humanity knowledge. Continuing his thoughts, 'why should neutrinos turn aggressive? There is no known recorded event in humanit history.' Twenty-four hour news channels were inundated with worldwide stories all saying identical information. 'Politicians were dying quicker that stamping on an ants nest.' Initial reports confirmed deaths in those buildings where politicians meet, the elite superior enough to tell ordinary, normal people how to live their lives while breaking all the rules themselves. 'We, the elected representatives know better than the people who elected us.' How many of these politicians fight elections with positive thinking. No! Much easier to say negative information whether 'true' or 'false'. Within moments a world without governments now in the hands of those who really run a country, 'civil servants,' 'state employees.' Neutrinos for a few moments selective in their journey through the Universe, what message were they delivering to humanits? Would humanits listen if they were told? No, just carry on as before, or will the military fill the vacuum?

For the general public, Mr and Mrs Ordinary, it was not the deaths of the political elite (as welcome as that was) that people talked about. No, more of a question, 'did you hear that sort or music that could be heard everywhere?' Children started to 'hum', 'mimic' the sound.

An eerie silence descended upon all those buildings where the political elite had worked, whose remains were now pools of fluid with bones. Poor ordinary working staff left with a predicament of what to do, no authority to give instructions, something needed to happen quickly with numerous fly infestations feeding on those elite remains. Instantly difficult to provide names to those nondescript fluids, bones, producing an overwhelming feeling of sickness. Who is in charge? Who can tell us what to do? Imagine silence in every United Nations building, a silent White House (USA), Duma (Parliament of Russia). Almost total silence within building after building in Brussels, a city filled with European Union unelected civil servants; that real source of political power governing Europe, no one could see any blue blood. Do the political elite really matter? More than once, speculation has provided a belief that humanits are ruled/governed by a small, united group of Founding Fathers, who could, might be, so-called aliens. Some extend their theory, suggesting all humanity is nothing other than a giant experiment. That Earth is a giant 'goldfish bowl' and that humanits were created for and then planted on it some 500,000 years ago. Those believing in such a theory explain that is why humanity cannot get out of Earth, (Yes, a very few in the form of astronauts/cosmonauts). Gravity keeps humanity upright with its feet firmly on Mother Earth, able to jump only a few metres into the air before falling backwards, hopefully without breaking any limbs, arms, legs etc. Humanity is forever a captive of Earth. Mother Earth a prison for humanity.

Still, the children humming that unusual music, brain washing, hidden messages within? Could there be music elsewhere from that great-unknown Universe? Ask the astronauts of Apollo 10, with a recording of music they made on the 'Dark Side' of the Moon.

As on the Moon, 'The Disappeared,' went missing again, now transported to those Parliament buildings of the countries they were born into. Within moments someone was back in charge. No time for sentimental burial, just sweep all the remains together into black plastic bags into communal, unidentified, burial places. In some countries a decision was made for mass cremation, everyone mixed up together in another mass grave. Pity those badly paid cleaners having to do that horrible work, facemasks with protective clothing a must (unfortunately not in every country). Families in disbelief with no way of mourning their deceased relative, but that is how it has been for ordinary families in every war/military conflict, often referred to as 'cannon fodder.' Why does this small planet we call Earth have so many military/armed conflicts?

For some unknown reason, that music which the children were humming everywhere produced a 'calm,' an acceptability that those 'The Disappeared' were politically in charge. Even the military and the security services accepted they were now in charge. Perhaps fear occupied their thoughts over what they had previously inflicted on 'The Disappeared.' First action: to stop all military action. All 'The Disappeared' on the same side, no advantage to fight. All food exports were prevented, food was to stay in the country of production. Could that help cure those who are without adequate day-by-day food? Not a good start for the new leaders with Western supermarkets starved of fresh fruit and vegetables. An answer to Western populations, to tell them a 'truth,' 'people go hungry because they are not allowed to purchase these foods that are for export only.'

A first attempt to rid the world of 'these young people without political experience,' happened after just 40 hours had passed. Again, those beyond-wealthy rich with their ocean-going yachts that Amos from Mossad continued to follow, they had no doubt they would run the world with great success (for the World or themselves?). Their hastily conceived plan involved the entire group acting together; who between them had affiliates and subordinates owing them a favour, all around the world? Military action out of the question, assassins needing to kill the two 'The Disappeared' at the same time; fatal injection, poisoning; given 'The Disappeared' needed to eat and drink. Motor vehicle accident: too messy with a possibility of survival. Sniper killing shot: enough contacts around the world to organize with relative ease: all somewhat conventional with no guarantee of total elimination.

One of those super-rich with substantial computing interests had long taken an interest in that ability 'The Disappeared' had to communicate without speaking. Since first hearing of that ability a team had been established to try and obtain this ability for him/herself, perhaps easier some form of interference to intercept those signals. Perhaps a development to literally blow brains out. Out of such research a type of sonic radio wave had been developed, with no way to test except in an actual event, no knowledge if it worked.

Attempting some equality in food production then distributing within a country was proving unbelievably difficult, as if humanity had no interest in those without adequate food. They wanted a full-table for themselves, forget anyone else. Then, some foods grown were not normally eaten within that country of production, food only produced for diets as prescribed by Western affluent world supermarkets, consequently fresh foods would begin to deteriorate, Mary very disgusted.

Mary immediately decided on a quid-pro-quo barter-type

exchange, all those specifically grown fruits and vegetables had to be exchanged for food manufactured/produced in a recipient country. Now that is much more difficult than can be imagined for many countries with a small agricultural industry. Mary found it hard to understand such absolute selfishness, self-interest. Who really cares if a baby dies in Eritrea as long as strawberries and creams are for teatime? With a little give, more take; Mary originated greater food supplies to those areas of minimal existence around Mother Earth. Much against what she intended to achieve in certain places medicines were more needed than food, so you keep people, mainly babies, alive, then food is needed. Mary often reiterated an ever-growing concern of what were the religions of the World doing to assist with these fundamental food crises? Very little was always her view.

Often she recalled how her grandfather (Mary grew up within 'The Horn of Africa') would talk about missionaries. How with little resources they taught people how to produce food, how to look after animals for food, particularly the benefits of egg producing chickens. What happened to those dedicated missionaries? Have they been replaced by professionally run charities where administrative costs eat into money given/donated or provided by inter-government agencies? Do you ever see administrators of a charity dressed in sackcloth and ashes, or is it best hotels, executive travel with 'never mind the cost?' Have another money raising event. How can these multi-national charities be run cost-effectively? Instead of big business hierarchy with all the incumbent perks, Mary decided enough was enough and disbanded into a country-only basis, workers only within that country where a charity is based. No cozy administration in England looking after Sub-Saharan Africa.

Discussions continued as to how to rid the world of 'The Disappeared,' to get them all in the same place at the same time, by far and away option number one. A publicity campaign started, 'Who are these unelected people?' directing that they were unaccountable to anyone, at least all politicians had been accountable through the United Nations, primarily in New York.

This started a bandwagon of public opinion driven by all those who decided their commercial/political well-being could be in jeopardy. Newspapers, television companies, all of media, decided to back this movement. Their fear, if everyone developed telepathic ability their days were numbered, who would need news media?

Within 'The Disappeared' they knew well about the 'unelected people' movement, but for once were in some disagreement as to what direction to take, not helped by constant messages from Amos from Mossad of Israel alerting 'The Disappeared' of this imminent danger to all their lives. Retaining a mixture of views, could a sense of fear be entering their DNA? Not what was expected of them, not what they had been selected for? Are they beginning to enjoy power they did nothing to obtain? Has selection gone wrong, nothing natural in their selection?

With those super-rich busily transferring money around the world, with payments to those who were being paid to do their dirty work, 'tax havens' were busy, so much money hidden in these tax havens. For many questions, 'what do these tax havens do with all the money deposited in their banks?' or 'are those world banks with 'tax haven' branches?', again, 'what do they do with those bags of money? Is that where money laundering takes place? Dirty washed into clean, then useable.

Money laundering, there is a story circulating that a stamp dealer was selling a block of four Penny Blacks for 3 million sterling. The story goes that when a customer inquired who spent that sort of money, with some disdain, had a reply, 'probably a money launderer. Who is going to stop a person leaving a country with 4 stamps in their wallet/handbag?' Could there even be a buy-back agreement? But the story may be fiction not fact.

Banks in those 'tax havens' started having difficulty making those instant bank transfers now made possible by modern technology, nothing serious, only slightly slower, as a little tired after a late night. Perhaps staff thought it was as a result of transfers going to obscure destinations, not those more normal financial centres, New York, London, Frankfurt, Hong Kong. Some staff joking, 'they didn't even know that such a place existed.'

Still the system moved even more slowly. IT departments now working overtime. Unlike old European banks, computing systems, were modern, not fifty or sixty years old, like Cobol Computing Language from 1959. Regardless of IT department efforts, it was as if a battery was running down. There were certainly no electrical supply problems, anyway, back-up generators were connected for an instant switch over, to a human eye really impossible to see. Then as if the battery ran out, systems collapsed in every bank in every 'tax haven' with one employee joking, 'all that dirty money has clogged up the washing machines.'

A little later banks discovered 'virus' entered the system as the slowdown started, those 'viros' continued devouring primary and secondary operating processes even after computers themselves ceased to function, hungry to devour any dirty money trails, eventually (hours) no records left, no ability to make transfers. Insurers at Lloyds of London awaiting substantial mind-boggling amounts of compensation claims, for once nothing to do with 'The Disappeared,' they reported.

What can those people who use dirty money expect when their deposits are not accessible? What parts of the world economy will suffer? How secure are banks? How secure are their foundations? Humanity happily builds building after building, the higher the better, with greater prestige, building on what, bedrock? How deep is bedrock? Reinforce with 'piling' techniques, making extra foundations that is obvious. Why then in Kaliningrad, for the recent 2018 Soccer World Cup, did they build a new soccer stadium that officials knew would sink? Is there a point when the absolute weight of buildings causes bedrock to sink? All building takes place upon that part of Mother Earth called crust, it varies in thickness from 0 (yes zero) to 60 kilometres thick, not much when you compare that to the mantle that is some 2900 kilometres thick, then the inner core, solid made up of iron and nickel, with temperatures of up to 5,500 degrees centigrade.

Humanity therefore exists on a very thin (in relation to the size of the Earth) crust that in certain circumstances could be ripped away. Does humanity know what lives under that thin crust (to which scientists provide that comforting answer 'of nothing can exist in such super-hot temperatures')? Then some other scientists will say, 'we know more about space than the Earth under our feet.' There in exists a fundamental problem with language. 'Earth under our feet,' when in reality it is a liquid of iron and nickel plus eventually a solid core, so scientists believe, of course no-one has been to such a place with its temperatures around 5,000 degrees Celsius. Humanity would fry into a little ball of liquid before evaporating.

Does humanity know more about the Moon than inside its own little planet in the Universe? Is it through all this burning heat, solid core that those neutrinos travel, emerging out the other side from the entry. Impossible to comprehend (could there really be a black hole under humanity feet?) that having travelled through, no tunnel is left behind for others to travel through. How can that be? A lorry driver will travel behind another lorry in an area of calm as the first lorry punches its way forward, slipstream, just like a motor car racing driver preparing to overtake that racing car in front. Scientists still to decide if neutrinos can carry germs/infections/pollution, if we do not know, will we understand in 300 years time, assuming humanity has not poisoned itself to death? Will that 300 years plus be fully dominated by a world controlled by whoever has those unbreakable systems of cyber security, able to knock out other systems while a 100% system safe from all? A world without conventional military forces, no army, no air force, no navy, no submarines? Rather like futuristic films of today, drones fighting drones, cyber space full of destroying messages. What happens to those mass employers of military manufacturing, what happens to their employees? Will they all be employed in those new cyber-space industries? (Sell shares in today's military companies.)

Devastating news from those places (islands) where tax havens had established effective control of all commercial business. Banks were going under, literally going under, sinking, ground underneath them giving way, already first floors submerged which meant that the 'vaults' were already inaccessible. Dirty money stinking into where, why, how? Definitely sinking, panic as those with billions/millions deposited unable to access or use. Desperate efforts to evacuate employees, as floor upon floor disappeared: no managers acting as captains of their sinking bank. Roll accounts established no one left on board as buildings sank and were immediately covered over by Mother Earth. Unemployed, distraught, Lloyds Insurance of London frantically checking if any members (syndicates) had exposure to such a mass loss of buildings, of investments. They say of Lloyds of London they will ensure every risk, premiums could be extremely high, however, insurance can be purchased. Lloyds has an unusual annual accounting routine, accounts drawn up years later. As now, with all unexplained events, it always fell at those feet of 'The Disappeared,' to be the organisers.

Children continued to hum, whistle; sing that music continuously much to continued annoyance, complaints from adult world. What had entered their minds? Imagine taking an instant whirlwind worldwide travel experience, no matter where, when, what time, children were fixated with repeating, repeating, repeating those few musical notes, strung together with no apparent meaning. Throughout governments worldwide, questioning if this could be attributed to subliminal messaging? If so, where and for what purpose?

Different political regimes engaged in assorted methods of trying to understand what was happening to young humanits. Psychiatrists suddenly entered those realms of the most wanted status: study these young people. 'What is happening? More fundamentally, is my country in danger?' As normal, self-interest, not global co-operation. As usual, an advantage in commercial military ideas; if such ability could be turned to a greater good, again, meaning self-interest.

Free holidays on offer to Florida (USA) Disneyworld for one thousand children aged from 7 to 14. That manufacturer of breakfast cereal, directed by White House officials, and deluged with would be participants. Modern computer technique profiling, the new favourite profession of psychiatrists established, producing a cross-section of the population meeting all criteria. Hastily prepared questionnaires which participants had to complete, then rewarded with one theme park experience, individual questioning about that experience, followed by another paper of questions followed by another theme park ride. Parents accompanying their children, relaxing poolside enjoyed holiday life free from constant nagging, "I Want,' children.

In China, much more authoritative, immediate state selection, parents told where to take, where to leave their children, with a small inducement of free university education. State officials from the beginning accepting that a proportion of those selected were not of university standard, therefore a small agreement specifying a monetary alternative for parents.

Within a so-called South American democracy, in effect a military hierarchy, state officials given an opportunity to provide their children with an incentive of receiving a share of knowledge obtained, no shortage of volunteers.

In one of those precious Western European countries, nothing would be allowed to happen to children that could cause long-term harmful damage, those health and safety do-good-liberals. Forgetting children spend hour upon hour upon hour within a world of computer games, of instant chat rooms. With illegal drugs easily obtained from someone's friend at school, if not from a drug-dealer handily parked somewhere close to the school entrance/exit gates. But those do-good-liberals insistent that this 'experiment' must do nothing to damage those precious children. Of course, no rewards offered to participants, they are doing it for the good of humankind, and yes, participants could keep precious mobile phones with them. Somewhere along this selection process it had been decided that removing 'mobiles' would produce inaccurate results. Such remains liberal-do-gooders power.

In Mary and Joseph's homeland, an incentive of extra food for a participant's family, a simple, effective encouragement. An Asian country member from within that Former Soviet Union decided only those good at sport would participate, not just obvious sports; athletics, football, tennis, also including judo, boxing, horse-riding, karate, wrestling. Their criteria, to excel at sport, required dedication, a none existence self-indulgence. All sport of course enhances a worldwide reputation.

Effectively all countries making choices to enhance self-interest. Much amusement within the ranks of 'The Disappeared' at a lack of communal good, perhaps with an exception of Mary and Joseph who were enraged with food being used as bait.

On social network sites, groups of children performed that music as if in choirs. Within America's State Department, an instruction was issued to establish any connection with those sounds heard and recorded from the Apollo 10 space mission around the Dark Side of the Moon. Could that which was dismissed of no importance all those years ago actually be a pre-run of that which was now happening? Still, that relentless music invading lives, brain washing, again high in vocabulary usage.

With modern techniques of brain scanning, many investigating centres observed a smallest of particulates lodged within brains in that area receptive to musical sounds. Not at random, rather in a precise, defined position, nowhere near sharing information, each centre had brain surgeons, (now-seconded) puzzled while at the same time, excited by what the particulate might be. Theorists immediately offering reasons in plenty, hospitals immediately directed when undertaking brain scans on children to send results to a particular place. Accordingly, quickly established that particulates were not random, all within that age group carried an imperfection, in precisely that identical positioning.

For many years automobile manufacturers have understood those particulates that exit motor vehicles (diesel) through exhaust pipes into breathable atmosphere. In that period, late 1990's to say, 2010, governments have placed an excessive belief in diesel engines reducing carbon dioxide emissions, therefore, 'saving the planet.' If research had been undertaken into diesel particulates emissions, that knowledge remained the purview of the automobile manufacturers, not the public, although the government probably knew (would they admit to the fact? Only if another person/party made such a decision). Particulates now commonly accepted as a primary cause of health problems within urban regions, specifically (or as known at present) breathing and chest infections.

Now being asked by brain surgeons involved in the ongoing projects, 'how can particulates' enter a young person's brain?' 'Is this particular 'one' a forerunner of greater problems?' Again, now more pressing than ever, 'what did automobile manufacturers know about diesel emissions?' 'Why did a major world manufacturer of motor vehicles go to such great lengths to install equipment to provide inaccurately 'low' readings for their vehicle emissions?' 'What did they know some twenty-five years ago?'

Having, in medical opinion, now discovered what had appeared in the brain, medical personnel started to discuss together via the Internet, in an open forum, what medical procedure could be undertaken for the removal of what they now called 'the musical particulate.' In reality only a question of time before Chinese or American surgeons conducted a first experiment, perhaps a Mexican child separated from parents, or street children of South American cities, or a child from the high mountains around Tibet.

Surgeons were too late, reports from Samoa as morning school approached, that children, without exception, were sitting on roads outside schools. Parental hysteria at day break in

New Zealand, Australia, as they were unable to drop children off at school, deep, physical hysteria as children got out of vehicles then sat around their parents, or friends cars, vehicles could only move by running over children. Police arrived, hundreds of children to move with just a few police. Around this third planet of an insignificant star, children everywhere were sitting outside schools.

At school closing time, children in Samoa got up out of the road and went home. Parents missed work and all those things done when their dear children are at school looked after by other adults. Is that what education is really about? Getting rid of children all day? Could parents teach their own children? Imagine all those car journeys saved, no need for two-car families. Scientifically, that would be good for health, not so many particulates, children walking would improve that child's health, alright, reduce overweight inactivity. A second day started exactly the same, now governments showed concern. Obvious response from parents, keep children at home, a more obvious response, as children walked or ran to school, again sitting in roads. More than one teacher commented they did not eat all day, no one child needed toilet facilities during school time. In some countries as school time arrived, military personnel were guarding roads into schools. What does a soldier do when surrounded by none-moving children? Pick them up and move a child at a time, or shoot them, or defy military commands? Who would blink first, children, or military?

Without question, it was those 'The Disappeared' causing this defiance. How could anyone explain children sitting on roads all school day long, constantly repeating the music, that music all day long? Once scientist decided to make a name for themselves, suggesting this is a particular particulate generated within 'entertainment systems' contained within motor vehicles, no proof, a logical conclusion. Going on to say it is a proven fact that particulates enter blood streams. Why would they not lodge within a human brain? Other scientists suggested that 'animal kingdom' must also be affected, receiving many a farmer saying, 'no testing on my livestock.'

Meteorologists started communicating within their worldwide organisations that unusual activity had started within 'jet streams' altering from normally accepted patterns. (The main jet streams are located near the altitude of the tropopause and are Westerly winds flowing west to east, the strongest jet streams are the polar jets at 30000-39000 feet above sea level.) These jet streams effect air travel as flight times can be dramatically affected by either flying with the flow, or against, which results in significant fuel and time saving for airlines.

Airline pilots began reporting problems with finding normal jet streams, those flying from America were reporting that without jet streams flight times were being substantially extended, again, fuel would be a problem, lack of fuel to complete Trans-Atlantic journeys. In opposite directions, pilots were reporting quicker flight times with 'not having to fly into the jet stream,' their primary concern, too much fuel left to make a safe landing. Immediate temporary measures, Shannon Airport in Ireland would have to be refueling staging point for America to Europe aircraft, Europe to America would need to dump fuel at sea prior to attempting a landing. Airline timetables in turmoil with airports packed with angry passengers. Real danger of a number of airlines unable to reach destinations, problems of airlines made headlines around the world, an explanation much too technical for mere normal Earth people to understand.

Airline travel affects many people and of course, air forces, worldwide. Meteorologists on the Pacific Coast of the USA were shocked to see a dense black cloud (totally insufficient description), a total Pacific Coast movement of dark matter moving as if it was a series of interconnected jet streams. Visibility, nonexistent, then absorbing sunlight, turning everything black. Instantly blackness engulfed farthest America, scientists quickly identified the blackness, particulates from Earth atmosphere were falling as if clinging fog, everything, everywhere coated in thick, choking particulates. As one scientist stated, 'as if Earth atmosphere could absorb, carry the weight no more, humanity may have it back.'

Impossible to see, no driving, no walking, only one safe place to be, prisoners in home, unable to escape. Choke outside; stay inside with every window, door closed, all right until the weight of particulates brought down power lines, then blackness. A few prepared people had candles ready, sewerage systems failed with particulates blocking up the system, and causing a supply failure for water. Events did not improve as movement continued into Europe, scientists predicting Asia, Australasia, would not be effected as the immense volume already deposited would leave nothing left to fall in those areas. Predictions were wrong, no reduction in particulates falling. A first day passed, a second day began. Particulates as if like snow, two feet, three feet, just like snow drifts. Unlike snowdrifts, impossible to build particulate men (snowmen).

Like everyone else, 'The Disappeared' suffered, were affected, but to people everywhere they were still responsible.

Come a third day, meteorologists reported a movement with jet streams, at sea level, hurricane or typhoon formation activity. For many, food was running low, having had a lifetime of only keeping enough food for a few days, always shops, supermarkets open within a short car drive. Long gone in many affluent countries drying meat, fish to keep during long winter months, pickling fruit, pickling vegetables as a normality. So called less affluent countries without a day-to-day reliance of the 'fridge' coping much better, could they survive when rich countries suffocated?

Meteorologists ran out of those names given to identify hurricanes and typhoons, with so many in formation numbering proved inefficient, they were forming in large columns as if foot soldiers moving forward to enter battle. Mindanao (Philippines) claimed distinction as first landfall. Within winds, within rains, rubbish from oceans began to be dumped back on humanity on land, instantly, a choking, sickening smell. All land mass received rubbish back from seas, even landmass never before having been affected by those hurricanes or typhoons. Mother Earth turned into one huge cesspit of humanity waste, rubbish, excesses of a society without a real thought for another day, another tomorrow, another generation, not even a tomorrow for their own children.

Oceans of Earth had a number of recorded 'garbage patches,' accumulations of humanity made rubbish (garbage) patches another pretend nice description as friendly as, 'my garden has a cabbage patch.' Your vegetable patch will not be as large as the great Pacific garbage patch, also called the 'Pacific Trash Vortex,' in the central North Pacific Ocean. This debris is found halfway between Hawaii and California. Estimates of size vary from 700,000 square kilometres, about the size of Texas, to more than 15,000,000 million square kilometres, about the size of Russia. Whatever a precise size, lots of dirty, man-made garbage taking over a world of sea-life. This is not an isolated garbage area; two more have been identified in recent times, one on the South Pacific Ocean, and the other in the North Atlantic. Is humanity now discovering those feelings of marine life with tons of rubbish above their heads? What do they think, feel, and understand? Especially as many have an ancestry much older, longer, than humans, as jellyfish who have been around for more than 500 million years. Anyway, those 'Disappeared' people have caused all those problems; statistically one or two of them should have died by now. Humanity now attempting a life buried under its own used, produced, cesspit of stinking, rotting, garbage. Rats were having a field day. All this rotting stuff as if 'manna from heaven.'

Could such an event be the system of regeneration used by Mother Earth when those inhabiting her surface cause the damage? Is that what happened with the dinosaurs, protecting her way of life? Is it just by an accident that she positioned herself exactly at a distance from her star which enabled life to exist, did she have a competition with her brother and sister planets as to which could produce life? Did she need a moon to assist?

Blame all these terrible events on 'The Disappeared.' Were they a last attempt, at a warning for humanity? Now they cannot be found, where have they gone? How have they escaped? Who on Earth knows where they have hidden.

It is a great relief to have a blame game where self is responsible for nothing bad. 'I am humanity in charge of my Earth. How can I cause it damage? Earth has been flying around forever. When did humanity take for granted its gift? Humanity did nothing to make Earth (or whatever others call it.) All that humanity had to do was preserve, protect. Look how Earth preserves, protects, it continues with imperceptible deviation on a long journey with the knowledge that as its sun burns out then Earth will die. Without drunken fits to wobble humanity upside down, without anger, starting a war as between the Western hemisphere, against the Eastern hemisphere, racing continents around so as they crash into each other. If humanity had been created to look after Mother Earth, humanity has done a fabulously pathetic, self-interested, bad job, marks out of ten, less than none, zero, nothing.

Did humanity make errors from its beginning, its creation, did its very first action damage Earth. Would you move into a new house, immediately knocking brickwork away? Did it go wrong when humanity attributed value to precious stones (who decided they were precious?) to landownership, to gold, to silver, to physical possessions, when did a value become attributed to diamonds, who decided gold was the best store of wealth/money? Did any life prior to humanity destroy our only homeland, as humanity has achieved? Might there have existed humanity that there is no knowledge of because it destroyed itself?

Did it go wrong with the beginning of the Industrial Revolution, pre-empting the flight into town and city, life starting great big city conurbations? (Must live in a city for all the amenities, breathing in every moment polluted air.) City life must be good, as everyone likes being a city-dweller. Early days of pollution, factory chimneys, constant 24 hours a day smoke full of rubbish. Long working days, only Sunday free, no guaranteed holidays, when factory owners were so important.

Most historians agree that two Industrial Revolutions exist, perhaps 1760 to 1830/40, then starting a second phase to 1870, all agree it started in Great Britain, the Black County, Lancashire Cotton Mills, coalmining, black, filthy black, a colourless life for worker ants.

That industry moving into America, China, Russia; huge technological change, but dirty filth everywhere. Little wonder those deep depths of particulates and rubbish. Into mass transport, all, everywhere wanting a motor vehicle, a sign of affluence, to be followed by 'everyone has' mobile phones. Is that, and this, the period it all went pollution mad, little more than 250 years leading into mass pollution? Did not clever people see that an ending would arrive?

'The Disappeared,' where on Earth are you? Please come back. Save us from our self-inflicted, humanity made, hell on Earth'; our children are dying.

Who created this new mass extinction, first the dinosaurs, then so-called humanity? Could it be the living creatures of Earth, a response to their mass extinction of thousands of species by humans? Could it be neutrinos concerned that each had become too dangerous, too polluted to travel through, Earth with a 'keep out' sign? Could it be a directing force from the Universe? Could the directing force conclude the Earth existence had failed? Could it be humanity itself because no person would stop the pollution, the race to extinction?

Will you, a human controlling the destiny of your only home planet cease to drive a car? Cease to use air travel, trains, public transport? To use legs only to commute to work? To walk to school, university? Cease to use plastic bags and food coverings? Cease to use supermarkets, unless within leg distance? Create your own carbon zero emissions environment? Produce your own and family carbon free electricity, gas, no nuclear power? Cease to create sewerage – consume less meats, butter, cheese?

Why should I? No one else will. I will be taken advantage of by

Michael Cooke

those thinking only of themselves.